MAN OVERBOARD

Greeley held up a hand, which stopped the overman in his tracks. The other two tightened their grips on Mason's arms and moved him back just enough to give him a taste of what it might feel like to topple backward into the water.

"Do you know how these men earned their names?" Greeley asked.

Mason's eyes darted back and forth in their sockets to get a look at the men who had ahold of him. "You mean . . . overmen?"

"That's right."

"I've heard a few things, but I don't know for certain which are true." Mason had heard more than a few things, but he didn't want to discuss them at that particular moment.

"Part of their duties involves ridding my boat of troublemakers," Greeley explained. "To do that, they pitch undesirables over the rail and into the water."

"I suppose that makes sense."

"Cheaters are tied to the side of the boat, way down low, and dragged for a few miles over rocks, through mud, and across a couple sandbars until their bones are turned to powder."

"I didn't cheat!"

"I know," Greeley said. "Men who can't pay their debts aren't dragged, but they are also tossed over. Only difference is that they're tossed into the paddle wheel."

Ralph Compton

STRAIGHT TO THE NOOSE

A Ralph Compton Novel

by Marcus Galloway

SIGNET
Published by the Penguin Group
Penguin Group (USA) LLC, 375 Hudson Street,
New York, New York 10014

USA | Canada | UK | Ireland | Australia | New Zealand | India | South Africa | China
penguin.com
A Penguin Random House Company

First published by Signet, an imprint of New American Library,
a division of Penguin Group (USA) LLC

First Printing, May 2015

ISBN 978-0-451-47237-3

Printed in the United States of America
10 9 8 7 6 5 4 3 2 1

The Immortal Cowboy

This is respectfully dedicated to the "American Cowboy." His was the saga sparked by the turmoil that followed the Civil War, and the passing of more than a century has by no means diminished the flame.

True, the old days and the old ways are but treasured memories, and the old trails have grown dim with the ravages of time, but the spirit of the cowboy lives on.

In my travels—to Texas, Oklahoma, Kansas, Nebraska, Colorado, Wyoming, New Mexico, and Arizona—I always find something that reminds me of the Old West. While I am walking these plains and mountains for the first time, there is this feeling that a part of me is eternal, that I have known these old trails before. I believe it is the undying spirit of the frontier calling me, through the mind's eye, to step back into time. What is the appeal of the Old West of the American frontier?

It has been epitomized by some as the dark and bloody period in American history. Its heroes—Crockett, Bowie, Hickok, Earp—have been reviled and criticized. Yet the Old West lives on, larger than life.

It has become a symbol of freedom, when there was always another mountain to climb and another river to cross; when a dispute between two men was settled not with expensive lawyers, but with fists, knives, or guns. Barbaric? Maybe. But some things never change. When the cowboy rode into the pages of American history, he left behind a legacy that lives within the hearts of us all.

—Ralph Compton

Chapter 1

Mississippi
1869

The *Delta Jack* was one of the most luxurious riverboats to float down the Mississippi. If one were to look at her plush carpets, sample the fine selection of liquor served in one of many bars, or taste the food prepared by its well-paid chefs, one might guess the riverboat to be exclusive to rich men or prominent gamblers. That couldn't be further from the truth. Everyone was welcome aboard the *Delta Jack*. All a man needed to become a passenger was enough money to sit in at one of the gambling tables scattered throughout its three decks.

Such a man didn't even need to be rich. He could stay aboard as long as he kept gambling. The *Delta Jack* made frequent stops, and as soon as a man's bankroll ran out, he was promptly escorted onto dry land. If he didn't want to separate himself from the *Jack*'s many hospitalities, he could always apply for a line of credit from the boat's owner. Cam Greeley was always willing to consider such an application so the man in need of funds could remain on board for a while longer. It was generally a good arrangement, if only for one of the two parties involved.

Games played on the *Delta Jack* ran the gamut from gin rummy and simple rolls of the dice all the way up to roulette and backgammon. But most men didn't board the *Jack* to play anything but poker. If all those other games were appetizers and dessert, poker was the steak and potatoes served in between. Some men dined for days on that steak. Others choked on it.

Abner Mason was one of the better-known faces on the *Delta Jack*. When he left his small but elegant cabin on the middle deck, he was greeted by friendly smiles by everyone from the young men hired to sweep the halls to the young women hired to convince certain players to stay on board for just a bit longer. At the moment, Mason's rounded face reflected every hour of the last twenty he'd played five-card stud before he'd gotten three hours of sleep. His light brown eyes were slightly bloodshot and black stubble sprouted from his chin. Even so, he did his best to return the smiles he was shown with one of his own, which was always well received.

"A good mornin' to you, Emma," he said to the young lady who walked toward him.

She was a fresh-faced little filly with blond curls and eyes that told a man she could teach him a thing or two. Having already taught some of her lessons to Mason during his many stays on the *Jack*, she smirked and nodded. "Afternoon is more like it," she said.

Mason wore a rumpled blue suit that had obviously doubled as pajamas. Since one hand was being used to keep his jacket hooked over his shoulder, he used the other hand to fish a watch from the pocket of his vest. The hallway was too narrow for both of them to pass each other while he stood facing her head-on, so Emma stopped as he flipped the watch open to check the time.

"Why, you're absolutely right," he said.

Remaining less than two inches away from him, she replied, "I may not know a lot of things, Abner, but I know how to tell the time."

"You know plenty, sweet thing," Mason said with just a hint of a Mississippi drawl.

"Up for another lesson?"

"Not just yet. I need to have breakfast."

"You mean lunch," she said.

"Not hardly. I'd never skip over breakfast. After all, even a man in my condition needs his coffee and bacon."

"And a woman in my condition," Emma said as she placed a hand on his chest to give him a little push, "needs to keep her schedule."

Allowing himself to be moved to one side like a door in a rumpled suit, Mason said, "By all means."

Emma traced her hand along his chest as she passed him. Once she'd taken a few more steps, she broke into a stride that caused her golden curls and a few other things to bounce in time to her gait.

Mason watched her strut all the way down the narrow hall. "A fine day indeed," he muttered before checking his watch once more and snapping it shut. "Or afternoon."

A good portion of the second deck was set aside for amenities to keep passengers comfortable. Apart from the small sleeping cabins, there was a dining room, a kitchen, and even a barber. It was to the latter that Mason went, and he wasn't the only one. When he arrived, there was already a man in the barber's chair. Mason helped himself to one of the newspapers that had been picked up when they'd last visited New Orleans and stepped outside again. There were chairs on either side of the door to the barber's cabin, but no other customers waiting for a trim. Grateful that he wouldn't have to make any polite conversations for a few minutes, Mason sat down, opened the newspaper, and pulled in a deep breath of warm air.

It was a balmy day with no shortage of insects buzzing around the chugging riverboat. Mason flipped through the ink-covered pages, skimming through the outdated stories without actually reading any of them. The words bounced off his swirling mind like flat rocks upon the water's surface. Finally he folded the paper up and placed it on his lap.

"Hell of a day, ain't it?" asked the freshly shorn man who emerged from the barber's cabin.

Mason looked up at him and replied, "I suppose so. You planning on playing more faro today? Or will you be taking another crap game to the cleaner's?"

"How'd you know all that? Did we meet during a game?"

"We sure did," Mason said, even though he only remembered the man's face after walking past the faro tables so many times the previous night. "You had a good run of luck."

"There's more to it than luck, my friend. Don't let anyone tell you any different!"

Mason got to his feet and tucked the newspaper under one arm. His jacket was draped over the back of the chair and he picked that up to drape over the same arm. "Is that a fact?"

"Sure is." Squinting, the man scratched his smooth chin and said, "I don't seem to recall your name."

"Abner Mason. We were both slightly inebriated at the table, so it's no wonder we're in rough shape. Don't feel bad, though. I can't remember your name either."

The man smirked and nudged Mason's shoulder as he stepped up to the railing to get a look at the green riverbank sliding idly by. "Virgil Slake's the name. Next time I see you, I'll buy you a drink."

"And I'll buy the next one!"

"Well, all right, then." With that, Virgil extended a hand so Mason could shake it. Mason did so with exuberance and Virgil was on his way.

Mason knew plenty about faro players even though he rarely played the game any longer. Like most gamblers, he'd gotten his feet wet by bucking the tiger. The day he chose gambling as a profession instead of a pastime, he swore off faro and the terrible odds that came along with it. Faro players, who always made a habit of drifting toward dice games as well, would always hold a spot in Mason's heart. They had to be wide-eyed, gullible, or full of themselves to keep playing a game that so clearly favored the house. Oftentimes, they were a smattering of all three, which meant they frequently lined the pockets of men in Mason's line of work. What's more, they were often drunk while at the table. Mason had been banking on that fact when he lied to Virgil's face about standing beside him at the faro table the night before. Because Mason had been correct in his assumption, Virgil didn't know enough to call his bluff and would most likely greet him like an old friend when they crossed paths again.

Smiling to himself, Mason turned on his heel and walked into the barber's shop. "Looks like I'm next," he announced.

The barber was sweeping his floor and didn't look up. "You're next," he said. "Just as soon as I'm done cleaning and have some lunch. Come back in an hour or so."

"Then maybe I should just go to the place down the street. I hear they're more accommodating to their guests."

"Down the street? What are you . . . ?" Finally looking up from his broom, the barber smiled broadly when he saw his customer's face. "I should've known it was you, Abby! Most other men wouldn't look like they just rolled out of bed at this time of day."

"Most men who sleep on this boat as often as I do roll out of bed even later than this, Dell."

"Yeah, but they look better than that."

"Fair enough," Mason said. "Can you help me freshen up or not?"

"For you, I'll postpone my lunch." He swept the pile of clipped hair toward the door and, when Mason stepped aside, through it. A few more strokes from the broom sent the clippings under the railing and over the side of the boat. Dell then turned around and marched back into his shop, where Mason was already making himself comfortable in the barber's chair.

"What can you tell me about Mr. Slake?" Mason asked.

"You mean the fellow that just walked out of here?"

"That's the one."

Shrugging, Dell replied, "Not much, apart from the fact that he likes his hair cut shorter on the sides than on top. Why?"

"No reason."

Dell draped a large white cloth over Mason's chest and tied it around the back of his neck. "Something tells me I'm not the only one that'll be fleecing that man."

"Fleecing? Such an ugly term. You're much better at your job than that!"

"I wasn't referring to my job," Dell said as he picked up a shaving brush, dipped it in lather, and painted it across Mason's face. "I was talking about yours."

"Oh. Well, then . . . you'd be correct."

Picking up his razor, Dell said, "In that case . . . I may remember a thing or two about that fellow. Standard arrangement?"

"Five percent."

"Make it seven."

Everyone who worked on board the *Delta Jack* had at least one story attached to their name. Even the boy who dumped the chamber pots over the side was rumored to have taken part in some bit of nastiness involving a wayward soul. There were plenty of rumors swirling about in regard to Dell and his dealings with various men who'd sat in his chair. Having become acquainted with the stout man sporting a curved waxed mustache, Mason knew for certain that some of those rumors were true. Others, however, were simply too unsavory to fit a man of Dell's character. Seeing the look in the barber's eyes as he opened that razor, Mason thought he might have to reconsider some of his previous conclusions.

Mason raised an eyebrow but was careful not to turn his head. "Seven percent? He just looked like another faro player who comes aboard the *Jack* for a night or two of the sweet life."

"Then you haven't been paying attention. He mentioned a thing or two about some good money he brought along with him that was turned into something even better."

"Surely you've worked on this boat long enough to

know better than to believe the boastings of men who sit in this chair."

"He flashed a fat wad of bills when he paid me," Dell said while commencing his shave. "And he had no problem peeling off a mighty healthy gratuity for a simple haircut and shave."

"Doesn't exactly mean he'll be so generous to another player. Even one as amicable as me."

"No," Dell admitted. He scraped a bit more from one cheek and then moved on to the other side. "But it does point to the idea that he may have even more money than that stashed away somewhere nearby. Maybe," he said as he evened out Mason's long sideburns, "even on his person or in his cabin."

"Cabin?"

"Mmm-hmm."

Looking into the mirror on the wall in front of him, Mason watched the barber work. "Maybe he's traveling with someone else who might have loaned him that money or could be watching over it for him?"

Dell shifted his attention to Mason's neck. After making his first pass, he glanced up to meet his reflected gaze. "Didn't bring anyone with him. As for the company he kept, that was limited to one of Greeley's girls."

"Which one?"

"Emma."

Mason grinned.

When he saw that, Dell smirked as well before turning his focus back to his job.

"You sure it was Emma?" Mason asked.

"Oh yes. She was all he could talk about. Even mentioned the little heart-shaped mole on her— "

"That's Emma all right. This is some good information, to be certain, Dell. Now that I've got it, though . . ."

"What makes it worth an extra couple of percentage points?"

"The question does seem like a good one."

"First of all," Dell replied as he set his razor down to pick up a pair of scissors, "there's the implied trust between a man and his barber." He began snipping Mason's sideburns, getting close enough to severing an ear that a chill worked through Mason's spine. "Have I ever steered you wrong, Abby?"

"Not yet, but you can do me a favor and stop calling me that."

"Calling you Abby? It's short for Abner."

"I don't care what it's short for," Mason said. "Actually nobody calls me Abner either."

"Keep your mind on what's important, friend," Dell said. "I believe our Mr. Slake is sitting on enough money to make a couple extra percentage points more than worthwhile. And I haven't told you all there is to tell."

"What else is there?"

"His schedule, for starters. I've also got the names of a few friends of his that are sporting men."

Keeping still as hair was clipped along the side of his head, Mason asked, "How might that be worth any extra pay?"

A man in a black suit walked past the door to the barber's cabin. He had a slender redhead on one arm and barely took a passing interest in the little barbershop as he escorted her along the deck. Once those two were out of sight, Dell said, "I'm sure that kind of information can come in handy to someone who might want to know about any dealings Mr. Slake might be involved in that aren't exactly . . . aboveboard. Perhaps . . . the same man who was talking him up not too long ago?"

Mason sighed. "You heard me talking to him outside?"

"Ears like a hawk, my friend," Dell said as he tapped the side of his head.

"And a nose for business to go along with it."

"You think any man can earn a decent living in a shop this size without making himself useful?" Dell asked.

Even when he was asleep, Mason rarely felt his thoughts slow to anything less than a roar inside his head. He'd imagined ways to wring some cash from Virgil Slake starting from the moment he'd seen Virgil's enthusiasm at the faro table. There were few men who didn't get measured up that way soon after crossing Mason's path. Being on board the *Delta Jack* only made those wheels turn faster, which was why Mason loved being on that boat almost as much as he liked sleeping in his very own bed back home.

Getting on a stranger's good side wasn't much of a chore. Without that particular skill in his arsenal, Mason wouldn't have lasted very long in the sporting life. Having an edge in that regard, be it some personal bit of information or the name of a trusted reference that couldn't be easily checked, was as good as gold. If Slake truly did have a healthy stash of money somewhere on the *Jack*, Mason figured he could chalk up one mighty fine mark in the win column.

"Seven percent, huh?" Mason asked.

"Not a penny more," the barber replied.

Chapter 2

Less than an hour later, Mason was again stepping out of his room on the upper deck. This time, however, stubble no longer covered his chin and his hair was neatly arranged. The suit into which he'd changed wasn't only pressed, but was a darker shade of blue and his vest bore narrow horizontal stripes. A lively tune was on his lips as he walked down the hall and went to the outer walkway that skirted the entire middle deck. Once he could feel the damp air against his face, he slid one hand jauntily inside his jacket pocket and kept the other free to tip his hat to anyone he might meet on his way to the Missouri Miss Restaurant.

Since the *Delta Jack* had stopped briefly while Mason was changing his clothes, there was a good amount of activity on her first two decks. A few of those bustling about were workers putting away supplies that had been acquired, but most were men and women taking in the riverboat and trying to decide which comfort they would sample first. Mason could recall being one of those setting foot on the *Jack* for the first time, but just barely. Since he was more interested in his next meal than surveying potential targets, he maneuvered as quickly as possible through the milling crowd until he arrived at a long room toward the aft end of the boat.

The Missouri Miss wasn't the fanciest restaurant on the *Delta Jack*, but it was preferred by most gamblers who called the riverboat their home away from home. There were no tables. There was just a single aisle between two counters that ran the length of the place and a door at either end. One counter was lower than the other and had several chairs where customers could sit to enjoy their meal while looking out the window toward the starboard side of the boat. The other counter was the same height as a saloon's bar. Behind it was a pair of stoves and a chopping board where food was prepared. Any customers sitting there did so on stools, which was where Mason planted himself as soon as he walked in.

Less than half the seats were occupied at the moment, which meant he didn't have to wait long before a tall woman with her hair tied back into a long braid acknowledged his arrival with a familiar smile. "You just wake up or just about to go to bed?" she asked.

"Just up," Mason said.

She turned to the cook, who was a tall fellow wearing a greasy apron. Judging by the lack of meat on his bones, the man didn't sample much of his own food. The woman with the braid said to him, "Bacon, grits, and burnt toast."

Only then did the cook look up from the stovetop he was scraping clean to ask, "That Mason?"

"Sure is."

The cook gave Mason a curt upward nod before wiping his hands on the front of his apron and stooping to retrieve a few strips of bacon from under the counter.

"Have any luck last night?" the woman asked.

Mason took off his hat and placed it on the counter to

his left. "You weren't with me, Bea. How could I get any unluckier than that?"

"You could've spent all day with her like I did," the cook said.

Bea turned to look over her shoulder at the man standing by the stove. "Nobody asked you a thing!" Turning to Mason, she dropped her voice to something of a purr and said, "Go on."

"I could go on all day long," Mason replied. "But I doubt it'd get me anywhere with a beauty like you."

"Never know until you try."

"I'll keep that in mind. Right now all I can tell you is that I'm useless before I get my breakfast."

She scowled at him before walking down to the other stove where a kettle was brewing. "Let's start with coffee. After that, we can continue with all the sugary lies."

"My pleasure," Mason said.

After pouring him his coffee, Bea went around to top off the mugs of other customers before settling back into her regular spot a bit farther down the counter from where Mason was sitting.

When he looked down at his mug, Mason found that a single egg had been placed on the counter beside it. Picking it up, he looked over to Bea and was given a knowing smile along with a nod. Mason placed his other hand over his heart as his way of silently thanking her before cracking the egg against the rim of his mug and mixing the raw egg into his coffee.

Ever since the morning after he took his first sip of whiskey when he was fifteen, Mason had heard plenty of supposed cures for the headache following a night of overindulgence. Most of those cures involved consuming something that was so disgusting that it made a man consider forsaking liquor altogether. Some were nothing more than concoctions sold from the back of a crooked salesman's wagon. All of them, however, had someone who swore by them, and the only one that Mason could swear to was the one he drank now.

Bea had introduced him to it on the same night he first introduced himself to her. Mason could carry his headaches well, but she'd had no trouble spotting the pain behind his eyes. Without any explanations needed, she'd given him some coffee and cracked an egg into it.

"Drink it," was all she'd said.

When Mason drank it, he nearly spat it right back up again. "That is horrid!" he'd exclaimed. "It tastes like it's at least a day old and . . . there's egg in it!"

"Of course there's egg in it. You watched me put it in there. And it's not a day old. It's three days old. Just drink the rest down and stop your whining."

For some reason, Mason had done what he was told. By the time the mug was empty, he thought for certain he would vomit all over the counter. A minute or two after that, he was right as rain. From that point on, he swore by the unusual cure for his headaches.

Mason was still stirring his coffee when another man walked into the restaurant and took the stool beside him. When Mason lifted the spoon from his mug, a viscous string of egg connected it to the thick tarlike brew.

"Whatever that is," said the man beside Mason as he pointed to the egg concoction, "don't try to serve it to me."

"What would you like?" the cook asked.

"Steak. Rare."

"You want steak?" the cook replied. "Go to the steakhouse on the first deck."

"What can you give me?"

"How about some beef stew?"

"Fine," the man grunted. "Just make it quick."

Mason took a long sip of his brew, swallowed it down, and then forced himself to have some more. "You want some advice?" he asked while letting that last gulp slide down his throat.

The man next to Mason looked over to him and said, "Yeah. I'll take some advice."

"Have a more cordial tone when you're speaking to the man who's fixing your food."

"Thanks. I'd like something else while you're at it."

Mason took another drink and set the cup down. He'd recognized the man next to him as a player from one of the many card games the previous night. Propping an elbow on the counter, Mason shifted on his stool to face him.

"I'd like the money you owe," the man said.

Squinting as he concentrated a little harder, Mason was still unable to come up with anything more than what he had done the first time. "Money? If I recall, both of us walked away from that table on the square."

"You were drinking like a fish."

Holding up his mug, Mason said, "I'll admit to that much and am paying for it in spades." When the other man didn't crack so much as a portion of a smile, Mason said, "I'll also admit to forgetting your name."

"Winslow. Dave Winslow."

"Pleased to meet you, Dave. Meet you again, that is." Once more, Mason cracked a joke and laughed at it. Once again, Winslow stared back at him as if he were watching a patch of weeds sprout in his garden.

The cook broke some of the tension by stepping up to

the counter directly across from Winslow and setting down a bowl of stew. He then dropped a spoon into it before grunting, "Anything else?"

"Not from you," Winslow replied without taking his eyes off Mason.

The cook wasn't about to be intimidated by the gruff tone in Winslow's voice or the fire in his eyes. He simply grunted under his breath and got back to the pot that was steaming on the stovetop.

Now that Winslow's food had been delivered, Mason thought he'd be granted at least a moment or two before having to resume the awkward conversation. Apparently that was setting his sights just a little too high.

"You owe some money," Winslow said. "A healthy amount of it too. I reckon a man like you would remember as much, no matter how many whiskeys he tossed back."

After downing the last of his thick, yet effective headache remedy, Mason put the mug down and said, "You're absolutely right. I would remember something like that. If I have debts to pay, I pay them. Just ask anyone who knows me. As for you, however, I know for certain that I don't owe you a thing."

"You got me there, mister. You don't owe me."

Mason was taken aback by that, but more than a little relieved. "Oh. Well, then, I suppose that's cleared up."

"Not yet, it ain't."

"Of course not," Mason sighed as he stared down at the dark muck coating the bottom of his mug. "Nothing's ever that easy."

"The money you owe is to a friend of mine," Winslow said.

"Then tell him to find me and I'll be sure to straighten this out."

Winslow used his spoon to poke at his stew. After lifting a dripping portion to his mouth, he dribbled some onto his beard and then used the back of his hand to wipe it away. "You'll deal with me."

Mason shook his head and looked around. One of the things he normally liked about being on the *Delta Jack* was that most of the people on there with him were other gamblers who all lived by the same code. Unfortunately part of that code was that a man was left to tend to his own business whether it wound up good or bad. If things with Winslow took a turn for the worse, Mason would be on his own.

"At least tell me the name of this supposed friend of yours."

Lifting the spoon to his mouth, Winslow said, "Ed Gifford," and then took a bite of his stew.

"Ed Gifford?" Mason scoffed. "I never heard of . . . oh, wait. Does he go by Giff for short?"

"He does."

Mason held back a wince as he recalled that he not only owed that man some money, but had won it from him under somewhat dubious circumstances. Keeping a straight face, he said, "This matter is between me and Giff, then. I'll have a word with him later tonight and settle up with him myself."

"That ain't gonna happen. He was put off the boat at the last port."

"Sorry to be callous, but that's really not my concern."

Winslow stood up and peeled back his jacket to reveal the gun strapped around his waist. "That's where you're wrong."

Chapter 3

Mason stepped out of the Missouri Miss Restaurant and into the same balmy air he'd been enjoying not too long ago. This time, however, he was much too distracted by the man following behind him to enjoy the scenery.

"You don't want to do this, friend," Mason said. "Trust me."

Winslow walked behind him with stew in his beard and a Colt in his hand. "I ain't your friend and I sure as hell don't trust you."

"How long have you known Giff?"

"Long enough for him to ask me to collect this debt for him."

When Mason turned around, he was jabbed in the belly by the barrel of Winslow's Colt. For added measure, he was prodded hard enough to keep him moving toward the back end of the boat. "You don't strike me as the sort of fellow who'd shoot an unarmed man."

Winslow smirked. "You tellin' me you're unarmed?"

"I was merely having a drink to soothe my aching head. Why would I be—"

Mason was interrupted when Winslow reached out to pull open the jacket to Mason's silk suit. The holster strapped under Mason's left arm was clearly visible, as was the .44 Remington kept there.

"Not armed, huh?" Winslow grunted.

"I didn't actually specify that I was the unarmed man in question. I just said I was there to soothe my aching head."

"Yeah," Winslow growled as he reached out to claim Mason's weapon and drop it into the holster at his side. "And it'll stop aching real quick once I break it open. Keep walking."

As he turned and walked toward the aft end of the boat, Mason looked for anyone who might step in on his behalf. The deck was mostly deserted since the stages on the lower level were now featuring some of the prettiest dancing girls in the South. Any of the men Mason spotted were racing to claim their seat at one of the many card games being played throughout the riverboat. He knew he'd have better luck asking for a dog to kindly let go of a piece of raw meat, but he tried to appeal to one passing fellow's sense of compassion by moving aside so he could show him the gun in Winslow's hand. The man, another gambler whose name Mason couldn't remember, merely shrugged and ducked through a door that took him into a blackjack parlor.

"Do you recall how much I'm supposed to owe Giff?"

"Four hundred dollars," Winslow replied.

"And what if I pay the money directly to you?" Mason asked. "We can part ways as friends and Giff won't be any the wiser. Surely he's no stranger to being disappointed when one of his plans doesn't bear any fruit."

"Ain't that simple."

"It can be," Mason assured him.

"Not if I ever want to get any more work like this."

And then Mason understood what was going on. This wasn't the performance of a friend or even a hired gun. It was an audition.

By this time, Mason was standing at a portion of the walkway that was as far back as one could go without dropping over the side. The serenity of being on the river was washed away by the churning rumble of the giant paddle wheel turning directly in front of him. After adjusting his jacket so it once again closed over his empty holster, Mason angled his hat to keep as much of the spray from the wheel out of his face as possible. "You want to be an overman?" he asked.

"Pay's good," Winslow replied. "Better than gambling anyway."

"But the work itself is pretty nasty. You sure you're cut out for it?"

"That's what I'm here to find out."

Overman was the name given to a small group of gunmen who kept the peace on board the *Delta Jack*. By necessity, every gambling boat had its own enforcers to put teeth into whatever house rules were in play. Without them, men running the games might as well hand their money out to any thieves who were bold enough to stick out their hands. An enforcer's job was to cut those hands off at the wrist. The enforcers working on the *Delta Jack* had earned a reputation so fearsome that losing a hand or two had become infinitely more desirable than crossing them.

"So, who is Giff to warrant such special attention?" Mason asked. "Part owner of this boat?"

"Not hardly," Winslow scoffed.

"An investor, perhaps?"

"Just give me the money."

Having crossed his arms, Mason placed a finger on his chin and made a face as though he was contemplating one of the world's great mysteries. "He must be someone important to catch the attention of a man like yourself."

"I'm here to collect a debt. You either got it or you don't."

"How do I know you're not just here to get the money for yourself?"

Winslow reacted to that question in much the same way that a large machine reacted to a wrench being tossed into its gears. "I already told you I was here for money. Are you deaf?"

"No. I mean, how am I supposed to believe that you're here for *Giff's* money? For all I know, you overheard him talking about the debt I owe to him and came along to pass yourself off as a collector. Saying you're a prospective overman could just be a way to lend some credence to your story."

As the wrench still worked its way through the machinery in his head, Winslow grimaced and grabbed hold of Mason's throat. "I don't give a damn what you decide about me. You'll hand over that money right now!"

"Or what?" Mason asked.

"You're trying my patience, mister."

Despite the fact that he was dangling from an ever-tightening fist, Mason somehow managed to smirk as he said, "If you intend to police men like myself and others on this boat, you're going to have to be well versed in making threats. If I was to grade your performance right now, I'm afraid I'd have to—"

Pinching Mason's windpipe shut, Winslow snarled, "You're about to be in more pain than you ever thought possible. That threatening enough for ya?"

"Actually," Mason croaked, "that's not bad." After saying that, he grabbed hold of Winslow's wrist with one hand while kicking the other man's knee using the heel of his boot. When Winslow grunted in pain, Mason used his free hand to relieve him of his Colt. Rather than fire a shot with the pistol, Mason thumped it against Winslow's ribs to loosen his grip.

Once he was able to pull free, Mason filled his lungs with a deep breath. "One should never harm another unless the situation calls for it," he said while rubbing the tender skin on his neck. "Bad luck."

"I'll give you bad luck!" Winslow grunted as he charged forward like an enraged bull.

All Mason had to do was take a large step to one side to clear a path. As Winslow rushed past him, Mason dropped the pistol's grip down like a hammer between Winslow's shoulder blades. It was a quick, glancing blow that did more damage to Winslow's pride than anything else. It also made his next few steps so wobbly that Winslow nearly tripped over the side and into the cold water below. Mason kept that from happening by quickly reaching out to grab the larger man's belt.

"You might want to reconsider your employment options," Mason said. "Seems you're not exactly cut out for this sort of thing."

Winslow placed both hands on the railing and pushed straight back. Since Mason still had a solid grip on his belt, Winslow found himself pulled off balance once more when he was swung toward the closest wall. He bounced off, staggered for a step or two, and then wheeled around to face Mason. Gritting his teeth through the pain that accompanied his next breath, Winslow said, "I'm gonna kill you!"

With a snap of his wrist, Mason sent the Colt he'd taken sailing through the air. A second later, the pistol hit the water with a heavy *plunk*. "You can try," he said, "but it won't be so easy."

Winslow's first instinct was to reach for his holster where he'd put Mason's Remington for safekeeping. Mason lunged for that holster as well and got to it just as the Remington cleared leather. Both men struggled to gain control of the weapon, swinging the pistol toward a nearby window looking into a roomful of card tables before it was forced in another direction to point toward the river. Winslow grunted with the effort of pushing the gun back toward Mason, who quickly snapped his head aside so the gun was no longer pointed at his face. Instead it was pointed at the face of a portly gambler on the other side of the nearby window, who gawked at the gun barrel and promptly dropped to the floor and out of sight.

Mason could hear some small amount of commotion behind the wall that Winslow had run into a few moments ago, but he knew better than to think any help was on its way. At least, none that would arrive quickly enough to do him any good. Shifting his grip on the other man's wrist, Mason dug his thumb into a tender spot as deep as it could go.

"Owww!" Winslow hollered. In less than a second, he couldn't help opening his hand and letting go of the Remington.

As soon as the pistol hit the deck, Mason kicked it away. Although he eased up on his grip somewhat, it was only so he could twist Winslow's arm around and bend it against the swing of the elbow.

When Winslow opened his mouth to let out another anguished groan, no sound emerged. His eyes were wide and his lips curled into an ugly sneer until he finally managed to suck in enough breath to clear some of the fog from his head. Winslow clenched both hands into fists. While he might not have been able to do much with the arm being held by Mason, he had plenty of options where the other was concerned. First, he delivered a chopping uppercut to Mason's stomach. Then he cocked back that arm to swing a hooking punch to Mason's jaw.

That second punch snapped Mason's head to one side, but hurt him less than the first, which had forced a good portion of the breath from his lungs. He tried his best to hang on to Winslow's right wrist. That proved to be impossible, however, when Winslow grabbed onto his own hand and pulled it back like a lever. He quickly pried himself loose and took a few staggering steps backward.

Since his holster was empty, Winslow reached for the other hip, where a hunting knife hung from a scabbard. By the time he'd taken hold of the thick bone handle, another smaller blade was already whistling through the air. Mason's arm had snapped forward like a whip and the little blade flew from his hand as though it had been shot from his fingertips.

Winslow might not have been able to see the blade as anything but a glinting flicker, but he could feel it as it sliced through the meat in his forearm. Out of reflex, he jerked that hand to the side, which also caused him to toss the hunting knife he'd just pulled. The larger blade clattered noisily against the deck while the smaller one stuck into the railing a couple of paces behind Winslow. In response to the surprised expression on Winslow's face, Mason smirked and shrugged one shoulder.

"I've got enough blades on me to do this all night long if that's your game," Mason lied.

Apparently his bluff was good enough to keep Winslow from trying to make a grab for the knife he'd inadvertently tossed. Instead he dropped to one knee and pulled up the cuff of his pants to reveal a holster concealed in that boot.

Mason lifted his shirt from where it was tucked into the front of his trousers so he could get to the pistol that was stashed there. The handle and cylinder were that of a .44 Remington very similar to the one that had already been taken from him. When he drew the gun from where it had been stashed, the second Remington proved to be very different from its brother. It had been sawed off just over an inch from the trigger guard, which allowed Mason to move freely while it had been concealed. That freedom of movement, however, came at a price.

Mason pulled his trigger, aiming several inches to the left of the man in front of him. Rather than send a shot wide where it would either take a chunk out of the railing or possibly get lodged into the paddle wheel, the bullet tore into Winslow's shin just below his knee.

At first, when Winslow dropped his gun, he couldn't make a sound. All the color drained from his face and he gulped for his next breath. As soon as he grabbed his bloody shin, he found his voice and let it fly with a warbling cry. His head craned all the way back and then drooped forward. Crumpling like a wilted flower, Winslow flopped over onto his side. After that, he was in no condition to do much of anything as Mason stepped forward to search him for any other weapons.

"Y-you killed me," Winslow groaned.

Having found nothing of note on Winslow's person, Mason kept the sawed-off Remington in an easy grip while hunkering down to the other man's level. "I did no such thing," he said. "It just feels that way. Perhaps you'll reconsider what I mentioned before about you choosing another line of work."

"I—I need a doctor."

"You sure do," Mason said while walking over to the railing where his knife had been stuck. The narrow blade was a bit longer than two inches, and its double-ring handle was only slightly shorter. Once the knife was in his hand again, Mason slipped a finger through one of the rings between the handle and blade and set the dagger to spinning. It was a finely balanced weapon that was as familiar to him as part of his own body. With an occasional wiggle of the finger around which the blade spun, he kept it twirling in a glinting display of sunlight reflecting off sharpened steel.

"I'd recommend waiting until we get to the next port," Mason said. The dagger fit into a scabbard hidden at the small of his back. Once it was in its place again, Mason didn't even feel it there. "I'm sure the captain wouldn't mind making a stop at the next town whether it's on the agenda or not." Dropping his voice a bit, Mason added, "I'd avoid the boat's doctor if I were you. He drinks most of the laudanum in his stores and doesn't have very steady hands."

Winslow nodded meekly. "Yeah," he grunted. "Just . . . get me . . . offa this boat."

Tucking the Remington back into place beneath his belt against his belly, Mason asked, "Are those the extent of your manners?"

"Get me offa this boat . . . please?"

"There, now," Mason said as he began the process of lifting Winslow to stand on one foot. "That's more like it."

Chapter 4

Mason had rarely seen any of the genuine overmen. When they were called into service, it was only in response to the kind of situation that no man wanted any part of. Since gamblers were, by their very nature, instinctual creatures, they tended to find somewhere else to be when those kinds of situations arose. After some time had passed, the *Delta Jack* was indeed brought to the next port, which belonged to a small town that could barely be seen from the banks. It should have been large enough to have a doctor at least. Mason watched from the third deck as one large fellow in a pearl gray suit dragged Winslow down the gangplank.

"It was a lucky shot," Winslow said while hopping on his good leg to keep up with the other man. "I swear! Tell Mr. . . ."

Having reached the end of the gangplank, the man escorting Winslow stopped and spoke to him in a low growl. He stood at average height and had a solid build. On a strictly physical basis, Winslow was larger. Something about the other man's demeanor gave him a more imposing bearing that seemed to shrink Winslow down to a smaller size. Mason strained to hear what he was saying but couldn't make out much from his vantage point. What he did see, however, was the short club hanging from the man's belt that marked him as one of the *Jack*'s enforcers.

"I understand," Winslow said. Strangely enough, his voice cut through the thick balmy air just fine. "Will I at least get the pay I was promised for this job? After all, I did put the scare into him pretty good and nearly managed to collect some of the debt."

The overman straightened up and glared at Winslow. For a moment, Mason was certain Winslow was about to catch a beating. As a few more seconds passed, Winslow slowly recoiled. All the other man had to do was keep glaring at him to convince Winslow that he needed to drop the subject he'd just broached and just walk away.

"All right, then," Winslow said as he hobbled along the short dock leading into whatever town was nearby. "I'll be on my way. Never mind about my fee."

The overman stood at the end of the gangplank, silently watching.

"Give my best to Mr. Greeley!" Winslow shouted.

By now, a few locals had appeared on the road leading from the dock into town. When they saw the bloody, hastily bandaged wound on Winslow's leg, they rushed forward to help him walk. One of them shouted, "This man's been hurt! What happened?"

The man at the end of the gangplank shifted just enough to turn his gaze toward the locals. He held it there for a second and then showed his back to all of them.

The locals watched the overman walk away but had no interest in approaching him or even asking another question. Instead they spoke to Winslow, who quickly hushed them and did his best to hurry toward town.

Mason watched the whole scene while leaning with his elbows against the railing. He let out a low whistle and said, "I've gotta learn how to silence someone like that."

Once the overman was back on board and the gangplank was raised, the riverboat's engines turned the paddle wheel once more. The *Delta Jack* let out a whistle and was on her way upstream. One of the doors behind Mason was opened and a gentleman in a tan suit emerged from a room where a bawdy song was being played on a banjo.

The gentleman brought a cigar to his lips, took a long pull from it, and exhaled a smoky breath. "Were we stopped?" he asked.

"Just for a short spell," Mason said.

"What for?"

"Had to get rid of some extra cargo."

Taking another puff from his cigar, the gentleman asked, "Must be an awfully small town at the end of that road. Any fresh fish come aboard?"

"Nope."

Since he didn't have any new players to scout, the gentleman shrugged and shifted his attention farther along the deck to where one of the working girls was having a stroll. He approached her and was eagerly greeted, which marked the end of his interest in the *Jack*'s unscheduled stop.

Mason was fairly certain almost everyone else aboard the riverboat either cared just as little for the distraction or hadn't even noticed it at all. They had their own business to conduct and might not have noticed if the riverboat chugged past a raging battlefield. He reached into his pocket to check his watch. It was early evening, which meant the regular folks in the town where Winslow had gone would be eating dinner soon. The gamblers on the *Delta Jack*, on the other hand, would be eating their evening meal anytime between now and midnight. Time didn't mean much at a card table. At least, not in any traditional sense. There was simply a time to start playing and a time to stop. Mason's starting time was swiftly approaching. He felt it in his bones. The hands on his watch were merely there to let him know what schedule the rest of the world was observing. He snapped the watch shut and promptly put such things out of his mind.

"Damn," he said to himself. "I love my job."

Over the course of the next hour, Mason prepared himself for that night's work. He went to his room where he could splash some water over himself so he was nice and fresh beneath his expensive suit. To give himself a more formal appearance, he pulled on a coat that came down to just above his knees. The standard .44 Remington was tucked into a holster beneath his left arm, but that was mostly for show. Everyone on the *Delta Jack* was armed. In fact, the first thing most passengers looked for was what kind of firepower another man was packing. If they saw what was in Mason's shoulder holster, they would most likely overlook the other weapons stashed throughout his person.

The sawed-off version of his Remington was tucked against his belly.

The dagger went into its scabbard at the small of his back.

Mason paused while going through the carpetbag containing his belongings. Reaching inside, he found an old knuckle-duster that he'd carried with him since his earliest years on the gambling circuit. It was a crude, simple weapon made to slip over four fingers to reinforce his fist to deliver one mighty wallop. In addition to being a set of brass knuckles, the set Mason carried also had a short point on one end. When worn, the point extended from the bottom of his hand like a small dagger clenched in his fist. He slipped the weapon on, closed his fingers around the weathered metal, and smiled. That knuckle-duster had always brought him luck. And when his luck took a turn as it always did, the little weapon went a long way in getting him out of it.

Even though the knuckle-duster was very useful, he decided against taking it along with him this evening. Mason packed it away at the bottom of his bag, patting it with the tenderness someone might show a family heirloom.

There were other weapons in that bag along with various, less lethal, tools of his trade. Mason ran his hand over all of them in a specific order at a specific speed until he'd brushed his fingertips against everything in there. Feeling centered and calm, he closed the bag and stood up.

His room was small, containing a narrow bed, a dresser, and a washbasin. On any other day, he was anxious to step outside the confined space to get a breath of fresh air before delving into the cornucopia of sights and sounds filling the card rooms and saloons packed into the *Delta Jack*. Tonight, he welcomed the quiet of his room and the way his four walls muffled the sounds of music, shouting, and revelry coming from all three decks.

He closed his eyes and gave himself a moment for all of his senses to drink in whatever they could.

After taking his moment of calm, Mason opened his eyes. He set his carpetbag on the floor between his bed and the cabin's back wall where it couldn't easily be seen. Standing in front of his door, he straightened the lapels of his coat and shot his cuffs.

"All right," he said. "Time to go to work."

Chapter 5

Mason's feet carried him quickly and lightly to the stairs and brought him all the way down to the first deck, where the night's biggest games would be played. There was plenty going on around him along the way, but Mason would not be distracted.

The prettiest girls on board all came out in the evening and yet none of them could hold his gaze for any longer than it took Mason to smile and tip his hat.

In the middle of the main deck was the *Delta Jack*'s largest card room. Oftentimes, it served as a way to catch the eye of the freshest passengers to step onto the riverboat. Tonight, it lived up to the promises made by the expensive rugs, crystal chandeliers, polished brass along the bar, and lavish dresses worn by the soiled doves who'd earned the right to patrol that space. Mason cut straight through the room until he reached a wall of humanity formed by some of the largest men he'd ever seen.

In most saloons, those hired to protect the money on the table wore their guns in holsters or stashed beneath a long coat. These carried sawed-off shotguns in plain sight and scowled at anyone in their vicinity to make their cruel intentions known. One of them, a barrel-chested fellow with a mustache that connected to his brushy sideburns, stared down at Mason as if from atop a mountain. "Find a game somewhere else," he said. "This one's invitation only."

"But I have an invitation," Mason said.

"Let's see it."

Mason smiled. "You won't trip me up that easily. There aren't any invitations printed, but that is a good way to smoke out the impostors looking to sneak into this game."

"What's your name?" the guard asked.

"Abner Mason."

The guard looked over to one of his partners, who gave him a barely perceptible nod. "All right," he said while shifting to one side.

Even though the way had been cleared for him, Mason couldn't help feeling leery as he maneuvered between the hulking armed men. The bit of fear niggling at the back of his mind flared up when the guard spoke again.

"Not so fast," he said.

"Oh yes!" Mason replied cheerily. "I'll need some chips. Two thousand should be a good start. Let me just . . ." When he reached into a pocket for the money, all but one of the guards brought their shotguns to bear on him. Hammers clacked back, the sound of which caused many people in that room to take notice.

"Put your hands where we can see them," the guard warned. "Slowly."

"Of course," Mason said. Once he raised his hands and it became clear that he wasn't about to be cut down by the shotguns, the other gamblers observing from a distance went back to what they'd been doing.

The guard who'd spoken to Mason kept his eyes and aim locked on him while one of the others started patting him down.

Keeping his hands up as he was searched, Mason said, "Awfully nice weather we've been having. Makes for a better voyage."

None of the guards spoke or responded in any way to the sound of his voice.

Undeterred by the situation, Mason asked, "Is it called a voyage or is that term only for seagoing vessels? Perhaps this is just a trip or . . . cruise?"

The guard patting Mason down found the Remington under his arm first and took it away. The holster was peeled off in a brusque manner that left more than a few bruises on Mason's back and shoulders.

"Then again, I'm not even sure if bad weather affects the river the way it would hamper a ship on the sea," Mason continued. "I've been fortunate enough to have smooth waters most of the time while I've been on the *Jack*."

Mason's belly gun was found next, along with the knife at the small of his back.

"Perhaps I'm a good-luck charm for this boat?" Mason offered.

The guard actually let out a single grunt of a laugh at that one.

After patting down Mason's legs and inspecting his boots, the guard behind him stood up and said, "He's clean."

"Oh my," Mason said as a short brunette with ample curves wrapped in a tight corset stepped into his line of sight. "I didn't see you there."

She showed him a pleasant smile while holding a

large silver tray. On it was all the weapons that had been confiscated from Mason's person.

"I'll be wanting those back after the game," he said. "And in the same condition in which they were found."

She curtsied and turned away to take the weapons with her.

"That's what I like about this boat," Mason said. "Even when a man is being treated like a prisoner, it's still done with style."

"When you're a prisoner," the guard said to him, "you'll know it. Did you say two thousand in chips?"

"That should be enough to get me rolling."

Judging by the look on the guard's face, it wasn't the first time he'd heard a boast along those lines. He walked over to a small lockbox beside several stacks of clay chips. "Where's your money?"

"In my pocket," Mason replied. "I'm surprised your associate didn't find it already, along with my liver and kidneys." When he didn't get a reaction, he added, "Just a joke, of course. Very thorough search earlier." Finally he said, "I'll just get it now." The guards all had the utmost confidence in the search that had been conducted, because not one of them flinched when Mason reached under his coat this time. He removed a fat wad of cash that he'd been building since his arrival on the *Delta Jack* and peeled off the required amount. The rest went into his pocket, where he hoped it would remain for the duration of the game.

The guard took the money and handed over several stacks of chips in return. Having handled so much cash every night as part of his regular duties, he dumped the bills Mason gave him into the lockbox like a cook handling just another cut of pork. "Take your seat."

"Any seat?" Mason asked.

"Sure."

Half of the seats were already filled at the large round table. One chair was taken by a rough-looking man with a scar running down one cheek. Another by a thin young man with hair so light that it almost looked white and the third was occupied by a woman with a trim build, exotic features, and a long mane of flowing black hair.

"Don't mind if I do," Mason said as he settled into the chair between the two men. From that spot, he was directly across from the lady who idly shuffled a deck of cards. "I'm guessing you gentlemen are sitting at this table for the same reason I am." Tipping his hat, Mason said, "The magnificent view."

"Don't get any ideas," said the man with the scar on Mason's left. "I saw her first."

"Abner Mason."

"Clint Hayes."

"Nice to meet you, Clint. Sorry to say you'll be quite disappointed later when I'm enjoying the lady's company."

"Doesn't the lady have anything to say about that?" she asked from across the table.

"No," Mason replied with a grin. "That's how chivalry works. Ironically it's mostly between the menfolk."

"I'll keep that in mind. I'm Maggie, by the way."

"Do you have a last name, Maggie?" Mason asked.

"Yes." With that, she calmly continued to shuffle her cards.

"Glad to see her treat you like somethin' she scraped off her shoe," said the blond man to Mason's right. "I was worried I was the only one to get that from Her Majesty over there."

"Comrades at the bottom of the pecking order," Mason said before extending his hand and formally introducing himself.

"Dan Andrews," the blond man replied. "Good to meet ya."

Suddenly Maggie stopped shuffling and sat up straighter. "Someone's coming," she said with excitement creeping in around the edges of her voice.

"Did she act like that when I showed up?" Mason asked.

"No," Clint replied. "She did have a good laugh when you were getting searched, though."

"Nice."

The man who arrived at the table next did so without so much as a word from any of the guards. In fact, they parted for him like the Red Sea clearing a path for Moses. He looked to be right around Mason's height, but lighter than him by at least thirty pounds. Some of that difference came from a distinct lack of hair on top of his head. The hair that remained formed a ring from the backside of one ear all the way around to the other. His nose was just a bit too long and his eyebrows just a little too bushy. The clothes he wore were well tailored, however, which was something in his favor at least.

"Now I see why Maggie didn't pay us any mind," Mason said.

Squinting to get a look at the new arrival, Dan reached into his shirt pocket for a pair of spectacles, which didn't seem to help him very much. "Why?" he asked.

"Because not one of the three of us sitting here owns this boat."

As if to further prove Mason's point, Maggie stood up and quickly primped her hair before the skinny man in the nice suit made it to the table. "Evening, Mr. Greeley," she said.

The skinny man took the seat between her and Dan. Setting down enough chips to build a small fort in front of him, he showed the other players a crooked smile and said, "Good evening to you all. So glad you accepted my invite. Shall we play some poker?"

"It's what I live for," Mason said.

Chapter 6

Cam Greeley didn't look like a man who would own something like the *Delta Jack*. Instead he looked more like someone who would tend bar on the riverboat or possibly own a saloon somewhere. Mason had only met Greeley on a couple of occasions before that night. One was the first time he'd boarded the *Jack* and the second was when he happened to find himself on the riverboat during a holiday. It was either Christmas or New Year's. Whatever the reason, Greeley had made an appearance to raise his glass in a toast, shake a few hands including Mason's, and then leave for some other part of the boat.

"I'll raise," Greeley announced.

The current game had been going for a few hours by now, which was enough time for all the players to become comfortable with one another. Mason had always thought leaders of countries and heads of state should meet over a game of cards. A felt-covered table piled high with chips was a mighty good equalizer. There, all men were judged by their actions. That didn't necessarily mean every hand was fair or that each game ran strictly by the agreed-upon rules. Some men relied on their skill at the game itself or the fine art of bending the rules to suit any given situation. Much like a politician, the most successful gambler used a combination of both to win the most important hands.

And then there was the element of luck. Only a fool was unaware of the role luck played in any given situation at or away from a card table. Luck was an element that was always in play in a gambling den, the bedroom, the battlefield, or any other spot where more than one element came together to create a result. Luck was always present and could never be controlled, but that didn't mean it couldn't be swayed. That was where skill came into it.

If Mason thought about the vicious circle for too long, his head started to swim. But he had to think about it when he sat at a table. Otherwise he might become lost in the hopeless notion that he was adrift in a sea of random chance. By the time Greeley touched the mountain of chips in front of him again, the torrent inside Mason's head had slowed to a more comfortable flow.

"Two hundred," Greeley said before pushing in enough chips to make the pot right.

Dan was the sort of player who handed over too much of his game to luck. He had more than enough chips to cover the bet that had been posed to him, but not much more. Mason watched him from the corner of his eye while sliding one of his own chips around the tip of one finger. He guessed Dan was going to fold and all that remained was to see how long it would take. Of course, Mason was always ready to be surprised by something other than what he guessed would happen.

Surprises were good things. They kept life interesting. Dan gave him a small one when he called the bet.

"Two hundred to me?" Mason asked.

Greeley nodded.

Clint said, "That's the bet, Abner."

Maggie raised an eyebrow. Possibly she thought it meant something when he repeated the amount of the bet as compared to the times when he'd simply acted. The truth of the matter was that Mason was well aware of when he spoke and what words he used before making his play. It was a very careful mixture of talking or not talking when he was either betting or folding, weak or strong. To anyone looking for a glimpse into what was going through Mason's head or a tell to let them know what he might do, it was a trail that led nowhere.

Taking another second to make it look as though he was considering his options, Mason said, "Why not? I'll call."

" 'Course you will," Clint said. "Raise."

Mason wasn't exactly surprised by that, since Clint had proven to be the sort who liked to think he had folks figured out before he'd even met them. Still, he reacted as if he was taken at least slightly aback by the development.

"What do you say, Maggie?" Clint asked.

She drew a deep breath and tapped a finger against one stack of chips. Something about her seemed mildly annoyed, but that was most likely because Clint had been trying to get on her good side since the game started. "I don't have much to say until you tell us how much you're going to raise," she replied.

The tactic was a ham-handed attempt to see if he might get some reaction from the player who was next in line to act. Since it didn't work, Clint said, "Fair enough," and slid one stack of chips forward. "Make it another three hundred."

Of all the players at the table, Maggie was one of the tougher ones for Mason to read. He'd be doing her a disservice if he chalked that up to her gender alone. Women did have a knack for keeping their true intentions out of plain sight, but this one had yet to get rattled by turns of misfortune or even overly excited when things went her way. Mason found that to be more than just intriguing.

"Call," she said. When she put her money in the pot, she did it without remorse or anticipation.

It was Greeley's turn again. For a man sitting behind as many chips as he was to overthink a raise of that size would have been posturing. From what Mason had seen, he didn't think Greeley was the sort who did much posturing. After taking a few seconds to weigh his odds, Greeley scratched his chin and pushed in enough chips to call the raise. Mason didn't think the chin scratch hinted at much of anything, but he wasn't about to write it off just yet.

The game they were playing was five-card stud. It was the last round of dealing and every bet had been called, which meant there was only one more card due to each player. Clint was the dealer this time around and he got busy flipping each player his last hope for a victory.

Some might have found it odd to know how long it had been since Mason looked at any of the other players' cards or even his own. Anyone who would have thought that, however, was most definitely not a professional gambler. Each person at that table had one down card and three faceup in front. It was a lot to take in and digest but was actually the least complicated part of the game. If it was just about the cards, figuring out what to do on each betting round would have been a simple matter of mathematics and statistics. Like any player who made a living at a poker table, Mason studied the other players much harder than the cards he or any of them had.

Now that the last cards were being dropped onto the table, it was not the time to look at them. Instead Mason watched each person's reaction to the card as soon as the player saw what it was. Since the other players were doing the same thing, he had to pretend that he was looking at his cards so the others would actually take a gander at theirs. If there wasn't so much money in the middle of the table, the entire charade would seem rather funny.

Mason had a pair of sevens showing in front of him and not much else. The card in his hand was a ten, which matched the ten of hearts that he'd just been given. Considering what else was out there, it wasn't enough to get his blood pumping.

Maggie already had him beat with the set of deuces she had showing. Her fourth card was the nine of diamonds, which she barely looked at for half a second. She bet her deuces by opening with fifty dollars tossed into the middle.

Next in line was Greeley. While he didn't have any pairs showing, all of his cards were clubs. Mason hoped against hope for some sort of reaction from him when that last card was dealt. No reaction would have most likely meant that his flush was already busted. Even the slightest twitch in the corner of one eye would have been enough to let Mason in on the victory dance the other man was doing in the back of his head. Greeley gave nothing away. From a man who'd risen to his level in the gambling profession, Mason wouldn't have expected any less.

"Raise," Greeley said as he pushed in another fifty.

Dan had two pairs: threes and sixes. Every card he'd gotten throughout the night, no matter what it was, had been regarded with the same amount of mild disdain. It wasn't the most original tactic but was effective enough to keep his head above water thus far. He called the hundred-dollar bet without saying a word.

That left Mason with two options. He could fold a hand that was already beat by at least one other player or he could put the rest of the table to a test. "Two hundred more," he said. When he put his money in the middle, Mason considered it an investment. If he got anything more than another look at what the other players would do, he'd consider it a bonus.

Clint didn't have much of anything in front of him, but there were some interesting possibilities for his hold card to put something together. If he held an ace in his hand to match the one showing, he had nothing but a pair. If he had a queen to fill out a straight, he was in pretty good shape. So far that evening, he hadn't seemed interested in doing much bluffing. That didn't mean that Clint hadn't bluffed. He could just be very good at it. So far, Mason couldn't tell which it was and he watched carefully for anything that might sway his opinion one way or another.

"I suppose I should bump it again," Clint said. Instead of matching his previous raise, he raised two hundred. Afterward, Mason detected a glimmer of something in his eye. It looked an awful lot like a man saying good-bye to a loved one.

When Maggie looked over at Clint, she didn't seem

very worried. Almost certainly, she'd caught sight of the same thing that Mason had. One by one, she studied the other men. Finally she let out a haggard sigh and tossed her card onto the pile of discards. "You all can fight for it," she said. Now that she was out of it, Maggie allowed herself to relax. When she leaned back in her chair, she looked up and caught Mason staring at her.

She brushed a few stray wisps of hair from her face and kept her eyes on him.

As much as Mason wanted to keep her in his sight, he wasn't about to be distracted in one of the oldest ways known to mankind.

"Raise," Greeley announced in the same tone of voice he'd used when adding fifty dollars to the pot. This time, however, he shoved six hundred toward the middle of the table.

Having a rich man try to buy a pot wasn't new. Having someone like Dan bump it up again without so much as a flinch, on the other hand, was enough to raise more than a few eyebrows.

"You sure you wanna do that?" Greeley asked.

Dan chuckled nervously. "Would you let me pull it back in if I said no?"

Greeley let that go without a word and shifted his gaze toward Mason.

"I'd like to take a stab at this," Mason said. "But I'm guessing one of you would only try to steal the buttons from my suit."

"You're out, then?" Greeley asked impatiently.

Sliding his hold card away like a child refusing to eat what was left on his plate, Mason said, "That's right."

"Take it," Clint groaned.

"That leaves me, does it?" Greeley said.

Dan shifted in his seat. "Unless there's another player sitting here that I haven't seen yet."

"You make that full house?"

"Even if I didn't," Dan replied, "what I got beats the trash you've got on the table."

"Depends on what I'm holding here," Greeley said as he tapped the card that lay facedown in front of him.

"Yes," Dan said calmly. "It most certainly does."

Chapter 7

Mason tried to read Dan's face as if he were the one faced with Greeley's decision. As with a scholar studying any subject, it was always a good idea to partake in hypothetical problems when he wasn't hip deep in the real thing. Thus far, Dan had presented himself as a typical cautious player: quiet, conservative, predictable. Mason hadn't allowed himself to be lulled to sleep by that, but he hadn't seen much of anything to refute it either. Now Dan was taking a bold step.

If he was bluffing, he was doing a fine job of it.

If he had a hand, he was committing himself to it wholeheartedly like a captain running several paces in front of his men with saber drawn during a charge.

Either of them was an impressive sight to behold.

Greeley took a deep breath and began sorting his chips. First he cut off enough to cover the raise. He looked at that for a few seconds, looked up at Dan, and then looked back down again. Next, he started slicing off smaller pieces of his pie. As each little pile of chips joined the call, Greeley scowled as if he were letting go of a beloved pet.

Everyone at that table knew it was an act. Mason was

certain of that much. If any of them truly thought the owner of the *Delta Jack* could be that concerned about money, they would have been plucked clean and hung out to dry long before now.

"I'm raising," Greeley said.

"Obviously," Dan snapped.

The quickness of Dan's reply, combined with the inflection in his voice, gave Greeley a sliver of information.

After counting up the chips he'd sectioned off, Greeley took another stack and pushed them in to the middle of the table. "Two thousand more," he said.

Without hesitation, and wearing a flicker of a grin that lasted for less than a heartbeat, Dan pushed everything he had in front of him. "And another twenty-two hundred seventy on top of it."

Greeley didn't know what to make of that.

Mason wasn't so sure either. In fact, he hadn't felt more grateful for anything in a while than he did for not having to be the one to make the decision that had just been put to the *Delta Jack*'s owner.

After staring at the chips Dan put in the middle of the table, Greeley said, "That's not enough to cover a raise that size."

"I have a line of credit here," Dan said. "This may be putting me to my limit, but it should cover it well enough."

"Credit?"

Dan blinked. "Yes. Credit issued by your cashier. You do still honor your own credit, right?"

"Of course I do," Greeley said with an angry edge to his voice. At least, Mason thought it was anger. So far, he'd never heard the *Jack*'s owner when he was angry. He'd heard stories about such instances, which were enough to make him certain he didn't want to be on the receiving end of it. Watching from a distance, on the other hand, was worth pulling the strings necessary to be invited to this game.

Keeping his eyes on Dan, Greeley raised one hand and snapped his fingers. One of the men guarding the table strode over to him like any well-trained attack dog. "Yes, Mr. Greeley?" he said.

"Have a word with Tilly," Greeley told him. "Ask her how much credit has been extended to Mr. Andrews here."

"Yes, sir."

The guard turned and walked away. As he passed the other guards, he handed over his shotgun and kept moving toward a cage at the back of the room where the boat's cashier and accountants performed their duties. Holding two shotguns instead of one seemed perfectly natural to the guard who remained behind.

Mason had to shift his focus back to Greeley. He would have assumed that Greeley knew the accounts connected to any of the players in front of him, but now he wasn't so sure. Greeley seemed genuinely flustered as he tapped a finger against his chin while staring daggers at the man to his left.

As for Dan Andrews . . . it seemed he was close to dozing off for a spell.

For the next several moments, the only sounds to be heard were those that drifted in from the rest of the room. Other games were in full swing. Girls laughed at men trying to woo them. Drunks told jokes or groused about something or other. In one of the other rooms on the deck above, music was being played.

Glancing toward the closest window, Mason said, "Hell of a nice night out there." His tone was friendly, but his voice came so suddenly that it hit the table like a brick tossed through a pane of glass. It might have been somewhat childish to purposely give the other players a start like that, but Mason simply couldn't help himself.

Clint suppressed a chuckle, but just barely. "It sure is," he said.

Maggie rolled her eyes.

Dan chuckled under his breath while idly drumming his fingers against the table.

Greeley leaned back and crossed his legs. Although he wasn't being so obvious about staring at Dan, he was still studying him.

It was easy enough for Mason to track the guard through the rest of the room. The man had a bulky build, but that wasn't what caused everyone he encountered to step politely back to clear the way for him. Even from a distance, Mason could feel the relief pouring out of those folks once it was clear that the man in the infamous gray suit wasn't coming for them. Mason had suspected that all the guards at that game were overmen and now he felt comfortable in changing that suspicion to a certainty.

When he arrived at the table, the guard collected his shotgun and walked straight over to Greeley's chair. "Seventeen hundred and seventy, Mr. Greeley," he said. "That's how much credit is left on his account."

Greeley didn't insult the other players by trying to make it look as though that was any sort of revelation to him. He merely nodded.

"Tilly wanted to know," the overman continued, "if the credit should be suspended."

"No need for that," Greeley replied.

"She also wanted to know if you wanted it extended."

With the lilt of an eyebrow, Greeley passed that proposition over to Dan.

"One hand at a time," was all Dan had to say to that.

Suddenly Greeley's mood seemed to improve. That was undoubtedly a surface affectation, but it was a good one all the same. "A smart way to live, sir," he declared. To the overman standing nearby, he said, "I'll let you know if Tilly needs to be informed of anything else. Run along, now."

Dismissing the overman as if he were shooing away a lapdog was even more impressive than any other display thus far. Mason, along with anyone else at that table, didn't need to be reminded of the guns at Greeley's disposal, but it was quite another matter to be shown firsthand.

Mason shifted his weight, careful not to make any noise.

"Your play," Clint said. Perhaps he'd wanted to show he wasn't frightened by the muscle being flexed by the overmen nearby, but it was still out of turn and Clint knew it.

Greeley would have been well within his rights to put Clint in his place, but he didn't. All he needed to do was snap his eyes across the table for a second and Clint backed down with an apologetic shrug.

Times like these were why Mason preferred to play from the position of a man who simply knew what he was doing and had a decent amount of funding to back it up. Being someone with Greeley's stature brought with it a whole other set of concerns. If he looked weak, there were any number of sharks in the water poised to take a bite out of him. If he looked heavy-handed, some of the more delectable fish in the water might get frightened away and leave him hungry.

If Greeley folded, he could look weak. Even worse, if he folded and Dan showed a bluff, Greeley would look like a fool.

If Greeley called and Dan was bluffing, he would look brilliant while Dan would be reduced to ashes. If Greeley called and Dan wasn't bluffing . . . well, that wasn't very favorable for a man in Greeley's line of work.

It was a tricky quandary, which was why Mason intended to retire someplace quiet once he pulled together enough money to call it a fortune instead of buying his own casino.

"You want me to call?" Greeley asked.

Dan continued drumming his fingers. Expecting him to jump at the chance to answer that question was hopeful on Greeley's part. Despite the cynical nature of gamblers, they were still strangely hopeful in a desperate situation.

Finally Greeley made his decision. "What the hell?" he declared. "It's only money. I call."

At that point, Dan wasn't about to string Greeley along. He tipped his hand to Mason before showing his hold card, however, when he glanced over to the row of overmen stationed a scant number of paces away from the table. Not that Mason could blame him. If he was about to take that much money away from someone like Cam Greeley, he'd be nervous too.

Dan flipped over his card. It was the six of clubs, which gave him a full house.

"I'll be damned!" Clint said.

One corner of Maggie's mouth turned upward as if she was not only seeing Dan in a new light, but enjoying the sight.

Mason was impressed as well but preferred to keep that fact under his hat for the moment.

"Nicely done, sir," Greeley said.

Graciously Dan replied, "Thank you."

"I had suspicions that you were holding something good, but I just had to see for myself."

"I understand. Done the same a few times myself," Dan said while raking in his pot.

"Would you like the balance credited to your account or would you prefer cash?"

"Credit will be fine, Mr. Greeley. I know you're good for it."

Greeley barely had to shift in his chair to summon an overman. When the scary fellow stepped up to the table, Greeley reached into his jacket pocket for a small notebook bound in leather. "Take this to Tilly," he said while scribbling on the pad with a little pencil. "Have this amount added to Mr. Andrews's account."

The overman took the piece of paper and folded it in half without looking at what had been written on it. He then turned and made his way through the crowd once more to the cage at the back of the room.

Even as he stacked all those chips while surely thinking about all the credit being written beside his name in Tilly's ledger, Dan barely cracked a smile. He seemed satisfied, but not overly so. Pleased with himself, but not to the point of arrogance. As Mason watched him, he knew he'd misread that man in a big way. He was just happy that it had been Greeley and not himself at the end of the move that had just been made.

"Let's deal the next game," Greeley said while clapping his hands together anxiously. "Next round of drinks is on me. Sorry to keep you all waiting during that last hand."

"No hard feelings," Clint said. "That was a hell of a show."

Mason had to concur with that sentiment. In fact, he was certain things would only get better from there.

Chapter 8

The next couple of hands went fairly well. Obeying one of the many unspoken rules in poker, Dan kept his head down and mouth shut for a while after taking such a large pot. Clint was happy just to be in the game again, which loosened his purse strings a bit. Greeley played the part of a good host and consoled himself by attempting to gain some ground with Maggie. Since she wasn't interested in either of the men beside her, she kept her eyes pointed straight ahead. Mason was sitting right there in her line of sight, happy to be the lesser of the table's evils.

Just to test the waters, Mason raised a hundred dollars based solely on the pair of nines in front of him. He had nothing in his hand and there were still two cards left to be dealt, but Dan and Maggie were already out and neither of the other two men had cards showing that could beat a pair.

"Raise," Clint announced as he pushed in just a bit too much money.

"I've got a few matters to tend to," Greeley said. He pitched his cards and stood up. "I won't be long. Care to join me, Maggie?"

"You want me to join you while tending to business matters?" she asked.

"Pleasure," he said while opening his arms as if to embrace his entire boat, "is my business. And it would be my pleasure for you to join me."

Greeley had been drinking along with everyone else and could very well have been playing up his intoxication, but any man with a pulse would have made a similar offer to Maggie if he was in Greeley's shoes. To her credit, she did a very good job of spurning his advances when she said, "I've still got a lot of ground to cover to make up my losses. Maybe some other time?"

"Most definitely." With that, Greeley left.

It wasn't one of the larger pots of the night, but Mason wound up taking it by calling Clint's ill-advised raise. "Anyone care to change things up a bit?"

"What's on your mind?" Clint asked.

"How about a few hands of draw instead of stud?"

"Sounds good to me. I could use a change of luck. Anyone else have any objections?"

It was Dan's turn to deal and he gathered up the cards to start shuffling them. "No objections from me."

"What about you, Maggie?" Mason asked.

"I don't like draw," she said.

"Maybe you just haven't given it a chance. You know, it's unfair to judge something unless you've given it a try. I may be able to open your eyes to some things you'd quite enjoy."

Scowling to let him know that she was aware he wasn't just talking about poker, Maggie said, "I think I'd rather take my chances with five-card draw."

"Suit yourself. Danny," Mason said while lifting his

hand in a mocking tribute to the way Greeley summoned his overmen, "you may deal when ready."

Dan shuffled one more time and then started flipping the cards out one at a time.

Collecting his cards under one hand, Mason perked up a bit when he saw the row of overmen all turn toward a central point. He couldn't see what they were looking at, but he could hazard a guess. "Looks like we've got another player coming," he said.

"About time," Clint grunted.

"Did you know someone else was due to arrive?"

"No, but there's been an empty chair beside me all night long and I figured someone was bound to fill it."

"Good," Maggie sighed. "Maybe that'll make it harder for you to leer at me whenever you think I'm not looking."

"If you didn't want a man looking, you shouldn't give him so much to look at."

Maggie's neckline did drop to an enticingly low point, and the bodice of her dress most definitely hugged her figure in a way that could be distracting. Rather than do anything to cover herself up, she turned her head while running the tip of her tongue along her bottom lip and said, "I'm only interested in interesting men."

"What about rich men?" Dan asked.

She, as well as Clint and Mason, was surprised to hear such a bold comment coming from someone who'd been content to remain so quiet. Mason raised his glass to him and said, "A fair question, sir!"

Maggie looked at him with a warmth in her eyes that could melt butter. "Rich and soft-spoken. That's an irresistible combination."

"Eh, just deal the cards," Clint groused.

The other three at the table had a good laugh while

Dan finished his deal. Before taking a look at what he'd been given, Mason took another glance at what was happening with the overmen.

"Definitely another player," he said. "And he seems to have passed muster."

The others at the table all looked in that direction as the guards stepped aside to let the new arrival through. He was dressed in a suit that was well fitting, if not impeccably tailored. The brown bowler on top of his head was removed to reveal a short crop of light brown hair. His having just endured a vigorous search, his jacket was open and slightly rumpled. Mason couldn't see any shapely girl with a silver tray of weaponry, so he guessed the slender gambler had come to the game unarmed.

Clint pulled out the chair that Mason hadn't noticed before and even went through the motions of dusting it off. "Have a seat," he said. "We just started a hand, but you're more than welcome to join us on the next one."

"Obliged," the new player said in a mildly grating voice.

Introductions were made all around and when it was his turn, the man in the modest suit said, "I'm Jervis Crane. Pleased to meet all of you."

"Likewise," Dan replied.

The first round of betting commenced with a paltry wager made by Maggie and everyone else tossing in enough to call.

"How do you know Mr. Greeley?" Mason asked.

"I've been making the rounds for half a dozen years now," Jervis said. "Mr. Greeley played in a tournament in New Orleans. A tournament I won. He invited me to come aboard the *Delta Jack* sometime, and when I got here, I was to look him up. I did and wound up getting invited to this game. Not a very exciting story."

"You can always embellish," Mason said. "We sit at tables like these for quite a long time. Embellished stories are always appreciated."

Jervis nodded. "I'll remember that."

Judging by Jervis's ramrod-straight posture and tightly wound features, Mason had no doubt the conversation would indeed be remembered word for word. In the meantime, he placed his chips in separate piles and went through great lengths to make certain they were all of equal height and distance from one another.

If Jervis embellished any other stories while they played through the next few hands, he did a miserable job at it, because they were only slightly better than his account of meeting Greeley. Mason and Clint picked up the slack by spinning some yarns of their own. After two hours had passed, even Maggie was laughing along with the rest of them. At least, Mason guessed the noises Jervis made were laughter. It was either that or he'd gotten something lodged in his throat and was trying to shake it loose.

Mason was just about to ask if anyone thought Greeley was coming back to the table when he got his answer. The boat's slender owner walked to his row of overmen with each arm draped around a different girl, wearing a smile that was bright enough to light up the room with enough left over to reflect off the water outside.

"Here comes our host," Mason said. "Looks like he took a bit of time for himself."

Looking over to Maggie, Clint asked, "What about you, darlin'? Want to take some time for ourselves?"

"Sure," she replied. "I can get away from you for a while and then meet back here to win some more of your money."

"Very funny."

Greeley said his farewells to the women accompanying him by kissing one on the ear and swatting the other on her backside. Both of his companions giggled, waved, and went in separate directions to find their next customers.

"It looks like you all have kept busy," Greeley said as he sat down. "And I see you've met Mr. Crane. Hopefully you're all getting along."

"Famously," Mason said. "We were just about to deal the next hand. The game's changed to five-card draw."

"But I am more than willing to play another," Jervis said.

Greeley waved that off. "Nonsense. Variety is the spice of life."

A comment regarding Greeley's variety in feminine companions sprang to Mason's mind, but he decided not to let it fly. There was no reason to rock the boat, especially with the man who owned the boat.

They dealt the cards and Greeley was in high spirits for several hands. Although the rest of the table quieted down considerably, it wasn't out of deference to the rich man's arrival. Having another player, especially one of Greeley's caliber, changed the whole complexion of a game, and everyone needed a short while to adjust.

Mason generally considered draw to be a game better suited for timid players. Not having any cards showing left a lot to the imagination. It was, however, an excellent forum in which to bluff. Because of that, he'd managed to pull in enough pots to put himself more than a little bit ahead for the night. He wasn't certain what time it was and didn't bother to check. When a game started to flow, time didn't matter very much and Mason liked it that way. He would keep going for as long as it took. Let the rest of the world do whatever it pleased.

"I raise," Greeley announced. One of the girls he'd been with during his absence was a short brunette with curves that could stop a stampede in its tracks. The upper portion of her dress was so loosely constructed that she only seemed to be covered by strings of wispy shadow. She was walking in a section of the room where she could be seen from Greeley's seat and he waved to her before moving his chips into the pot. Since he didn't announce how much he was raising and didn't cut off his chips as he usually did, Mason was certain Greeley was sifting through some more pleasant memories instead of focusing every bit of attention on the game.

It was the first round of betting for that hand, and Greeley was third to act. So far, his was the first bet made and he was too busy watching that brunette blow him a kiss from the other side of the room to notice Dan calling the raise. Mason wasn't holding much of anything, but there was a chance he could make either a flush or a medium straight. The raise was small enough for him to call it and hope for the best.

Clint bumped it up a little bit more, which wasn't a surprise to anyone who'd played with him for more than three hands in a row. Maggie made some sly comment and called.

The shapely brunette was speaking to a man at another table, but she'd positioned herself in a way that she could give Greeley an awfully good show as she leaned over to address the man in front of her. Mason took a quick look over there and was immediately glad he did. From where he was sitting, thanks to the brunette's low-cut dress and ample bosom, she might as well have been naked from the waist up.

"Oh," Greeley said absently. "Is it to me? I'll call."

Mason was fairly surprised that Greeley counted out the correct amount of chips. Then again, he was the man who not only employed that brunette but had also seen a whole lot more of her not too long ago.

Since everyone was in, they made their discards and waited for the replacements to be dealt. Maggie was the one doing the honors this time around and she'd proven sometime ago to be adept at flipping cards to the exact spot where they needed to be. Also, the snapping motion of her wrist caused the rest of her to shake in a way that Mason couldn't help noticing.

"Stop it," she growled.

"Stop what?" Clint asked.

"You're staring at me," Maggie said as she glared over at him. "Stop it. Now."

"Yes, ma'am."

Apparently Mason wasn't the only one who'd noticed Maggie's enticing little movement. He rubbed his eyes and vowed to himself not to have another drink for a while. Mason wasn't exactly drunk, but he'd had enough whiskey for some of his baser instincts to rise to the surface. He'd order cold water next time the glasses were refilled. If that didn't get his head back in the game, he would step outside and dunk it into some river water.

From what he could tell, nobody was overly excited about their hand. Then again, Mason wouldn't expect to see much reaction from players sitting at a table like this one. He looked for some of the signs he'd already picked up on from the folks around him, and since no cards were showing, all he could see was a silent war brewing between Maggie and Clint. Yet another reason why Mason didn't much care for five-card draw.

"Twenty," Greeley said while tossing in a chip.

Dan looked at his cards and thought it over for a moment before calling. His luck had run pretty dry ever since his big haul. Even though he was a long ways from broke, he wasn't stupid enough to try to stoke a fire under his game by tossing more cash onto the flames. Unless Mason was very wrong, he guessed Dan would be chased away by an above-average raise.

He had every intention of doing just that, if only to take a stab at a modest pot, when Mason finally looked at the two cards he'd been given to replace the ones that had been thrown away. He'd decided to hope for the straight, thinking he had a better chance of getting a pair or two instead. What he got was exactly what he'd been hoping for, and it was an exercise in restraint to keep from letting everyone know about it.

"Make it fifty," Mason said, praying to the Lord above that someone would try to make a move of their own.

Clint couldn't drop out fast enough. As soon as his cards hit the table, he excused himself and walked straight over to one of the working girls who'd caught his eye. A blonde in a pink dress was all too happy to take his arm and laugh at whatever he said to her.

Jervis called without any fanfare.

Maggie took a moment to think before running one finger along the edge of a stack of chips. "Raise a hundred," she said.

"Make it three hundred," Greeley countered.

As Greeley put together enough chips to back his play, Mason took quick stock of his cards. Sure enough, his prayer had been answered. As long as he didn't trip over himself to wring some more chips out of the players who remained, he should be in for a very interesting night.

Chapter 9

As far as Dan went, Mason had been completely right. After the raise that had been made, Dan folded up his tent and was out of the hand. Since Mason wasn't absolutely certain that Jervis or Maggie would raise, it was up to him to do the honors. The only question was . . . how much?

Now that the number of players still in the hand had been trimmed down a bit, Mason didn't want to scare away any potential contributors to the pot he intended to win. Too big a raise could very well take a bite out of his own profit.

Too small a raise would let the others off the hook. For a gambler, anything that took money from his pocket was intolerable.

"Raise," Mason said after one last moment to think it over. "Five hundred."

Jervis had clearly made some sort of hand, because he stared at his cards as if they were speaking to him. It was also possible that he was simply aching to play. After all, he hadn't been in the game for as long as everyone else and was most likely just getting his feet wet. That was the time when any gambler wanted to keep rolling. If he didn't have something worth playing, he would have been more than happy to dump his cards already. Eventually he shrugged and put the money in.

Maggie, on the other hand, didn't have such a dilemma. She'd reached a decision, but it had nothing to do with her cards. "I'm out. In fact," she added while getting to her feet, "I'm going to get some fresh air." She left the table, walked past the overmen, and made a straight line toward the closest door.

"Five hundred, is it?" Greeley asked in a voice that wasn't nearly as distracted as it had been the last time he'd used it. "What did you catch, Abner?"

"One good way to find out," Mason replied.

"Eh, I'm not all that interested in seeing them cards."

Inside, Mason clenched. Even after his consideration, he still could have overplayed his hand.

"I'll just take it down right here," Greeley continued. "That is, unless you care to pay three thousand to put me to the test?"

Not only was Mason no longer clenching his guts into a twist, but he was back to trying not to look overjoyed when he reached for his money. He'd laid out the bear trap, and the biggest grizzly of them all had stumbled right in. It wasn't smart to poke the grizzly with a stick, but there was no way in hell he was going to let it out of the trap.

"Make it eight thousand," Mason said in what would surely drive the other man to the hills.

"Twenty."

"Twenty thousand?"

Greeley nodded.

Mason was back to clenching.

His first instinct was that Greeley was posturing. He had to have still been stinging from taking the loss from Dan. Even though he'd played it off like the benevolent host and gone away to let off some steam with a few of his girls.

All those hours, Mason had been studying Greeley, using every observational instinct he'd honed during his years of sitting at poker tables across the country. He'd picked up on more than a few signs that Greeley was trying to represent a hand instead of actually having one. Greeley had been distracted before and was too proud to admit as much now by laying down his cards.

Instead of admitting he'd been outplayed again, Greeley meant to buy the pot. It was not only a common tactic used by rich men, but was also one that annoyed Mason the most. Rather than rely on skill or even dumb luck, a rich man could crawl into the bottom of his wallet and hide like a coward in the dark. Mason, along with any other gambler on the circuit, had lost hands to men like that simply because the player in front of him had a better family name or a bigger inheritance. They could afford to put a man's livelihood at stake just to save face. And once again, rich men got what they wanted simply because they threw enough money in a certain direction.

"I call," Mason said through gritted teeth.

Greeley leaned back in his chair, looking to Mason like just another rich man trying to play the part of emperor. "You sure you want to do that?"

"Yes, I'm sure."

"Do you have enough to cover a bet like that?"

"No offense, but we've already gone through all this before," Mason said. "Are you honestly going to bring the game to a stop every time someone makes a big bet?"

"I'm just making sure you can back that mouth of yours," Greeley said.

"Don't you worry about my mouth."

Leaning forward, Greeley placed one set of fingertips on the table as if he was making a spider with his hand. "If you can't back up your bet," he said in a low voice that sounded more like a rake being dragged across dry slate, "there'll be consequences."

"You don't have to teach me the rules of this game, Cam. You made a bet and I'm calling it. Right now you're the one who needs to back yourself up."

"You're sure?"

"Tell you what," Mason said. "Let's just play the game and take it from there. Isn't that why we're here, after all?"

Greeley leaned back again. "You're right. On all counts, you're absolutely right. You called my bet, that's part of the game, and the game is why we're here. What have you got?"

Strictly speaking, Greeley was the one who needed to show first. At that point, however, Mason was glad to put an end to the matter before he let his temper get the better of him by saying something he might regret. He turned over his cards, spread them for all to see, and said, "Straight to the eight."

Everything Mason had put together in his mind thus far told him he had Greeley beat.

Everything Mason had observed told him that Greeley was in a prime position to be steered into a trap. All that was needed was a hand big enough to do the job, and a straight was pretty big.

Everything Mason had put together and observed was proven wrong the instant Greeley showed his hand.

"Flush," Greeley said coolly. "King high."

The clench Mason felt at that moment was worse than all the previous ones combined.

Much, much worse.

Chapter 10

"What's the matter, Abner?" Greeley asked. "Need a drink?"

Mason nodded.

Raising his hand to summon one of the girls circling the vicinity of the table, Greeley said, "Get this man a drink."

Although Mason heard those voices, they and the rest of the sounds in that room became muddled as if his ears had filled with water. He maintained his composure, even when a cold sweat broke out beneath his starched shirt.

When the drink was brought to him, Mason took a sip and let out a breath.

"Hurts, don't it?" Greeley asked.

"I've had worse," Mason said, suddenly all too aware of how many eyes were on him just then. Maggie and Clint were still away from the table, but the remaining players all looked at him as if they were waiting to see if he would fall from his seat. It galled Mason to be seen as such a fragile amateur. "I'm fine," he said in a much stronger voice. "Looks like I'm done for the night, though."

Mason stood up, started to collect his chips, and then

left them where they were so he could pull on his coat. He said his farewells to the other players, or at least he thought he did. In actuality, he felt more like a puppet just going wherever he was pulled. He went through the motions of leaving a game as he'd done so many times in the past and walked away.

For a second, he was sure he was going to be stopped by the wall of overmen guarding the game. Before he walked straight into them, however, they parted and allowed him to pass.

From across the room, Clint spotted him and started to say something. Maggie was nearby as well, but they both quickly decided against approaching him.

Mason didn't know what was causing all the special treatment and he didn't care. All he wanted was some crisp air on his face. He got it once he opened the door and headed for the closest railing he could find. His steps quickly degraded into a stagger, but he managed to halt himself by gripping the railing with both hands.

It was late in the evening, possibly even drawing close to dawn. Mason could tell as much from the cool dampness in the air and the inky texture of the sky. The shore drifting past was quiet and sleepy, which went a long way to helping him gather his thoughts.

It wasn't the first time he'd taken a loss. It wasn't even the first time he'd been completely cleaned out in one hand. It was, however, the first time he'd had such an easy time getting away from the table afterward. Of course, it wasn't as if he had many places to go.

"You're not gonna try and swim for it, are you?"

Mason recognized the voice right away. Even if he hadn't, he would have bet everything that he wasn't being allowed to make this walk alone. Of course, as of a minute or two ago, that didn't amount to much of a bet.

"Nah," Mason said. "I wouldn't get very far anyway."

Greeley stepped up beside him and leaned against the rail as if he were simply taking in the predawn stillness. "Wise choice. You'd be surprised how many men in your position have tried hopping over that railing and testing their luck with the river."

"No. I wouldn't be surprised at all."

"I suppose not." Pushing away from the railing, Greeley said, "Let's take a walk. We have some things to discuss."

The heavy hand that dropped onto Mason's shoulder was most definitely not Greeley's. When he looked at who was pushing him along, Mason found the overman who'd been the one to greet him at the card table and carry the notes back and forth to Tilly later on. He seemed even more imposing now, even though he still stood more or less the same height as Mason.

"Howdy," Mason said.

The overman nodded and gave him a nudge to keep him moving. Since he didn't have any say in the matter, Mason decided to at least put an end to the shoving by falling into step alongside Greeley.

"You prefer to be called Mason, right?" Greeley asked.

"Generally, yes."

"I could tell you didn't like it when you were called Abner. Nothing to be ashamed of, though. It's a fine name. I had a cousin named Abner."

"I'm not ashamed of my name," Mason said. "I just . . ."

"Don't like the familiarity?"

"Yeah," Mason replied while nodding to the man beside him. "That's it."

As he walked beside Mason, Greeley seemed very calm and even friendly. That might not have been an act, but it also wasn't any sort of friendliness in the usual sense of the word. It was the demeanor of a man who had not only the winning hand, but the only hand. "I understand fully," Greeley said. "There's a certain lack of respect that comes about when a man gets too familiar with someone."

Mason thought back to when he'd purposely addressed Greeley by his first name. He'd known what he was doing, but hadn't realized just how badly it could come back to haunt him.

They were walking along the deck, past several doors that led into the main card room as well as a few smaller ones. On the other side of those doors, people were enjoying themselves, enjoying one another, drinking, laughing. To Mason, they might as well have been on another continent.

"I've got one question for you." Greeley quickly shook his head and added, "Rather, I have one question that I need to ask you before the others."

"What the hell was I thinking?"

Greeley laughed once. "That's it. What the hell were you thinking?"

Having reached a set of stairs near the aft end of the boat, they stopped before beginning to climb to the next deck. Mason put his hand on the banister, looked up, and said, "I thought I could win. Simple as that."

"I was also going to ask if you thought I was a fool or possibly just a bad cardplayer," Greeley admitted. "But that would've just been to bark at you. I could always tell you had a good head on your shoulders and knew what you were doing. That's why I invited you to my private game. I like to play with the best." Clapping a hand on Mason's back, Greeley got them both moving up the stairs. "That being said, of course, there's still another matter that needs to be addressed."

"I can get your money," Mason said.

"We've had a pretty good conversation until now. Don't ruin it with lies or double talk."

"I honor my debts, Mr. Greeley. Ask anyone."

"I've already asked some folks about you. Back when you came onto my boat the first time and sent poor George Rey packing with nothing but dust in his pockets. You remember that?"

"I do," Mason said with a fond smile. George Rey had been a loud, overbearing blowhard. It had been nothing short of divine to wring him dry and crush his spirit just to watch him skulk away like a whipped dog.

"You've played many a game on the *Delta Jack*," Greeley continued as they stepped onto the second deck and rounded a corner to head straight to the next set of stairs. "You've never caused any trouble and you've kept your cheating down to an acceptable amount." Before Mason could jump to his own defense, Greeley held up a hand to stop him. "Don't worry. Every gambler cheats now and then. It's part of the game. As far as a fair competition goes, just having men like us play with most cowboys you'll find in a saloon is mighty close to cheating."

Mason chuckled as a courtesy.

"I like to bring on players who think they know what they're doing," Greeley continued, "but mostly as a way to feed the real professionals. Every now and then, the chum gets lucky. The reason I bring all this up is for you to know that I do not consider you to be chum that is fed to the barracudas."

"Thanks . . . I guess."

They made their way up the second set of stairs much quicker than the first. Once they were at the top, they stood at the pinnacle of the *Delta Jack* herself. Dawn was definitely approaching. Soon the sky would start to lighten. Mason just hoped he'd be allowed to see it.

"You're funny," Greeley said. "Very amusing. Did you know some gamblers come to the *Jack* just to play you in a game?"

"I didn't know that."

"It's true!"

In an odd sort of way, despite it being the worst time to think such a thing, Mason was flattered. When he started to turn to walk toward the bow, Mason was steered aft by the rough hand of the enforcer who'd been following them the whole time. Mason took a quick glance over his shoulder and saw there were now three overmen trailing behind them. It was no wonder the few other passengers they'd seen while on their walk had quickly turned and headed in another direction.

"This is all well and good," Mason said. "I appreciate the kind words and all, but it's really unnecessary. I said I'll get your money and I have every intention of doing so."

"I'm sure you do. The problem is that intentions don't fill a man's pockets any more than the dust you left to that asshole George Rey. I need cash and I'd like it right away."

"I can get it."

"All of it?"

Mason winced. He knew only too well that he didn't have that kind of money lying around. Greeley knew it too. Since saying so out loud wouldn't do either of them any good, Mason replied, "I've built up some credit with you throughout my visits."

"That's gone," Greeley said with a motion that made it look as if he were wiping an unseen chalkboard clean.

"Plus, there's what I had at the table."

"Which has already been taken and counted up. At least that is something you won't have to pay back. Keep in mind, whatever Tilly has in her books for you will be applied to this here, but you'll have to pay that back eventually. That's the devil of credit, as you know."

Trying not to get flustered, Mason snapped, "Yeah. I know about credit. I've got more cash in my cabin."

"Enough to cover your loss tonight?"

As Mason struggled to think of a diplomatic way to answer that question without getting himself shot, three overmen fanned out behind Greeley like a firing squad. They didn't have guns in their hands, but one had a rope. Somehow Mason would have preferred to see a gun.

"Truth be told . . . ," Mason said.

"Don't waste my time by saying something like that," Greeley said in a voice that was bereft of the friendliness he'd shown only moments ago. "Just tell me the truth. When you lie, I'll know well enough and one of these men behind me will knock some of your teeth down your throat."

"All right. What I was going to say was that I don't rightly know how much cash is in my cabin."

"That's a lie." Without another word, Greeley motioned toward the men behind him. One of them stepped forward and punched Mason in the mouth so quickly that it would have been impossible to do a thing about it.

"Every gambler knows exactly how much he has at any given time," Greeley said. "Otherwise he's not much of a professional, and as I already told you, I'm well aware of how professional you are."

Mason rubbed his jaw. No teeth had been knocked loose, but a few felt dangerously close. "I'm not lying," he said. "I've been playing a lot, drinking a lot. . . ."

Greeley scowled and nodded to the man who'd just punched Mason.

Before that beefy fist could thump him again, Mason hastily added, "I wasn't blind drunk and I know all gamblers drink plenty of liquor. All I meant was that I've only been using my cabin to take the occasional nap and sock away some of my profits. Generally I've been doing pretty well, so I haven't needed to dip into those profits, which means I don't have an exact count."

The overman standing with his fist cocked back looked to Greeley and waited.

After thinking for a second, Greeley nodded once.

The overman lowered his fist.

"Let me ask you this," Greeley said. "Do you think there's any way you have enough to cover the remainder of your debt?"

Mason's mind was swimming with so many frantic thoughts that he couldn't get a good feel for how much of the debt remained. Rather than risk another punch in the face by asking for a count, he admitted, "No."

"The truth. Good to hear." Greeley then stepped back and jabbed a finger at Mason.

The overman who'd punched Mason before did so a second time. His fist moved as if it were attached to a piston and snapped Mason's head back so hard that he was dizzy when he brought it up again.

Keeping far enough back for all three overmen to surround Mason, Greeley said, "That was for getting in over your head. You should've known better than to bet more than you could pay. It was a stupid mistake and you're better than that."

Mason agreed with those words so wholeheartedly that he didn't mind taking a punch to the face to drive them home.

"There's no need for this," Mason said as the overmen swarmed him. Two of them held his arms in an iron grip while another softened Mason up with a couple of chopping blows to his stomach.

"I'm not a man to be cheated," Greeley said.

"I . . . know that!" Mason replied as he was hit once more in the gut.

"I'm also not a man to be taken lightly where debts are concerned."

"Believe me . . . I know that too."

"I don't think you do, Mr. Mason. Otherwise you wouldn't have made a bet you couldn't possibly honor."

Now that he'd softened Mason up, the overman stopped punching him. The two hanging on to Mason's arms slammed him against the railing, facing straight back to the boat's churning wake. The third flexed the hand he'd pounded against Mason's face and torso before reaching for the coiled rope that had been set on the deck near his feet.

"I can honor my debt," Mason said. "Just not all at once. All I'm asking for is a few days to . . . What is he doing?"

The third overman had a bald head and thick black

eyebrows. Until now, Mason had been too distracted to get much of a look at him. Now that the overman was looping one end of the rope around his ankles, Mason couldn't focus on anything else.

Greeley held up a hand, which stopped the overman in his tracks. The other two tightened their grips on Mason's arms and moved him back just enough to give him a taste of what it might feel like to topple backward into the water.

"Do you know how these men earned their names?" Greeley asked.

Mason's eyes darted back and forth in their sockets to get a look at the men who had ahold of him. "You mean . . . overmen?"

"That's right."

"I've heard a few things, but I don't know for certain which are true." Mason had heard more than a few things, but he didn't want to discuss them at that particular moment.

"Part of their duties involves ridding my boat of troublemakers," Greeley explained. "To do that, they pitch undesirables over the rail and into the water."

"I suppose that makes sense."

"Cheaters are tied to the side of the boat, way down low, and dragged for a few miles over rocks, through mud, and across a couple sandbars until their bones are turned to powder."

"I didn't cheat!"

"I know," Greeley said. "Men who can't pay their debts aren't dragged, but they are also tossed over. Only difference is that they're tossed into the paddlewheel."

Chapter 11

The rope was wrapped around both of Mason's ankles and cinched tight. His boots clamped together and the two men gripping his arms hoisted him a few inches off the deck.

"I'll get the money!" Mason said. "There are people who owe me. I can collect on some debts of my own!"

"Where are these people?" Greeley asked. "Here on the *Jack*?"

"Some of them."

Greeley wasn't pleased to hear that and he motioned to his men. Mason was picked up like a scarecrow and hung over the railing. The only thing keeping him from falling was the solid grip those two enforcers still had on his arms.

"Not good enough," Greeley said.

"I've got money stashed. Not here, but I can get to it in a few days. Just give me enough time to get to it."

"Tossing a man into the paddlewheel ain't an easy thing," Greeley said. "The first one who went over this railing missed it completely. The second just bounced off and splashed into the water not too much worse off than if he'd been tossed over from any other side of the boat."

Mason's legs flailed but were being held by the rope tied to his ankles so he could only thrash like a fish. He bucked and twisted his body, knocking uselessly against the railing.

"In order to make the point I wanted to make," Greeley went on to say, "there had to be more of an impact . . . so to speak. That's when one of my boys here came up with the notion of tying a man by the legs good and tight." Greeley appeared in the corner of Mason's eye and gazed out at the huge, churning wheel behind them. "That way, he could be thrown out a ways to knock against the wheel for a bit. Of course, there was always the chance that he might just fall through and drop straight into the water without a scratch. Would you believe one lucky bastard got away from me by doing that very thing? Seems impossible, but it happened."

"I've got a watch," Mason sputtered. "Some cufflinks. A few tie tacks. They're worth something. That's what I meant when I said I needed to go and see what I had in my cabin."

"With the legs tied," Greeley said as if there had been no interruption whatsoever, "there's no getting away. Granted, it's a little barbaric. Maybe even more than a little. Still, it gets the job done. And if you think it hurts getting knocked around once or twice, that ain't nothing compared to getting knocked around after your legs or back have already been broke."

"I said I'll pay and I meant it. I can't pay anything if I'm dead!"

"You won't be dead, Mr. Mason. At least, not right away."

Mason had yet to go over the side, but he was being slowly moved into position. From where he was, he could already tell the overmen had more than enough combined strength to toss him past the paddlewheel if they'd wanted to.

"You know something? I gotta hand it to you," Greeley mused. "Going as far as you did for a low straight . . . it takes real sand." He turned to one of the men holding Mason's arm. "You should've seen him. 'Straight to the eight,' he said. Like there wasn't a chance in hell for him to lose."

Mason was through begging. The only tool at his disposal was his voice, and that obviously wasn't going to do him any good. If Greeley meant to kill him, he'd just have to get on with it.

"Plenty of others have found themselves in this same spot," Greeley said. "And they wound up here after losing with far better hands than your straight. I'm not sure whether that makes you look stupid or brave. Maybe you're just confident. Which is it, Mr. Mason? Stupid, brave, or confident?"

If Mason didn't intend to beg, he'd be damned if he would play along by answering a question like that. Instead he let out a hard breath and closed his eyes.

The man gripping his right arm gave Mason a shake. "You were asked a question," he snarled.

Still, Mason kept quiet.

"Maybe proud is another possibility," Greeley said. "I've got to say, none of these qualities put you in a very favorable light."

"If you won't listen to reason," Mason said, "then I don't know what else you want from me."

"Reason?" Greeley scoffed. "You make a bet that's worth more than you are ten times over and now you want to talk to me about reason?"

"I made a mistake. I'll admit that much. I already offered to set it right and you don't seem interested. You've got the men. You've got the guns. They're holding the rope. If you just want to watch me twist and then drop me into the river, then I'm not in much of a position to stop you."

"What are my alternatives, Mr. Mason?"

"You can let me try to make good on my bet."

"And what if you can't?"

"If I couldn't, there's no way I would have made that bet," Mason explained.

Greeley considered that for all of two seconds before he started to laugh. "That doesn't make a lick of sense."

"Sure it does. If I was going to make a bet that I had no intention of paying, that would make me either a cheat or a fool. You've already told me that you know I'm neither."

"Yes," Greeley sighed.

It actually did Mason some good to keep talking. The more he spoke and thought about what to say next, the less he worried about becoming better acquainted with that paddlewheel. "Therefore," he said, "I simply got overzealous and misread the lay of the cards. You show me one gambler who hasn't been guilty of that at least half a dozen times and I'll show you someone who hasn't placed more than a dozen bets in his life."

"Nobody could argue with that."

"So you must already have figured I'd be able to repay what I owe one way or another. Toss me over this railing and—"

This time, it was Mason who was silenced by one of Greeley's bony, swiftly upraised fingers. "Don't start telling me what I should or shouldn't do," he warned.

Mason knew when it was time to shut up.

For the next few seconds, the only sounds to be heard were muffled voices and music coming from the card rooms and the constant splash of water against the instrument of Mason's swiftly approaching demise.

Just like when Greeley had kept everyone waiting at the poker game, Mason was certain a decision had already been made. Greeley was just sifting through a few final points while letting his opponent twist in the wind.

Finally Greeley said, "Pull him up."

Mason let out the breath he'd been holding.

"But don't untie him," Greeley added. "Not yet."

The overmen set Mason down and held him in place as if they were afraid he might flap his arms and fly away.

"How many days were you thinking you needed to collect the money you owe?" Greeley asked.

"Maybe a week or two."

Instead of calling him out on the fact that he'd requested a shorter time before, Greeley said, "I suppose that's to get the funds from where you have them stashed."

"That's right."

"How much are we talking about once you pull all of that together?"

"Should be well over ten thousand."

"That's quite a nest egg. You sure about that sum?"

Mason wasn't anywhere close to sure about it, but he'd already committed to it, so he nodded.

"That's still not enough," Greeley pointed out. "Even with what you had on the table and with that line of credit I offered, to buy you some extra time."

"If I can't pull it together," Mason said, "you can always bring me right back to this spot. I doubt that wheel is going anywhere."

"You've got that right."

"I know a few men who can loan me some cash. I won't bore you with details, but just know that I can scramble for this money. I'll just need time. Once I see exactly how much I can get, we can further discuss terms for settling things between you and me."

"You want terms?" Greeley asked in a low voice. "I'll give you terms. We're due to stop at our next port tomorrow morning at ten thirty. You've got until then to pull together as much money as you can from your cabin or anyone else on this here boat that might be considered a friend."

"That's very generous," Mason said.

"I ain't through. That also gives me some time to put together a list of certain jobs I need done. Jobs that you're gonna do for me."

Mason's eyes widened a bit. "That's a great idea! We can work out a trade."

Greeley nodded. "You'll do these jobs without asking any questions and I'll be sure to check to make certain they're done. If they're not, I'll tack them on to the debt you already owe me."

"Sounds fair."

"I imagine it would. Especially since you were about to get ground into chuck steak not very long ago."

"It's amazing how a man's perspective changes after something like that," Mason said.

"And it's also amazing how quickly a man gets his smart mouth back after something like that." Turning to one of his overmen, Greeley said, "This is why I normally don't like to make deals once things have gone this bad."

"If I could remind you," Mason said carefully, "the only thing that went bad was me making one of the worst bets in my life. After that, I stood up to leave and . . . here I am. What did you expect me to do? Sit and keep playing with money I didn't have?"

"I expected you to find some way to get yourself out of this because you don't have the money. Don't make me repeat myself, Mr. Mason."

"So . . . what are these jobs you need me to do?"

"I've got a few in mind," Greeley said. "And before them wheels in your head start turning again, let me remind *you* of something." He put his hands on his hips and stood in front of his prisoner so he was the only thing Mason could see. "If I decide to give you the chance to work off this debt you owe, I won't just be turning you loose on good faith. If you step out of line, I'll know about it. If you try to slither away, I'll know. If you try anything at all that I don't much like . . ."

After a slight pause, Mason said, "You'll know about it."

Greeley tugged on Mason's tie and then cinched it just a bit too tight for comfort. "I knew you were smart."

"Were?"

"Tonight doesn't really help you in that regard, now, does it?"

"I suppose not," Mason said.

Taking a step back, Greeley motioned to his hired guns, who immediately began untying the rope from around Mason's legs. There had been a few other passengers out for a stroll on the deck, but they had quickly turned away when they saw the overmen standing guard.

"You go on and see how much you can scrape up to pay toward that debt," Greeley said. "Find me before we dock in the morning and I'll have Tilly work up the exact amount left for you to pay. After that, well . . . we'll see. How's that sound?"

"Not too bad."

"Good," Greeley said through an ugly smile. He then turned to walk back to the stairs that would lead down to the decks below.

"Mr. Greeley," Mason called out.

Greeley stopped and turned around.

"What sort of jobs will I be doing?" Mason asked. "I'm not exactly suited for some kinds of work."

"Any resourceful man can do these jobs. They're dangerous, but not impossible."

"Sounds like you already had this arrangement in mind before I made that bet."

The smile returned to Greeley's face, only this time, it was even uglier than before. "Why do you think I allow men like you to have so much leeway on my boat? Sooner or later, someone gets cocky enough to do something they shouldn't. When that happens, there are plenty of ways for them to redeem themselves. Same reasoning behind me offering credit to men in debt."

"Can't exactly profit from interest percentages unless you allow someone to get into a hole in the first place."

Greeley nodded. "I'm a firm believer in giving someone enough rope to hang himself. Speaking of which, I didn't tell you what happens to someone who lies to me. Instead of tossing him over the side or taking the time to inflict more creative pains, I take that rope and hang him from a smokestack. That one right there," he added while pointing to the closest stack extending from the top of the *Delta Jack*.

Mason watched a bit of smoke curl from the stack.

"Play your cards right, Mr. Mason," Greeley said. "Otherwise that straight to the eight you were so proud of will run you straight to a noose."

Chapter 12

The door to Mason's cabin swung open and he was inside by the time it smacked against the wall. It rattled on its hinges, slipping through his fingers the first two times he tried to get ahold of it so he could slam it shut again. Even after the latch fell into place, he kept his hand on it as though he thought the door might come open again just to spite him.

"Straight to the eight," he grunted. "What the hell was I thinking?" Mason closed his eyes, patted the door, and exhaled in a slow, steady sigh. When he opened his eyes again, he was no longer filled with the haze that had obscured his vision before. Mason wasn't the sort of man who got angry for long. That kind of temperament didn't suit a gambler. Men who got angry and stayed angry weren't generally around long enough to see the cards start falling their way again. The main thing that sparked and held Mason's ire was himself. He could stay angry at himself for a good, long time.

"Wasn't thinking," he grunted. "Not that it matters, though. Lost grip on the reins for a couple seconds, and that's all it took."

The hand that was pressed against the door curled

into a fist. He pulled it back a few inches, held it there, and then rapped it against the door just hard enough to make a sound. The anger had receded, spread out like oil on top of a lake. Lessened, but still there.

"Don't let it happen again, Abner," he whispered. "Simple as that, right?" He took another breath. "Yeah," he sighed while letting it out. "Right."

He was shaking his head as he went to the narrow bed. It wasn't much more than a threadbare mattress on a metal rack, which made it easy to take apart. Mason lifted the mattress, slipped a hand beneath it, and started feeling around under there while grumbling, "Straight to the eight. Straight to the noose. Real clever. Bet you came up with that one while you were skulking behind me like the skinny, bony vulture you are."

Upon finding what he was after, Mason pulled his hand out to where he could see it. The sock that had been under the bed was held together by more mold than stitching. He emptied the sock into his other hand and kept shaking it until the folded money stopped falling out. Even then, he dug inside to feel every disgusting fold in the hopes that something had been left behind. Something had, but it wasn't anything Greeley would want. Mason shook the brown grit off his hand and focused on the cash.

One hundred and fifty-two dollars. It was a good start.

Mason walked around to the other side of the bed and reached beneath the frame for the other sock. That one was even filthier than the first and was wadded up so tightly that it had practically become one with the floor. Stuffing money in hosiery was such a time-honored method that some crooks didn't honestly think someone like Mason would use it. The trick to deceiving the rest of the robbers who might try sifting through his room while he was away was to make the socks look as if they were there since the first week the *Delta Jack* had been afloat. Another good trick was the simplest of them all. He stashed two socks under there instead of just one. A matching pair. That way, they looked like something that had truly been lost instead of something that was only supposed to appear to have been lost.

Simple tricks like those were the essence of what Mason did for a living. Figuring out how the gears within people's minds turned and then using that to his advantage. He reminded himself of this invaluable lesson while shoving his hand into the second filthy, malodorous sock. Keeping his money from being sniffed out by common thieves wouldn't be all that different than surviving the wrath of Cam Greeley. All Mason had to do was keep his wits about him, remember what he'd learned, and put it to good use.

There was a hundred and four dollars wrapped within the sock. What Mason had told Greeley about not needing the money because of a string of profitable games had been absolutely correct. That last hundred and four dollars had been inside his sock for so long that the bills stank and had acquired a dusting of mold.

"So much for that string of good luck," he grunted.

Next, he moved on to his carpetbag. Mason was careful in opening that, simply because it had been left in plain sight while he was away. Opening it slowly, he gazed down into the darkened space and nodded. Someone had gone through the bag while he was away.

"Now, ain't that a coincidence?" he said under his breath while reaching into the bag with one tentative hand.

Whenever he left the carpetbag unattended, Mason was careful to leave everything inside it placed in a precisely random manner. Each item had its place, but those places appeared jumbled to any eye but his own. Even with both eyes closed, he could reach into that bag and know exactly where every single one of his possessions belonged. What he saw now was fairly close to the way he'd left it, but wasn't exactly how it should be. That meant someone other than him had looked through the bag and done a fairly decent job of leaving it intact.

Reaching past a few small weapons, Mason winced. He'd been so preoccupied with everything else that he'd forgotten to reclaim the knife and pistols that had been taken from him before the game. Putting that to the back of his mind, he found a pouch tucked into the corner of the bag that was only slightly skewed from where it should have been. Mason removed the pouch, opened it, and found his second pocket watch. This one was of a higher quality than the one he wore at the moment and was reserved for special occasions. It seemed peculiar that it hadn't been taken by whoever had gone through his things, but that could just mean the person had only been looking for cash.

"Damn," he sighed while opening the watch and running his thumb along the engraved cover. "I like this watch." Resigning himself to what needed to be done, he closed it up again and stuffed it into a jacket pocket.

The next pouch he found was smaller than the first but hadn't been moved from its rightful spot. Since the pouch was made from felt, it tended to stick to the lining of the bag, which made it tougher to find. Mason opened it and was pleased to discover the two sets of cuff links were still inside. One set was gold and the other was silver. Finally he tugged at the lining of the bag until part of it came loose. The stitching had been removed so the lining was tucked into place. That way, it could be peeled down by anyone who knew precisely where to look.

"There you are," he whispered once he saw the two stickpins that had been pinned to the interior of the lining. Neither of the pins was very big, but they each had a few small diamonds embedded in them.

Mason removed them and was about to put them in with the cufflinks when he paused to take a closer look. They were dented in several spots. The stickpins were bent here and there. One was even missing a diamond from its setting. The longer he gazed down at them, the harder it was for him to let them go. After a few seconds, he couldn't even bring himself to look at them any longer. They'd been given to him by his grandmother and just thinking of handing them over to Greeley was enough to make him feel ashamed.

Pinning the one with the missing diamond back to the lining of the bag, he sighed, "Not yet. Things are bad, but they're not bad enough. Not yet anyway." He tucked the lining back in place so the pin was hidden once again. "I'll know where to find you if I need to. Let's just try to keep it from getting that far."

The carpetbag was closed up and placed in its spot against the wall. As much as Mason wanted to stretch out on that bed and close his eyes for a bit, he forced himself to straighten up and head out again.

The sun wasn't quite up yet, which meant there were still a good number of people in most of the poker rooms on the *Delta Jack*. Mason made his way back to the largest of the rooms and saw the table where Greeley's game was still going on. Someone else sat in Mason's seat, playing his hand and having a grand old time. Before he ventured any closer to that section of the room, Mason headed for the bar and ordered a whiskey.

"Put it on my bill," Maggie said while approaching the bar to stand beside him.

Mason showed her a weary smile. "I'd politely refuse that offer, but I'm in no position to turn it down."

"I'm surprised you're still in a position to walk and chew solid food," she said. "That makes you pretty lucky."

When the bartender gave Mason his whiskey, it was on a tray that also held his pistols and dagger. Taking the drink he'd been given, Mason replied, "I'm a charmed man."

She already had a drink in her hand and tossed it back. Setting the glass on the bar, she asked, "What brings you back so soon? Seeing as how you're alive and still in one piece . . . you are still in one piece, right?"

"Near as I can tell."

"I would have thought you'd be resting or, at the very least, someplace away from this room."

"I left something behind. Apart from my dignity, that is." Mason signaled to the bartender, who came back with a bottle.

"I've seen plenty of men take losses like that one," she said.

"Maybe you're a jinx."

The comforting smile on Maggie's face dimmed considerably and she turned her attention to her drink instead.

"Sorry," Mason said while returning his weapons to their rightful spots on his person. "That was rude. Next round's on me."

"Can you afford it?"

"I've got a few dollars to my name. At this point, I'm buried so deep that sinking a bit more won't make much difference."

Smiling again, Maggie said, "There's a certain amount of freedom in that."

"I suppose that's one way of looking at it."

After she was poured her next drink, she said, "What I meant to say before is that I've seen plenty of men take beatings at the table. And you're right. Most weren't as bad as yours. Still, those other men took it a lot worse than you did. Some flipped tables over. Others started swearing or making accusations of cheating. A few even drew their pistols just to start a fight. From what Jervis told me, you stood up, dusted yourself off, and made a courteous departure. A bit unsteady on your feet," she added, "but courteous."

"I appreciate the comfort," he said. "And the drink."

"Is there anything else I can do?"

Mason emptied his glass and savored the warmth of the liquor scorching its way down to his belly. "Can you loan me twenty thousand dollars?" he asked.

"I can go as high as three."

"Really? I was just joking about the money."

"You need it and that's no joke," she said. "I wouldn't mind helping you out."

Leaning one elbow against the bar, Mason turned to face her directly. "Don't take this the wrong way, but . . . why?"

"Why help you?"

"I appreciate the thought, but we only just met. That seems like an awfully big favor."

She shrugged. "I've been on the gambling circuit for a while myself. I took a few losses that seemed they would be the end of me . . . in more ways than one. The worst of those seemed pretty close to hopeless. Frankly I thought I might be . . ." She trailed off and shuddered slightly. Watching her, Mason knew exactly how she felt. If he somehow clawed his way out of this hole, he was sure he'd shudder when looking back on it no matter how many years had passed.

Putting on a brave smile, Maggie said, "It was a bad time and someone helped me out of it. Someone I didn't know very well. Someone who came through for me when people I'd known for years only thought to run for cover."

"Sounds like you were in quite a pickle," Mason said.

"To say the least." She tapped the bar with her glass so the man tending it would return with the bottle again. "I'd thought the man who was helping me was only doing it so he could . . . so I would . . . well . . ."

"I understand," Mason said before she was forced to relive even more of what were clearly unsavory memories. "I've often marveled at how boorish men can be where the fairer sex is concerned."

The way Maggie laughed, it seemed she didn't know whether Mason was saying that honestly or was just trying to put on a kind appearance for her. Her features softened right before she looked away from him, and when she spoke, it was in a softer, more familiar tone. "I'm ashamed to admit, when I thought this man's motives were the same as almost every other man's, I was still ready to accommodate him if it meant getting the money I needed."

"Must have been even worse than I'd imagined."

She nodded, started to lift her drink to her lips, and then paused with the glass halfway raised. Then Maggie smiled. "Before I threw myself at him like an idiot, he handed over the money."

"Just like that?"

"Just like that. I asked why, much like you just did, and he told me he did it because he could."

"I've heard that explanation given before," Mason said. "Usually it's to justify wickedness instead of generosity."

"Yes. I've heard it too and I kept waiting for this man's wickedness to show through. It never did, though. He was no saint, but he meant what he'd told me and was true to his word. I took the money he offered because I couldn't afford not to. I repaid what I could and he moved on before I could settle even half of my debt to him. Before he left, he told me to do the same for someone else someday."

"I can't believe I'm the first man you've met at a card table who was in need of money from a generous stranger."

"Not by a long shot," she said. "But you're one of the few that deserve it. Also, you're the only one who deserves it and just so happened to be there when I have enough money to make this offer." Straightening up and speaking in a crisper, more businesslike voice, Maggie explained, "I did well tonight and I've got a few men in my sights who should enable me to do even better. Take the money, Abner."

For once, Mason didn't mind hearing his first name used in a conversation with someone who wasn't a blood relative. "How long will you be on the *Jack*?" he asked.

"I like it here. I don't have any plans to leave for a while."

"Good. I'll accept your more than generous offer, but on one condition."

"Name it."

"Don't go anywhere until I get a chance to pay you back. If you do have to disembark," he added, "kindly leave word for me so I'll know where to find you."

She lifted her glass. "From what I've seen of you in action, I'd guess you'll be back on your feet in no time."

"I do like the way you think, Maggie."

Their glasses clinked together and their eyes met in a very promising way. Before he could be too distracted, Mason spotted someone else who held promise of a different sort.

Being someone who was well versed in reading any man in front of her, Maggie immediately saw the change in Mason's face and followed his line of sight directly to what had caught his attention. "What's the matter?" she asked.

"You see that fellow over there?"

"Yes. The one at the craps table. Is he one of Greeley's men?"

"No, no," he chuckled. "Nothing like that. He's someone I've been keeping my eye on for a short while."

Maggie nodded. "Ah, I see. You heard he's had a run of good luck and doesn't exactly know how to keep a firm hold of his money."

Snapping his eyes back to her, Mason asked, "How could you possibly know all that just by looking at him?"

"That's Virgil Slake," she said, which surprised Mason even more. "Dell may not exactly be the best when it comes to cutting a woman's hair, but he does have a lot of interesting stories to tell."

"And here I thought he only told those stories to his best customers."

"He does. Considering how long he took while sweeping the few clippings from the front of my dress, I'd say I'm one of his favorites."

"What did he tell you about that one over there?" Mason asked while nodding in Virgil's direction.

"Pretty much what I told you. He wanted payment for any more than that, and I figured I could get information about another gullible little fish in this pond for free." Smiling in a way that would have warmed any man's heart, she added, "I was right."

"Yes, well, I did pay for the extra information and I believe I may be able to get my hands on some more of that money I needed."

"Mr. Mason, I hope you're not going to make me part of something illegal."

Mason winced at the tentative sound of her voice, which Maggie seemed to find very amusing.

"I've fleeced plenty of men before and not just at the card table," she said. "What do you have in mind for this one?"

"Something of a loan."

"Something of one?"

"Yes," Mason replied. "Except he doesn't know he'd be loaning it to me. I sincerely doubt he would be as kindhearted as you."

Just then, as if to bring Mason's point fully across, Virgil howled angrily before slamming a fist down on the craps table in front of him. When one of the other men there tried to have a word with him, Virgil responded by shoving the man back and tossing his beer into the man's face.

"I can see how one might not consider that one to be very kindhearted," Maggie said.

The next bets were quickly placed, the dice were rolled, and Virgil announced the outcome by howling again. This time, he raised his voice in celebration and clapped on the back the same fellow he'd just pushed.

"How do the blowhards find a way to be just as obnoxious when they're happy as when they're angry?" Mason groaned.

"It's a gift they all have," Maggie said. "The good thing is it makes it so much easier for people like us to knock them down a few pegs. Speaking of which, tell me some more about this loan you're proposing."

"Dell told me Mr. Slake over there has been doing significant damage to the faro table as well as that craps game."

"He's been here for days and he's still ahead? Just playing faro and craps? That's almost unheard of."

"Not if he's cheating."

Maggie nodded. "That would fall in line with what I heard as well. What would you like from me?"

"Think you could distract him for a while?" Mason asked. "Maybe for half an hour?"

She adjusted her posture so her natural assets were on even more prominent display. Pulling a few strands of hair to hang in front of her face and releasing her braid so the rest of it flowed over her shoulders, she said, "I think I can manage that."

Chapter 13

Maggie was so good at her appointed task that Mason wanted to stay in that card room just to watch her work. Since he had some work of his own to do, he pulled himself away from there and made his way to the next deck up. Along the way, he spotted a few overmen who watched him carefully without making a move to get in his way. Mason tipped his hat to the enforcers and moved along until he got to a short, narrow hallway filled with doors numbered one through ten.

Someone stepped out of door eight: a short man in a crisp black suit with a silver chain across his midsection. He nodded to Mason, checked his watch, and hurried down the hall. Not long ago, Mason had been that fellow with the uppermost priority being getting to the next card game. Soon he might be that fellow again. For the moment, however, he was the fellow who broke into another man's room with bad intentions in mind. Fortunately this wasn't Mason's first go-round in that role.

According to Dell the barber, the door Mason wanted was number six. He tried the knob, hoping against hope that his job would be easy. The door was locked. "Oh well," he muttered while reaching around to the small of his back. "Nothing good ever comes easy."

He pulled the dagger from its hidden scabbard without making a sound. The tip of the blade was scratched along a section that was less than an inch long, and when he stuck the blade into the door's lock, he imagined he'd add a few more imperfections to the metal. Rather than look at what he was doing, Mason shifted to stand sideways so he could watch the hallway in case anyone happened along at the wrong time. He didn't need to see his hands to know what was going on down there. He could feel the blade grinding against the lock's mechanism, which told him everything he needed to know. After guiding the dagger farther, he was able to twist it and open the door.

"Sometimes," he whispered while entering room six, "I wonder why anyone bothers to lock these."

Even though he'd been perfectly satisfied with his own room, Mason had been well aware it was small. Compared to Vernon's accommodations, his were spacious. The bunk folded down from the wall and was held in place by a chain at the upper and lower corners. Beneath the bunk and sticking out a little bit was a flat chest with a smaller lock embedded in its front panel. A small table folded out from the wall below a porthole like a miniature version of the bed, but was supported by a wooden post that fit into notches cut into the wall as well as the bottom of the panel. A small chamber pot was in one corner of the room, and that was all there was to see.

"No wonder he plays so much faro," Mason said. "He doesn't have enough room to stay in here for long." He rubbed his hands together and said, "All right, then. This shouldn't take long."

The first place where Mason set his sights was the chest

below the bunk. Of course, it helped that there wasn't much of any other place for someone to hide something in that cabinet of a room. Before raising the bunk, he lifted the paper-thin mattress and ran his hand along every inch of the frame. That took all of five seconds, but at least it put his mind at ease when he folded the bunk up and held it in place with a leather strap hanging from the wall that connected to a hook on the edge of the bunk.

Mason squatted down to get a look at the chest. It was about two feet wide and less than half of that in height. The size of the lock was suited for a key the size of one that might unlock a set of handcuffs. He knew how to pick a smaller lock like that one, but he didn't have the tools with him. "Eh, to hell with it," he grunted as he jammed the dagger's blade beneath the lid and used it as a lever to force it open. Inside, the chest was filled with some folded shirts, a few neckties, and some pairs of wool socks. Mason went for the socks, felt them, and found they were empty.

"Hope springs eternal," he sighed before putting the socks back.

Before he started emptying the chest, he felt along the interior of the lid. It was lined with a thin layer of felt, which brought a smirk to Mason's face. Using the dagger once again, he sliced along the inner edge of the lid so he could peel away some of the lining. Stashed under there were five gold coins stamped only with their weight in grams as well as several impressions made by the teeth of men looking to gauge their authenticity.

Since the felt had been undamaged before he got there, Mason guessed those gold coins were Virgil's holdout stash. If things went badly, every gambler kept a private bankroll tucked away to get them on his feet again. As far as he knew, none of the games on the *Jack* paid out in gold, which pointed once again to those coins being Virgil's backup. Mason set them down next to the chest and started emptying the clothing onto the floor as well. After removing the socks, two shirts, and three ties, he hit bottom.

"What the hell?" he grumbled.

The chest wasn't large, but it should have been able to hold more than that. Mason knocked on the bottom while looking at the outside of the container. By his estimation, only half of the chest's storage capacity was being used by the clothing. He shook his head.

"Virgil, Virgil, Virgil," he said while feeling along the edges of the chest's interior. "If you're going to give one of these a false bottom, you need to make the compartment a bit smaller. That way," he added as his fingertip grazed along a notch in the front edge of the chest's bottom, "it's not so easy to spot. I should have a word with you when this is through."

The tip of the dagger came in handy yet again. This time, he just needed to loosen the panel at the bottom of the chest to pry it loose. It came off with a small amount of convincing to reveal several neatly arranged stacks of money. Mason's heart skipped a beat. He put the dagger away so he could sink both hands into the treasure trove just to feel all that cash for himself. "I never get sick of this," he sighed. He dug his hands in a little deeper with the intention of pulling as much of the cash out as possible. Instead he found something else.

"What have we here?" Mason said as he removed a good portion of the cash.

It turned out the stacks of money had been piled in a way that created yet another hidden space. Situated on the true bottom of the trunk with stacks of cash all around were two devices. One was a rectangular metal box that was open on the top and had a steel rod running all the way through it. The rod was connected to a knob on one end and was built to hold two dice in place so they could be shaved.

"Very naughty," Mason said while running one finger along the dice. Sure enough, they'd both been shaved along specific edges so that when they were thrown, they were likelier to roll a certain way. Someone with enough practice could tip the odds significantly in their favor. It was a crude method of cheating that relied mostly on switching the shaved dice with the ones being used at the craps table being set up for a fall.

The second device was much smaller. A short ivory handle was connected to a small iron cage that was just large enough to hold a single die in place. Holes in the cage corresponded to pips on the die, and a small spike sharpened to a point at one end was used to bore a hole into the pip. That hole could then be filled with something heavy like metal shavings or lead and painted to look as it had appeared before. When the loaded dice were rolled, they would favor the weighted side, which meant the number on the opposing side would come up much more often than not.

No matter how many cons he might have run in his years of scraping by to earn a living, Mason couldn't tolerate someone who cheated at dice. Those were the same heavy-handed idiots who rigged roulette wheels or picked another man's pockets while he was busy with a woman. There was no skill involved. No finesse. No style.

Mason rarely needed to cheat any longer, but he knew the amount of practice involved with being able to sway those odds. The tricks needed to skew a poker game were similar to sleight of hand used by stage magicians, and those men were considered artists. Being able to shuffle a deck of cards while keeping them in the same order was a skill. Picking cards out using only a sense of touch that had been honed finely enough to detect the weight difference of face cards versus number cards was extraordinary. Rigging dice only required tools.

Since he was already squatting, Mason hunkered down a bit farther and brushed his hand against the floor. What could easily have passed for grit or flecks that had fallen from the bed frame or chains now struck Mason in a whole other way. Judging by the amount of scrapings and metal shavings lying around, Virgil had been quite busy in his room to improve his chances at the craps tables.

"Now, this explains quite a lot," Mason said. "Makes things a whole lot easier too."

Greeley had been correct when he said that most, if not all, professional gamblers cheated in one way or another. When a gambler got caught at cheating, he had to accept the consequences. For Virgil Slake, his consequences were a lot better than if he'd been caught by Greeley's overmen.

Outside, footsteps knocked against the floorboards.

"I'll leave your coins, Virgil," Mason said as he began stuffing his pockets with cash. "That way you'll at least have something to get by with for a while."

The footsteps came to a stop and someone in the hallway tugged on the handle of Virgil's door.

Mason hurried to collect two more fistfuls of cash before standing up. His hands were still in his pockets when the door was opened by a man who most definitely wasn't Virgil Slake.

Chapter 14

The man who'd opened the door wouldn't have drawn much attention no matter what room he was in. Mason only recognized him because he made it his business to watch and remember as many faces as possible whenever he was playing cards in a place for more than two nights in a row. Even though Mason had seen the short fellow with the short hair parted down the middle, that didn't mean he knew who he was. He did, however, have enough information to make an educated guess.

"What are you doing?" the man asked. His features, while normally bland and passive, took on an aggressive edge once he spotted Mason.

"I'm here to get the money Virgil needed," Mason said in a rush. "You must be Virgil's regular partner."

The man still looked suspicious but was now equally confused. "Yes," he replied. "I'm Bob. Who the hell are you?"

"Phillip Everly," Mason said, using one of his standard aliases. "Virgil has someone on the hook and needs some funds to cover a whale of a bet. He must've sent you to help me get this money to him."

"I never heard of you."

"But you're his partner, right?"

Bob seemed just as confused this time as the first time Mason had asked that question. The fact of the matter was that most cheaters who had to rely on machines and loaded dice also had to rely on partners to make their job easier. Plus, figuring out the identity of the man who had the key to Virgil's room wasn't much of a stretch.

Mason stood up straight and made no attempt to hide the money in his hands. It was too late to do that anyway, so he went so far as to keep stuffing what he had into his pockets. "Are you here to help me?" he asked.

"Put that money down," Bob said.

"Why? We'll just have to pick it up again."

"I said put it down!"

"Sure," Mason said while lowering his arms. He dropped most of the cash onto the floor. An instant before letting go of the few bundles left in his possession, Mason snapped his hands up to send those bills fluttering into Bob's face. When Bob stepped back and tried to brush the money away, Mason ran straight at him.

Leading with his shoulder, Mason lowered his head and rammed Bob squarely in the chest. The other man grunted as his shoulders hit the door behind him and the handle jabbed into his lower back. Bob swung his hands wildly in front of him, partly to clear the paper from his eyes and partly to get ahold of Mason before he could get past him. He was successful on both counts.

Mason had the end of the hall in his sights when he was pulled backward a couple of steps. If he'd built up any momentum, he might have been knocked off his feet when he was brought to a halt so quickly. Even though he kept his balance, it took him a moment to figure out he was being spun back around. By the time he got his bearings again, Bob was taking a swing at him.

Even though Mason started to turn away from the incoming blow, he wasn't fast enough to avoid it completely. Bob's fist clipped his jaw and sent him stumbling to one side.

"You're not one of Virgil's partners!" Bob said.

Like most second fiddles in a team of idiots, Bob wasn't very bright. What he lacked in brains, however, he made up for in aggression.

Mason reached for the gun at his hip, if only to put a scare into the man in front of him. Bob reacted quickly by bringing one knee up and snapping that boot straight out to pound into Mason's stomach. Thanks to the beating he'd taken that night, Mason was already filled with a dull ache from head to toe. One more kick or punch here and there wasn't about to make a difference. That kick did knock him back, however, which allowed Bob to reach for his own pistol.

Now that he stood at the end of the hall, Mason had an option open to him that gave him much better odds than testing his speed on the draw. He stepped back and jumped to the side, clearing the hallway altogether as Bob took his shot. The pistol's roar filled the hallway and hot lead burned into the wall. Mason drew his Remington and kept hurrying down the corridor and away from the hall. Another shot was fired that took a chunk out of the wall behind him. After that, Bob emerged from the hallway to get a better look at what he was shooting.

Mason fired from the hip. The Remington bucked against his palm, illuminating the corridor directly in front of him. His back was to a door to the outside deck and Mason reached with his free hand to open it. The shot he'd fired wasn't meant to draw blood and knocked a hole into the wall several inches away from anything with a pulse. Bob was either too brave or too stupid to care about the gun in Mason's hand, because he kept coming regardless.

"Damn," Mason growled as he stepped into the chilly air. There was still plenty of noise coming from many different sections of the boat, but not nearly enough to mask a pair of gunshots. The men who would be coming to see what was going on wouldn't be happy to see Mason's face again so soon.

He lowered his pistol so as not to alarm anyone else he might encounter while walking along the deck. Keeping himself against the rail, he watched the door he'd just stepped through, waiting to see who would come out next.

"What's wrong down there?" someone called from the deck above. "Was someone shot?"

"Keep your head down!" Mason shouted. He shook his head, hardly believing that his fellow passengers could take an interest in him now when he'd had to fend for himself in so many fights before. Rather than dwell on the strange situation, he opted to try to get out of this one with his skin intact.

"Come back with that money!" Bob shouted.

Keeping his Remington pointed toward the door that Bob was about to burst through, Mason tried to think of his best options. Killing Bob was the first one to spring to mind but wasn't very appealing at the moment. Even in self-defense, shooting a man on the *Delta Jack* would only irritate Greeley further. Odds were that he'd reconsider any arrangement he'd made with Mason and just be done with him in the quickest way possible.

"Where'd you go, you bastard?" Bob shouted.

Mason inched along the railing as his mind spun with possibilities. If he gave back the money he'd taken, Bob would most likely lose interest and find somewhere else to go. After that, it would just be a matter of lying low so neither Bob nor Virgil caught sight of him again.

The door was shoved open and Bob came out. He had the wide, round eyes of a dumb animal that had been spooked. One wrong move and it would attack whatever it could reach.

Mason's gun hand came up so he could sight along the top of his barrel. It was easy enough to line up his sights with Bob as his target. Squeezing the trigger was another story entirely.

This wasn't a matter of defending himself with less than a heartbeat to choose between life and death.

This wasn't a chance to keep someone else from getting killed for no good reason.

This was putting a bullet into a man who wouldn't see it coming. There were plenty of men on God's green earth who wouldn't have had much of a problem with something like that. Abner Mason wasn't one of them.

Bob wheeled around, unaware of the thoughts that had flickered through Mason's ever-churning mind like so many moths darting past a candle's flame. Unlike Mason, he didn't need any time to think before acting. Once he had his target in sight, Bob came straight at him.

"I'll give you back the money," Mason said in a rush.

Bob would cover the short distance between them in another second or two.

"What else do you want from—" Mason ducked below Bob's wild swing and snapped a quick punch to Bob's ribs. His intention wasn't to put his man down, but merely back him up a few steps. As soon as that happened, Mason felt his back touch the railing and planted his feet on the deck. "Let's work this out," he said. "See? I'll even holster my gun. This has gone far enough already."

Mason could tell by looking into Bob's eyes that the man wasn't about to gun him down where he stood. Unfortunately he didn't see anything in there to let him know Bob was about to rush him from such a close distance. If he had seen that coming, he might have been able to get out of the way before being knocked against the railing behind him.

Not only did Bob catch him full on, but his momentum took both him and Mason straight over the side.

Chapter 15

When he heard the wind rushing past his ears and his feet flailing in open air, Mason figured he'd merely passed out.

But he was on his way farther down than just the floor. Mason fell for a good couple of seconds, and when he hit, it was the river that was there to greet him.

His back slapped against the cold water hard enough to light a fire behind his eyes. Mason tried to pull in a breath, but was unable to send even a trickle of air into his aching lungs. When he could finally inhale, he got a chest full of river water for his trouble.

Mason kicked and swung his arms in a desperate attempt to keep his head above water. Very quickly, he realized he wasn't even completely certain which direction was up. Once he'd figured that part out, something pressed against the top of his head to force him back below the surface.

"Tryin' ta kill me?" Bob wailed.

Mason wanted to say something to that, but most of his face was still underwater at the time. He reached up to grab Bob's wrist and couldn't manage to pry it from the top of his head before his strength started to ebb.

"Who the hell *are* you?" Bob shouted.

His voice rippled through the water down to Mason's ears, giving him something to focus on apart from the fact that he couldn't breathe. Bob's voice, the hand holding him down, the bubbles rising from his mouth—all those things made it clear to Mason's fading consciousness which way he needed to go if he was going to survive the fall from the deck of the *Delta Jack*.

Mason reached out to find Bob with both hands. Instead of trying to fight him or even force him to let go, Mason pulled his knees in close to his body so he could plant one foot on Bob's chest. From there, Mason straightened his leg and drove his weight downward as if he was using Bob as a stepladder to make his way above the water. In a matter of seconds, the tables had been turned and Bob was the one being forced under while Mason gulped down as much fresh air as he could.

His eyes burned and his ears slowly drained as Mason bobbed on the churning river. The sound of the paddlewheel was almost deafening from down there, but at least it gave him a point of reference. Mason now had a good idea of which way he needed to go to get his feet back onto solid ground. Using a serviceable swimming stroke, Mason got himself moving toward the shore with Bob following close behind him.

"You tried killin' me, but it didn't work," Bob sputtered in between sucking in and spitting out mouthfuls of water. "Any real man woulda faced me with a gun in his hand or fought me in a brawl. Only some yellow cur tries to drown someone in cold blood!"

"First of all, you're barely making any sense," Mason said while continuing toward the shoreline. "And second, you're the one who pushed *me* into the water! How could you have forgotten that?"

"I didn't forget nothin'. Only reason I did anything was that you were in Virgil's room stealin' his money!"

"Well, you got me there. You want to arrest me?"

Bob's head was wagging back and forth as he dog-paddled toward dry land. "Soon as I get to some law, I just might."

"Great. Lawmen are usually in a town of some sort. All we need to do is find one of those and you'll be on your way."

"You talk real smug now. Just wait and see how smug you are once you get what's comin' to you."

Every so often, one of Mason's boots scraped against a rock or a thick patch of mud. A few seconds later and he could feel slimy ground beneath his boots. He slowed his kicking, allowed his body to float upright, and then tried to stand up. His feet sank a few inches into the muck, but he was able to support his weight.

When Bob swam close enough to him, Mason put his hand on top of the other man's head and gave him a push downward. Having already taken his hand away, Mason waited for Bob's head to break the surface of the water again before saying, "Stand."

"I . . . I'll give you . . ."

Mason sighed and pushed Bob down again with enough force that Bob finally managed to touch the bottom. By the time he got around to standing up, almost half of his upper body emerged from the water.

"See?" Mason said.

"You tried to drown me," Bob grunted.

"I just wanted you to find the bottom. You were flopping around like a damn trout at the bottom of a fishing boat."

"Boat? Boat! Aw, no!" Bob cried. "Where's the *Jack*?"

Mason pointed upstream. "Somewhere that way, I'd imagine."

"It left us behind?"

"Why wouldn't it? You think we're important enough to warrant a search party?"

It took a few seconds, but Bob finally stopped trying to spot the *Delta Jack* in the darkness. When he turned his eyes toward Mason, he asked, "Where's the money?"

"Can't buy your way out of this one, I'm afraid," Mason said.

"It don't belong to you."

"And it doesn't belong to you either. You stole it. You and Virgil both."

"We won it, fair and square," Bob said.

"Fair and . . . and . . . square?" Mason laughed. Each word he spoke was harder to get out than the last. "That's fine talk coming from . . . from a dice smith."

"Who's Smith?"

"You . . . really are . . ."

"What's wrong with you?" Bob asked.

Mason wanted to answer but couldn't think of any words to say. That alone was enough to cause concern. His next hint that things weren't right inside him was when his vision started to blacken around the edges.

He didn't recall much of anything after that.

Chapter 16

Mason dreamed he was falling.

Falling and toppling.

End over end.

After a while, the toppling stopped. Unfortunately it stopped when he felt he was upside down. Instead of rolling through space, he merely hung there and swayed in short arcs like a pendulum.

His body ached.

It was an ache that soaked all the way down to the bone until it became impossible to pin down the exact spot where it started.

His stomach twisted into a knot, wringing all the bile up to the back of his throat. At least he hadn't eaten much in the last . . . he didn't even know how long it had been. All he could say for certain was that whatever was inside him was on its way back up. He opened his mouth, which was all it took to get the wheels turning. Suddenly his entire body tensed and he reflexively reached out for something to grab in the inky darkness that had enveloped him. What he found was smooth and yet coarse. It was moving, just under the surface. Before Mason could figure out what he'd found, he emptied his stomach in a violent wretch.

"Aw, fer Pete's sake!" someone nearby groaned.

Mason tensed again, only this time there was nothing left to come up. Several dry heaves racked his tired body and when they subsided he felt surprisingly better.

"You make another mess on my saddlebags or did you manage to puke yer guts out onto the ground instead?"

The light that flooded through Mason's skull was nothing divine or unusual. It was simply his eyelids peeling open after being stuck to his head by a mixture of blood, dirt, and sweat. When he allowed his body to relax, he conformed to a wide sloping shape that had a very familiar odor. He blinked, cleared his throat, and waited for his vision to clear.

"You awake?" the nearby man asked.

Mason let himself hang for a spell, swaying to the movements of a horse's plodding steps. Before he could get used to the current state of affairs, an elbow was jabbed into his shoulder.

"Answer me."

Thc first attempt Mason made to respond was just a croak from the back of his throat. He coughed, winced at the taste of the remnants of what he'd just spat up, and tried again. "Yeah," he finally said. "I'm awake."

When Mason tried to move, he found that he could do so rather freely. His arms hung down to dangle against the horse's flank, as did his legs. Next, he attempted to shift the weight of his body. As far as he could tell from that small bit of experimentation, he was simply draped over the back of that horse. Placing his hands flat against the horse's rear haunches, Mason kicked his feet until he could slide off.

"Aw, now you went and done it!" the horse's rider said.

Mason's vision was slowly clearing, but his balance wasn't quite there yet. When his boots hit the ground, he remained upright for a second before his knees buckled and he dropped straight down onto his backside.

The rider brought his horse around, gripping the reins in one hand and a pistol in the other. Mason's pistol, to be exact. Upon seeing the gun in the man's hand, Mason slapped a hand against his belly.

"Won't find that sawed-off model," the man said. "You won't catch me with that one twice."

Mason blinked several more times and then rubbed his eyes. Between the haze in his head and the brightness of the sun, it had been difficult for him to focus on much of anything. With a little effort, though, he could make out the rider's face just enough to learn his identity.

"Winslow?" Mason croaked.

The rider smiled down at him. "You ain't forgotten my name after shooting my damn leg. I'm real touched. Now get the hell up."

"What's going on?" Recent memories came to him in a rush, sending a wave of panic through Mason's blood. "Where's Bob?"

"Bob?"

"He's the man . . . about my height . . ." Between the throbbing in Mason's skull and Bob's distinct lack of any memorable features, it was difficult for Mason to come up with much of a description.

"Oh, you mean the fella who fell off the boat with you?" Winslow asked, saving Mason the trouble of putting more words together.

"Yes."

"He's gone."

"Where'd he go?"

Winslow looked up to the clear blue sky. "Now, that's one of life's mysteries. I can tell you I shot him, though."

"He's dead?" Mason asked.

"Oh, that's for certain. It was messy."

Mason sighed. Part of him couldn't help thinking about how much easier things would have been if he had just taken the shot when he had it. If Bob was going to die anyway . . . but he knew better than that. Things wouldn't have been simpler. They would have been very difficult, but just in a slightly different way. Forcing himself to clear his head a bit more, Mason asked, "What happened?"

"Well . . . that Bob fella was mighty anxious when I found the two of you. He did something he shouldn't have and—"

"No," Mason cut in. "I mean . . . how'd I wind up here? How is it that you're here as well?"

"Get walkin' and I'll tell you the story." When Mason didn't move right away, Winslow thumbed back the hammer of the Remington.

Mason started walking before the inevitable threats were issued. The river was to his right, and to his left was a thick crop of weeds and trees. Gnats and mosquitoes filled the air, buzzing amid a symphony of cicadas. The more his ears cleared up, the more Mason wished for them to close again. Since there wasn't much of a choice of places to go at the moment, he walked in the same direction the horse had been pointed before. It must have been the correct decision, because Winslow flicked his reins to get moving that way as well.

Reflexively Mason reached for his watch. It wasn't there, so he asked, "What time is it?"

"What's the matter?" Winslow replied. "Got somewhere to be?"

"Actually, yes."

Coming up alongside Mason, Winslow made sure the man on foot could see when he reached into a jacket pocket to pull out Mason's watch. He flicked it open, checked its face, and said, "Looks to be a bit after eight in the morning. This might not be accurate, seeing as how this watch of yours seems to have gotten wet."

"Just tell me how I wound up on the back of that horse."

"Do you recall the last time we met?" When Mason turned to glare at him, Winslow said, "You seem out of sorts."

"I remember."

"Well, I was escorted straight off the *Jack* and into the office of a man who could barely call himself a doctor. He stitched me up, wrapped half a splint onto my leg, and meant to charge me as if he'd cured me of everything that ailed me. I told him to go to hell and I left."

"You were in a condition to walk?" Mason asked.

"Not as such, but I had a schedule to keep. You see, the *Delta Jack* may not be the fastest boat on the water, but I couldn't let her get too far away if I was gonna catch up to her again."

"You seem to be in an awful hurry to get tossed off the same boat again."

"I wouldn't have gotten tossed anywhere," Winslow said. "Not after I had a word with Mr. Greeley."

Mason laughed. It wasn't anything that could be heard from a distance, but it still hurt his aching joints. "You were trying to sign on as an overman, right?"

"Yeah. What's so funny about that?"

"What's funny is the thought of you as an overman."

"Oh, that's right. You and them have locked horns recently, huh?"

"Yes, and any one of the overmen I saw could chew you up and spit you out just like I spat out my last couple of meals back there. And," Mason added, "whatever was left would smell just as bad as the mess that was left behind."

"I've got leverage with Mr. Greeley," Winslow boasted while using the Remington to tap his chest. "You think just anyone is allowed to sign on as one of his men?"

"No, which means you're definitely out of the running."

"When I was put off the *Jack*, it was just to teach me a lesson and get my leg fixed. After that, I was to come on back and arrange some other way for me to prove my worth."

"Oh, so Greeley is going to make a special stop to pick up a prospective gun hand. A gun hand, by the way," Mason scoffed, "who's already failed at the single job he decided to take on."

"For your information, I wasn't supposed to kill you. I was just supposed to . . ."

"What?" Mason asked. "What were you supposed to do?"

"Forget it."

Mason pulled in a deep breath and let it out with a sigh. "All right, then. You still haven't told me how I wound up on that horse."

Winslow smiled, relishing the fact that he was back on friendlier ground. "The man who put me off that boat told me to come back when I was healed up, but I could tell he didn't really expect to see my face again. I could also tell he wouldn't have many good things to say about me the next time he spoke with Mr. Greeley."

As much as Mason wanted to throw another smart

comment or two at Winslow, he kept himself from doing so. Winslow seemed happy to keep talking, which suited Mason just fine.

"I wanted to talk to Greeley again sooner than that," Winslow continued. "And I thought if I could meet up with the *Jack* when she got to her next port, I should even be able to get another crack at you. Turns out I got out of that sorry excuse of a doctor's office quick enough to follow the river and catch sight of the *Jack* in no time at all!"

"I assume having the law nipping at your heels lit a fire under you as well," Mason said while shooting a sideways glance up at the other man. "That must have made it a bit easier to choke back on the pain from that leg."

Winslow twitched. "Law? What law?"

"You mean you stole that horse without anyone knowing?" Mason asked. "When I pictured you storming out of some doctor's office with your leg bandaged and a scowl on your face, I imagined you just grabbing the first horse you could find."

"That ain't how it went," Winslow said hesitantly.

"Really? So Mr. Greeley was kind enough to have a horse waiting for you? Or maybe you were carrying enough money to buy one?"

Scowling, Winslow said, "It wasn't the first horse I could find. Besides, ain't none of that will matter once I get Mr. Greeley to see what I bring to the table."

"Yeah? And what's that?"

"You!" Winslow was back to being full of himself as he puffed out his chest. "I been keeping up with that boat for the better part of a day, just waiting for it to dock or make another stop or even slow down so I might try to signal the captain. Even with this leg that you ruined, I woulda swum all the way out to that boat if I had to."

"Leg that I ruined?" Mason asked. Even though he knew nothing would come of it, he couldn't keep himself from questioning the other man's sorrowful words.

"You're the one that shot me, weren't you?" Winslow said.

"Only because you meant to kill me!"

"I wasn't gonna kill you. Hurt you, maybe, but not kill you."

"Oh, you're right, then," Mason said, sneering. "I'm a cad."

"I guess it don't matter none. Soon as I heard gunshots coming from the *Jack*, I thought for certain it wouldn't be long before the boat stopped. Maybe to let someone off or to toss off whoever was making that trouble. At least that commotion made it easier for me to figure out how far ahead she was.

"I rode along the river," Winslow continued, clearly enjoying telling his story to a captive audience. "There was a straight stretch and I could see the *Jack* up ahead. I thought maybe I might catch up to her then and there. Even though I didn't get close enough, I gained a lot of ground. Enough ground to hear more commotion and see some unlucky fellas fall over the rail."

As Winslow kept talking, Mason kept his eyes open for an opportunity to make good on an escape. There might be some path that he could take on foot that would slow a man down who was riding a horse. Perhaps he could spot a thick branch or a rock that was large enough to be used as a weapon. There were bound to be things like that around, but just none of them in the immediate vicinity. Not yet anyway.

Winslow had his eye on Mason but didn't seem overly concerned about him. The Remington was held in an easy grip as he kept right on spinning his yarn. "It wasn't easy finding the two of you," he said. "Something as big as the *Delta Jack* faded from sight in all that dark, so spotting two men in all that water wasn't no picnic. In fact, I missed you both on my first look. After I doubled back for another, there the two of you were. Washed up like a couple of drowned rats."

"And you just couldn't help yourself," Mason said.

"I didn't know who it was at first. That other fella . . . what was his name?"

"Bob."

"Yeah, Bob." When Winslow spoke that name, he did so as if he were a hunter talking about the most dangerous bear in the woods. "He was hoppin' mad when I found him. You know, I've heard that said plenty of times, but he truly was hoppin' mad! He was hoppin up and down, carryin' on like a lunatic when I pulled him off you."

"I thought you would've let him finish the job," Mason said.

"I didn't even know you were the other man that fell over. You was lyin' facedown like someone dropped you there."

Now that he'd had some time to wake up, Mason was remembering more and more from what had happened with Bob. Walking helped get the blood flowing as well. As near as he could recall, he'd simply passed out from sheer exhaustion. It hadn't been the first time that had happened. Normally, however, it was after days of sitting at a card table with nothing in his belly apart from whiskey and whatever greasy mess the saloon had cooked up that night. At those times, he wound up slumped in his chair, snoring while the other players snickered and tossed trash at his head.

This had been different. Mason had been put through the wringer a few times. He'd been beaten, chased, and then tossed off the *Jack* so he could swim for his life. Once he added in the fact that he'd been exhausted from lack of sleep to begin with, Mason was surprised he'd made it to dry land before his body gave out on him.

"Gettin' the drop on ol' Bob wasn't exactly a challenge," Winslow said. "All I had to do was climb down from my horse and walk over to him. He called me a gimping son of a bitch and I knocked him down with one good punch. I rolled you over, got a look at yer face, and convinced Bob to help load you on my horse."

"You two found something in common, did you? Wanting to do me bodily harm?"

"Something like that. Bob wasn't much in a talking mood, though. He surely didn't take kindly to me tellin' him to load up this horse. I changed his mind when I found your gun. He gave me some lip that I wasn't in a mood to hear and then knocked into my bad leg, so I pulled my trigger. The powder must've been wet, because it didn't fire."

"What a shame," Mason said.

"I hit him upside the head and kept pulling the trigger until I found one round that did what it was supposed to do. Bob actually looked surprised when it happened. Like he didn't think anything bad could happen to him."

"Bob wasn't exactly a learned man."

"Well, now he's just a dead man. Since you were on my horse and still asleep, I started riding down the river. Shouldn't be long before we meet up with the *Jack*. I think she was supposed to make a stop in Tennessee before too long."

She sure was. Mason had hoped to be on the riverboat when that happened, but a man couldn't get everything he wanted. Still, there was a bit of time before his meeting with Greeley. If he was going to make a move on Winslow, Mason had to make it good. As he'd learned through years of playing cards, the best way to pull off any move from a bluff to a giant raise was to preface it with a bit of groundwork.

"Any chance I can get back on that horse?" Mason asked.

"Oh, sure!" Winslow replied. "We'll take turns. If you like, I'll even let you hold the gun for a spell. Shut yer mouth and keep walkin'."

Mason was a long way from healthy, but he was in good enough condition to move faster than he was doing so at the moment. He also didn't need to limp so dramatically with every step, which he did to play up his fatigue to the highest possible degree. If he could pass himself off as weaker than he truly was, he should have an advantage when the time came to part company with Winslow for good.

Then again, since he was only escaping to meet up with Greeley, it was difficult for Mason to decide which option was more appealing. He could always run in another direction entirely and take his chances on his own. Mason quickly set that option aside. He was in too deep to just run away now, and he wasn't in good enough condition to get very far anyhow.

Sometimes Mason wished he couldn't see so many of the angles in front of him. There was a certain contentment that came along with shortsightedness.

Chapter 17

For the first short portion of their trip along the riverbank, there were several times when Mason considered making a run for it. He'd just be taking his chances with Winslow experiencing another couple of misfires with the Remington. No matter what happened, it would be better than staying with Winslow, who would not stop talking.

The majority of what Winslow said involved all the damage he could do once he became an overman and all the many benefits Greeley gave to his men. If half of what Winslow said was to be believed, the overmen were just a few pegs below royalty. While that might have held true on board the *Delta Jack*, anywhere else they were simply thugs.

But there was no reason to burst Winslow's bubble where that was concerned. Mason let him spout off for a couple of miles, since doing that allowed him to survey his surroundings and even pick up a few rocks and a sharp stick off the ground, which could later be put to use. Mason had yet to come up with a way those things would be useful, but he wasn't about to give up hope.

"What time is it now?" Mason asked.

"I told you already, this watch may be broke."

"Just tell me what it says."

Winslow sighed as if he'd just now lost the desire to keep flapping his gums about something or other. "Little after nine," he said.

"Any way of telling if that's accurate?"

"What appointments do you got, huh? Any schedule you're tryin' to keep, you can just forget about it. You wanna know why?"

"Because," Mason said as he wearily recited the same tired threat that had already been leveled at him several times in the last half hour, "you're the one holding the gun and I'm the one walking."

"That's right."

In the distance, a shrill whistle blew. Mason's head perked up as he looked upriver. There was a bend not too far ahead and the river past it was hidden by a thick patch of woods. In the sky above the trees, however, was a trail of smoke leading to a point that couldn't have been very far away.

"Where's the port you're headed to?" Mason asked.

Winslow stood in his stirrups to get a better look. "Don't know," he said. "Somewhere in Tennessee is all I heard."

"Are we in Tennessee?"

"Don't you know that much?" Winslow grumbled.

Mason decided he didn't need to know the answer to his question badly enough to keep begging for it. He stuffed his hands into his pockets and set his sights on the path in front of him. If he looked a bit harder, perhaps he could find the chance he'd been waiting for.

They rounded the bend, which revealed a larger stretch of river. The water rippled as if still feeling the effects of the *Delta Jack*'s passage. Farther along was a welcome sight for Mason's very sore eyes.

"There she is!" Winslow proclaimed. "I knew I'd catch up to her before long. How far do you think that is? Maybe two miles away?"

"If that," Mason said.

"Pick up the pace so we get there before she casts off."

"Or I could ride on that horse with you. We'd definitely make it then."

"Oh, you'd like that, wouldn't you?" Winslow sneered.

"Yes, I would!" Mason snapped. "That's why I said it. Get me up in that saddle so we can be sure to get back on board that boat!"

"Just so you can try to get me offa this horse? I don't think so."

"Then tie me up."

"Ain't got a rope," Winslow said. "Wait a second. We may not need to worry about walkin' or ridin' out to the *Jack*. We can float out to it." Scowling, he muttered, "Would that be quicker or not?"

Once again, Mason looked over to the gun in Winslow's hand and tried to figure the odds of him being able to hit a moving target. Even though Winslow had taken everything from Mason's pockets and holster, those items could be replaced. Not having to put up with the idiot for one more minute would be worth the cost of a few new weapons. Since Winslow's odds only improved with every bit of time the gunpowder in those rounds took to dry, Mason didn't have much time at his disposal.

"You're honestly thinking of swimming upriver instead of riding?" Mason asked.

"No. I thought we'd take that boat."

Mason looked in the same direction as Winslow. There were a few large rocks embedded in the riverbank about a hundred yards away, but he hadn't thought much of them. Now that he took a longer look, Mason could see what could have been the pointed bow of a rowboat poking out from behind the rocks. Being higher up would have given Winslow a slightly better angle as he stared toward the rocks intently.

Of two things, Mason quickly became certain. The first was that a small boat had definitely been stashed behind those rocks. The second was that he probably wouldn't get a much better chance to escape than when Winslow was gawking at that boat. Picking a spot on the ground in front of him, Mason dug his toe into the sandy dirt and stumbled forward.

"Ow, hell!" Mason groaned.

"What'd you do?" Winslow asked without looking back at him.

"Tripped over something."

"Keep walkin' anyway."

"I may have twisted my ankle," Mason complained.

Winslow looked over to him, but only for a second before looking back toward the rocks. "If I can get as far as I have with a shot-up leg, you can keep walkin' on a twisted ankle."

"It . . . may be broken." When he saw that Winslow wasn't about to budge from his spot, Mason hunkered down as though he was about to curl up like a shriveled piece of cabbage.

"You really are some kind of dandy," Winslow said as he brought his horse around to ride over to the spot where Mason was huddled. "You don't have soft rugs under your feet or fancy crystal chandy-leers over your head and you just go to pieces."

Although he appeared ready to fall over, Mason tensed every one of his muscles in anticipation of the perfect moment. His head was bowed, but he watched Winslow ride over to him. There was a fifty-fifty chance that Winslow would approach him in the direction Mason wanted. By the looks of it, this was going to be one coin flip that he might win.

Pulling back on his reins a few yards short of where Mason had pretended to trip, Winslow told him, "Get up."

"Just . . . give me a second," Mason replied through a strained breath.

"You already took a few seconds. Get up right now before I put you down for good."

Mason started to stand, but winced and dropped back down again. He knew he was laying it on a bit thick, which was the point, since he guessed that would get under Winslow's skin even more than if he played his role convincingly.

"You're not foolin' anyone," Winslow snarled. "I've got half a mind to drag you behind this damn horse!"

It seemed Mason's guess had been right.

Shifting his reins to the other hand, Winslow brought his horse a little closer to Mason. The anger in his eyes only grew when he leaned down to grab Mason's arm, because that was the same side as his hastily bandaged leg. "It don't even matter if you're sandbagging or not," Winslow said. "By the time I haul you over to them rocks, if your legs weren't busted already, they sure will have—"

Mason's hand dipped into his pocket to grab the stick he'd procured earlier during the walk. It had been snapped in half, which created a sharp point at one end. When Mason brought his fist down, he drove that point into the middle of the bloody patch where Winslow had been shot by the sawed-off Remington.

Winslow clamped his jaw shut and his face turned red with the effort of choking back the scream that leaped into his throat. He managed to contain himself for about half a second before cutting loose with a bellowing, profanity-laden roar. He tried once more to grab hold of Mason's arm, but blinding pain sapped him of a good deal of his strength. That made it relatively easy for Mason to slap away his hand.

As soon as he'd diverted the hand meant to drag him alongside the horse, Mason reached for the Remington that had been tucked under Winslow's belt for safekeeping. He might have gotten to it if Winslow hadn't suddenly reeled back in his saddle while tugging on the reins. His stolen horse pivoted around toward Mason, its hooves stomping the ground within inches of Mason's feet. The last thing Mason needed was a genuine injury that would render him immobile, so he abandoned his pistol and headed for the rocks at a dead run.

Winslow caught his breath and shouted, "You're dead!"

Mason's head filled with all the new angles he now faced. Rather than sift through them as he would normally have preferred, he just pumped his legs harder to run faster.

"You're . . . *ooowwww*!" Winslow hollered.

It was only then that Mason realized the stick was no longer in his hand. He must have left it in Winslow's wounded leg where it had just been pulled out. That bought Mason enough time to cover a few more yards of riverbank, but he figured he'd pay for it by having a much angrier man coming after him.

For the second time in as many minutes, Mason was right.

Before Winslow let his next obscenity fly, he sent a pair of bullets through the air to hiss over Mason's head. After that, the profanities flowed like water.

Mason was too busy running to worry about whatever nonsense Winslow was spewing this time around. His breath came in short, choppy bursts and his feet dug holes into loose dirt that had been washed up by winds and river water. As another shot whipped closer to him than the ones before it, Mason pushed his muscles to the point of burning to close some more distance between himself and those rocks.

The next shots that were fired sounded different than the previous ones. A more experienced gunman might have been able to tell the caliber of those rounds or maybe even the model of the weapon that had set them to flying, but all Mason knew was that they hadn't come from his Remington. At the moment, that was more than enough.

More shots were fired back and forth and fewer of those bullets were being sent in Mason's direction. After running for what felt like a good couple of miles, he made it to the large rocks stuck in the mud. In that same area, there was a rotting tree trunk and moldy planks from what could have been a boat or a cabin that had been blackened by a fire. Mason was pleased to see that there was indeed a rowboat. Unfortunately dragging a boat to the water and rowing away didn't seem like such a good idea with at least two armed men nearby.

Mason approached the boat and rather than try to push it into the river, he checked inside to see if its owner had left anything behind. Apart from oars fastened to the sides of the boat through metal rings, there were only a few articles of clothing folded and placed on one of the narrow seats.

Not too far away, the gunshots had stopped. Winslow's mouth, however, had yet to run out of steam.

"Whoever you are," Winslow shouted, "you picked the wrong man to cross!"

Despite having just searched the boat, Mason did it again in the hopes that he might have overlooked something the first time around. It didn't take much time for him to see that he hadn't.

"That's right, whoever you are!" Winslow hollered. "I see you. Just stay where you are!"

There could have been some useful items wedged beneath the boat, near the log, or in the mud around the base of the rocks. If Mason had had just a bit more time, he would have looked around to see what he could find. But, judging by the heavy thump of approaching hooves, time wasn't something Mason had in abundance.

Winslow rode into view. He had the Remington in hand but was pointing it toward the trees. "Come on," he said. "We're going."

"Who else is out there?"

"I don't know. I didn't get much of a look at them. Don't matter, though, because we're goin'."

The next time Winslow glanced toward the trees, Mason stuck his hand into his other pocket. "Why were they shooting at you?"

"They didn't say anything, so how should I know?"

"They? There's more than one?"

"Yes!" Winslow barked. He turned in his saddle and leaned over to grab at Mason's arm or possibly his shirt. "Just come along with me before I—"

Mason cut him short by pulling his hand from his pocket and punching Winslow squarely on the nose. The impact sent Winslow teetering in the other direction, where he wobbled and tried unsuccessfully to regain his balance. His eyes seemed focused on something that wasn't there as he slid from his saddle. If he hadn't been knocked out from the punch, he was certainly put to sleep when he hit his head on a rock after falling off his horse.

"Damn," Mason said as he winced in surprise. The horse had been startled by the loss of its rider and moved quickly out of the narrow space between the log and rowboat. Now that Mason had a clear view of Winslow, he hurried over to him to check if his punch had proven to be fatal.

Winslow was still breathing, but he wasn't a pretty sight.

"That you, Mr. Mason?" asked a man who had gotten all the way to the rowboat without making a sound.

Mason wheeled toward the sound of that voice. The burly man wasn't familiar, but the pearl gray of his pants and the club hanging from his belt were very distinctive. "Y . . . yes. I'm Mason."

Another man stood behind the first. Both had the sleeves of their starched white shirts rolled up to their elbows. They were missing their pearl gray jackets, which Mason had discovered neatly folded and placed on one of the seats inside the rowboat.

"You know who we are?" the man asked.

"Pretty sure I do."

"Good. Then you won't argue when I tell you to come along with us without making a fuss."

"Where are you taking me?" Mason asked.

"I thought you said you knew who we are."

"That's right, but . . ."

"If we wanted to bury you here, we'd already be digging the hole," the man stated. He looked down at Winslow and asked, "What did you intend to do with this one here?"

Mason opened his fist and allowed the rocks he'd collected earlier during his walk to fall from his hand. "I intended to hit him in the face with a fistful of rocks. Seems like that plan worked out pretty well."

"Who is he?"

"You don't know?"

The overman took another look down at Winslow and grunted. "Looks familiar, but I can't put a name to his face."

Mason couldn't help smirking. "Now, that truly is funny."

Chapter 18

When Mason rode the rest of the way to where the *Delta Jack* was docked, it was on the same horse that had brought him this far. This time, however, he was the one sitting in the saddle. One of the overmen who'd found Winslow rode alongside him and the other rowed the boat to the dock. The gunman in the boat was so thick through the chest and arms that he made the task seem relatively easy.

Mason was escorted back onto the riverboat at a little after ten in the morning. Surprisingly enough, he was given until the agreed-upon time to clean himself up in his own cabin. Fighting the urge to lie down and catch some sleep, Mason gathered up everything he needed, splashed some clean water onto his face, and changed into fresh clothes. Those simple things alone made him feel like a new man.

On his way down to the main card room, Mason walked around to the starboard side, where the rowboat had been hauled up from the water by a pair of hooks. He leaned over the edge and saw Winslow still lying in the little boat like a piece of forgotten baggage.

* * *

The card room wasn't quite as full as it had been during the middle of the night, but there was still a respectable number of gamblers at the tables. Most of them had gotten even less sleep than Mason, and the ones who had brighter eyes carried the bulk of the conversations. The biggest difference at that hour was the number of working girls standing at the bar as opposed to sitting in men's laps. At that time of day, even for the truest night owls, breakfast was in higher demand than sweet talk from a pretty set of lips. One of the ladies not at the bar spotted Mason and came right over to him.

"Where have you been?" Maggie asked.

"I got tossed overboard," he said.

When she looked him up and down, only to find a clean set of clothes wrapped around his lean frame, she clearly wasn't feeling any sympathy. "The least you could have done before catching a nap was let me know you were done in Virgil's cabin."

"Did he give you any trouble?"

"Not a bit. He got awfully presumptuous the longer I kept him distracted, but I've managed to shake free of worse than him. Did you find what you were after?"

"Not enough to settle my debt," Mason replied, "but enough to give me a good running start at it."

"Speaking of that," she said while reaching into a pocket stitched into the bodice of her dress. "Here's some of that money I offered."

"This is very generous. Are you sure you can part with it?"

"I'm not parting with anything," she said. "It's a loan. Save your gratitude until after I let you know what the interest will be."

Mason let his eyes wander up and down over her figure. "I can tell you where my interest lies right about now."

She smiled at him in the same way she would smile at a precocious boy. Patting his cheek in a similar fashion, she said, "That's very flattering, but I doubt you could handle any vigorous pastimes right now. You look like one big bruise."

Although he wasn't sure how he looked, Mason did know he could feel the playful touch of her hand against his face as if it were an angry slap. He did his best to hide his wince and said, "Sometimes the best thing for a man to help recover from his wound is a mighty good distraction."

"You really don't let up, do you?"

"Nope."

"If you had showed me this side of you while we were playing cards," she said, "I might not have considered lending you this money."

"I do like to make a good first impression," he said.

"And the impressions after that?"

"A man can only hold back his instincts for so long."

Maggie let out an exasperated sigh. There was something in her eyes, even as she was rolling them, that told Mason she was enjoying the conversation at least a little bit. "I wasn't about to carry all that money with me," she said. "I can get to the rest real soon. Instead of handing it over in a roomful of card cheats and gamblers, why don't I bring it to your cabin?"

"That sounds like a good idea. It's number twenty-four."

Turning her back on him, she tossed a disinterested wave over her shoulder and said, "A bath couldn't hurt, you know."

"For me or you?"

She shook her head and quickened her pace to get away from him.

"Or us?" Mason added.

Maggie didn't respond to that. She could have heard him, but she also could have been too far away to catch his comment. He put the odds at an even fifty-fifty between the two. He was more interested in something else, however. Something that could prove to be much more promising than any wager laid down at a poker game.

He leaned back against a wall, partly to appear as though he didn't have a care in the world and partly to support the weight of a very tired body. "Come on, now," he said under his breath. "Don't disappoint me."

Maggie kept a purposeful stride as she went to the door leading out of the card room.

"Come on . . ."

There was no possible way she could have heard the words that Mason spoke quietly to himself. Even so, she honored his request by turning to look back at him one last time before walking out of the room.

He was right there watching her and tipped his hat to the lady. "Much obliged, ma'am," he said.

Mason went back to his cabin, his steps carrying him as if he were fresh as a daisy and ready to grab the world by the throat. Once he got inside, however, he relaxed his guard and let out the breath that had been keeping his chest puffed out all the way from the main card room. He unbuttoned his jacket and then his vest, peeling them both off to lay them on his bed. There was a small shaving mirror hanging from the wall above the washbasin, which he'd mostly ignored up to this point. He'd seen his own reflection plenty of times before and hadn't been anxious to see the state of it after all the hell he'd gone through recently. After what Maggie had told him, though, he was curious as to how bad it could be.

"Good Lord," he groaned when he got a look at the bruised and battered man staring back at him from the looking glass.

His eyes were sunken from sheer exhaustion, as were his cheeks. Bruises covered his face like blotchy paint, and one side of his jaw was swollen. Cuts marred him even further, making him look every bit the wreck that Maggie had hinted at. Since he was already surveying the damage, Mason unbuttoned his shirt to get a look at the rest of the picture.

There were at least five different shades of black and blue smeared along his rib cage, mixed with a generous portion of red and yellow. Part of Mason's reasoning for not setting his eyes on what he'd figured would be an ugly picture was that he might be able to convince himself that it wasn't so bad if he couldn't see it. To some extent, he'd been correct. Now that he was looking straight at the calling cards left by all the punishment he'd taken recently, the pain throughout his body seeped in that much deeper.

Inch by inch, Mason tested his ribs and worked some of the kinks out of the joints in his upper body. Every movement was followed by a wince. And with every wince, there came a fresh jolt of discomfort. He might not have been able to recall each time he'd taken a punch or was otherwise knocked around, but he could feel every last one of those encounters etched into the fiber of his aching body.

"How the blazes are you still standing?" he asked the reflection in the small circular mirror.

Mason went to his bed and sat on the edge of the mattress. If he was going to keep his appointment with Greeley, he couldn't stretch out or make himself very comfortable. Even closing his eyes for too long put him in danger of sleeping through the rest of the day. Mason split the difference by putting his elbows on his knees and allowing his head to hang forward while his eyelids drooped until they only allowed a sliver of the outside world to make it through.

Even with the precautions he took, Mason began to feel sleep encroaching on all sides. Like a stalking predator, it intended to bring him down and wasn't about to be discouraged. It was, however, frightened away by a sudden sharp sound that came from the door.

Mason's head snapped up and he rubbed his eyes. As he was trying to figure out whether or not he'd imagined the noise, it came again. It was just a knock and still it had sped his pulse up to keep him from collapsing. He went to the door and opened it just enough to get a look outside.

"Did I wake you?" Maggie asked.

"If you did, I'm grateful," he said. "Come in."

She stepped inside. The sunlight seemed brighter than it had when he was last out of his room. Whether that was due to the advancement of hours or the sensitivity of his eyes, Mason did not know. He was simply grateful to shut the door again.

Maggie carried an envelope that was folded shut but not sealed. "Here you go," she said. "The rest of that money I offered."

It wasn't until that moment that Mason realized he

hadn't even counted the first bundle of cash she'd given him. He took the envelope and reflexively hefted its weight in his hand. "I'm grateful," he said. "Very much so. Thank you."

Her features took on an expression of exaggerated pity as she said, "You look awful."

Suddenly very much aware of his partial state of undress, Mason shrugged. "Not exactly what a man wants to hear when his shirt is off, but I suppose you're right."

Having walked past him to stand near the porthole, Maggie stepped closer to him. "Actually, for a man who's been tossed overboard after being dangled a couple of inches from a moving riverboat's paddlewheel, you look very good indeed."

It seemed the story regarding Mason's encounter with the overmen on the third deck had made the rounds throughout the *Jack*, but had become slightly exaggerated. Since she seemed to be responding well to the embellishments, he wasn't going to split hairs over details.

"It was quite the harrowing affair," he said. "I did, however, fare much better than most other men who might have found themselves in a similar position."

"I would say none the worse for wear," Maggie replied while tracing her fingertips gently along his bruised chest and midsection, "but that wouldn't be entirely accurate."

"Perhaps I should spare you the sight of my injuries by more properly attiring myself."

"Or . . . we could tip the scales in the other direction."

Mason brought his hands up to the portions of her blouse that hung low on her shoulders. He gently pulled them down before diverting his attentions to unlacing Maggie's bodice. She made no move to stop him and smiled warmly as her dress loosened enough to be removed.

"Aren't you concerned with keeping your appointment?" she whispered.

"I was," he said. "Not so much anymore, though."

Chapter 19

"You're late," Greeley said as Mason stepped into one of the backrooms of the *Delta Jack*'s main theater.

Even though it wasn't as large as a traditional theater, the stage and the number of seats in front of it were impressive for something floating down the Mississippi. It was in that very room that well-known singers and dancers performed for the *Jack*'s audience. On any given night, the most beautiful girls in the county kicked their heels up for the audiences in front of that stage. There was even a small orchestra to accompany all those acts.

Some folks said Greeley kept his office there on account of all the noise. If a man was beaten or even shot so close to all that music and carrying on, hardly anyone would be able to hear it. Surely, those were just more rumors circulated to occupy idle minds between poker hands, but Mason couldn't help thinking about them now.

"Apologies," Mason said while straightening his waistcoat after having his weapons taken roughly away from him. "It's been a hard couple of days."

Greeley hadn't seemed very accommodating before, but he nodded and stood up from behind his desk. "Care for a drink?" he asked.

"I should get pummeled more often," Mason chided. "Every time I see someone anymore, they offer me a drink."

"And are you likely to refuse?"

"Not on your life."

Greeley's desk was small but well crafted and highly polished. The office was slightly smaller than a regular saloon's backroom, consisting of the desk, three chairs, and a cabinet that folded out to become a bar. Greeley went to that cabinet, removed two glasses from inside, and then took out a decanter of liquor.

As always, there were armed men wearing pearl gray suits in Greeley's immediate vicinity. Mason had had so many encounters with the overmen by now that they were all beginning to look familiar. None of them had formally introduced themselves, however, and he doubted that was likely to change anytime soon. The overman who stood nearby was one of the men who'd dangled Mason over the side of the upper deck. He looked to be in a better mood than he had been then, but not by much.

Handing over one of the glasses to Mason, Greeley said, "I hear you've been busy since we last talked."

"What have you heard?"

"That you jumped ship when you were supposed to be gathering up enough money to pay your debt."

Mason quickly started to defend himself, but was motioned to keep quiet for the moment.

"No need to explain," Greeley said. "It didn't take long for a couple different stories to get to me. No matter how you left the *Jack*, however, I had to send some men out to fetch you. I didn't want to miss this chance to continue our conversation."

And Mason was certain Greeley wasn't about to pass

up the opportunity to show he could back up the promise he'd made regarding the futility of anyone trying to get away from him when they had bills to pay.

"It didn't take long for those men to catch up to you," Greeley continued. "They were a bit surprised to find you weren't alone."

"Not more surprised than I was to see who'd bagged me and tossed me over the back of a stolen horse."

Greeley chuckled and sipped his drink. "Winstead, I think his name is."

"Winslow."

"Whatever. The man's got rocks for brains. He proved that well enough by thinking he could be on my payroll doing anything more than scrubbing the decks or shoveling coal."

Mason took a sip of his drink. It was a rather fine brandy that must have cost a pretty penny. On any other day, he would have savored it. Now, however, he longed for the harder impact of a good, cheap whiskey. "Speaking of him, is he . . . uh . . . still with us?"

"On the *Jack* or on this earth?" Greeley asked.

"Either."

"Yes to both, I'm afraid. Some of my boys want to have a word with him about the shots he fired at them when they found you. They'd prefer to have him awake for the experience. Considering how badly he wanted to join my men, I would assume shooting at them was some kind of mistake. Then again," Greeley added with a shrug, "that fellow is quite stupid."

"I can't argue with you there, but I will point out that a man like that could work pretty cheap."

"Are you campaigning for him?"

"Let's just say I don't want to see him dead."

"After all them times he tried to harm you?" Greeley asked. "I can't say that I understand your reasoning."

"If anyone should have killed him, it was me," Mason said. "But since he may also be the one person on this boat who's hurting more than I am, perhaps he deserves a touch of sympathy."

"A gambler with a heart," Greeley said while lifting his glass. "Never thought I'd see the day."

"Me neither," Mason sighed before taking another drink.

"To be perfectly frank with you, that idiot's fate depends on how friendly he is when he's up to talking again. If he begs good enough, he may just draw breath for another day or two. If he's still got some fight left in him, well . . ." Greeley shrugged and set his glass down. On his way back to his desk, he opened a drawer and removed a bundle of familiar weaponry. "I believe these things belong to you, Mr. Mason?"

"They do. I don't suppose I'd be overstepping if I asked for the return of my property?"

"Not at all! In fact, you're gonna need it."

While he was grateful for the prospect of getting his guns and knife back, Mason didn't much like the sound of that. "What will I need them for?" he asked. "That is, apart from the normal perils of day-to-day existence."

Greeley took his seat. Resting a hand on the sawed-off Remington, he asked, "How much money do you have for me?"

"Seven thousand fifty-six dollars," Mason replied. "I could scrounge up some pocket change to add in as well, but I doubt that would help much."

"Considering the situation you're in," Greeley said through a sharklike smile, "every little bit helps."

"Yes, well, there was over three thousand in chips at my spot when our game was ended."

"Three thousand two hundred, to be exact."

"Really?" Mason said. "I thought there was more than that."

"Afraid not."

Mason reached into his waistcoat's inner pocket for an envelope and then reached into the pocket on the other side for a second envelope. Holding one in each hand, he said, "Here's what I've got so far."

It was a sizable chunk of money, even for someone who made a living playing games where large sums of money frequently changed hands. When he handed it over to Greeley, Mason felt a painful twinge inside him that had nothing at all to do with the injuries he'd weathered of late.

Greeley took the envelopes, opened them one at a time, and flipped through their contents. He then held them up until the overman at the door stepped into the office to collect them both. The armed man tucked them away beneath his pearl gray jacket, which was undoubtedly a safer spot than the vaults at most banks.

"There's still a ways to go in clearing things up between us," Greeley said.

"Yes, but I told you before I wouldn't be able to collect the whole amount right away."

"I know," Greeley replied in a voice that was as dead as the wood composing his desk. "I ain't deaf."

Mason wasn't the sort of man to beg anyone for anything. It was a simple matter of survival instinct, however, to know when to back down a step or two. "I collected this amount in just a scant couple of hours," he reminded him. "That's got to count for something."

"Of course it does. It counts for ten thousand, two hundred and fifty-six dollars. You still owe a lot more than that, which counts for something as well. If you want a pat on the back for taking a chip out of the debt you incurred, then you'll have to look somewheres else."

Choking back on the urge to stand up and leave that office before being degraded any more, Mason nodded slowly. "I told you before I would find a way to pay my debt, and that's still my intention."

"Good, because I've put together a list for you."

"List?"

"That's right," Greeley said as he reached into another of his desk's drawers. "Remember my proposition regarding certain tasks you could perform to settle things between you and me?"

"Of course," Mason replied.

"Here it is." With that, Greeley placed a folded piece of paper on his desk and slid it toward Mason.

Mason picked it up and unfolded it to find a list of three names. After turning the paper over to see if there was anything on the other side, he asked, "This is it?"

"You want me to think of some more?"

"No, I just thought . . . well, yes, actually. I thought there'd be more. How am I supposed to know what these names even mean?"

"They're names of men, Mr. Mason."

"I can see that. Are they men who owe you money? Are they long-lost friends or relatives? Do they have one of your pets that you'd like returned? I could go on all day long and still not have any idea what you want me to do."

"The first name on that list," Greeley said. "Read it to me."

"Randal Simons."

"Right. He started off owing me money. He ducked me for a few years and then turned up in San Antonio with some story about how he'd needed to tend to some family tragedy, which was why he never called on me."

"I see. You found out there was no family tragedy?" Mason said. "I've heard plenty a man give that tired excuse."

"No, there was a tragedy," Greeley said. "His aunt and three cousins all died from a pox outbreak. Their homes were going to be taken away for some reason as well. I don't remember exactly." He grunted with a dismissive wave of his hand. "That don't matter. Everyone has bad things happen and the world don't stop turning on their account. It sure as hell don't stop when I run into a stretch of bad luck."

"That's . . . true," Mason said in the most sympathetic tone he could manage for such an unsympathetic tale.

"Even so, I showed him some compassion by not letting my boys cut him to pieces bit by bit starting with his toes and working their way up. Even gave him an extra couple of weeks to get his payment to me. You wanna know what he did in those weeks?"

"No."

Greeley leaned forward as if he was about to leap over the desk to strangle whoever was in front of him. "He surrounded himself with whatever was left of his family, got drunk, and told everyone that'd listen how he soaked me for all that money and didn't have any intention of paying me back."

"Oh. That's . . . that's not good."

"It sure ain't. And when I sent a few of my boys to get it from him, they found out that they'd been branded as horse thieves and a price had been put on their heads. My men ain't even thought about stealing no horses. That lazy coward just did that because of the bounty hunters that drift in and out of that town where he's at. Any man with his face on one of them notices finds himself staring down the barrel of a gun less than an hour after he arrives."

Mason couldn't help himself from chuckling. The laugh started in the pit of his stomach and threatened to burst out of him. Being exhausted didn't help matters any, but he did manage to stifle most of it. Unfortunately *most* wasn't enough.

"Something funny?" Greeley snarled.

"Not at all."

"Then why were you laughin'?"

"I wasn't laughing. I just . . ." Mason took a breath and shrugged. "Sorry. It's just that, you've got to admit, that's a rather amusing way to defend oneself."

"It wouldn't have been amusing if my men had been shot or killed."

"They weren't," Mason said right away.

"And how do you know that?"

"Because you would have said so right away. Also," Mason added, "I doubt you'd need help from any outsider to settle up a score that large or that you'd trust a task like that to someone like me."

Slowly the icy glare on Greeley's face began to thaw. "You're a smart fella, Abner. Real smart."

"Not smart enough, sometimes."

Greeley nodded. "Took the words right outta my mouth. Anyway, you're right. None of my boys was killed, but not from Simons's lack of trying. He's made a nice little home in that town of bounty hunters and crooked lawmen."

"Crooked lawmen?"

"All lawmen are crooked to some degree," Greeley said. "Or if they ain't, one of their partners is. Not that this town has much law anyways. From what I understand, the law's got an arrangement with the bounty hunters where wanted men are concerned. They're set up by one and taken down by the other. Only part that concerns me is that Simons's sister's husband is one of them crooked lawmen and one of his cousins is a bounty hunter."

"He's got quite the system going there, it seems."

"You're right about that."

"And you want me to find a chink in his armor?" Mason asked.

All that remained in Greeley's glass was enough liquor to slosh around the bottom as he idly waggled it back and forth. "Yeah," he said. "And then I want you to kill him."

"Kill him?"

"You heard me."

Mason sat forward. Whatever had been inside him that wanted to laugh was long gone. "I'm not a gunman," he said.

"You've made that real obvious a couple times since this mess has started," Greeley said smugly.

"Then I fail to see why you'd want me to do this. Especially when you've got so many gunmen on your payroll already."

"Is that all you think my boys are?" Greeley asked.

Since he was in this deep already, Mason didn't see any reason for prolonged niceties. "Yes," he said. "Everyone knows that's what they are."

Rather than try to feign being offended by Mason's words or tone, Greeley shrugged and said, "I suppose that's fair."

"Then send some of them," Mason said. "Hell, you've got a man lying around here somewhere who's dying to prove himself to you. That is, unless you've already dumped Winslow somewhere."

"No, he's here . . . somewhere." Looking over Mason's shoulder, he asked, "Right?"

The overman posted at the doorway nodded once.

"Yeah, he's here," Greeley continued. "You wanna take him with you?"

"No. I don't want to go at all."

"Well, I can't send my boys. I already told you about the arrangement Simons has with—"

"Yeah, yeah," Mason snapped. "The law and bounty hunters. I recall."

Not only did Greeley allow Mason to cut him off in the middle of a sentence, but he seemed more than a little amused by it. "You want another drink?" he asked.

"I want to know about the next name on the list," Mason said. He held up the paper, but needed a moment to stare at it before his racing mind could make sense of what was written there. "Seth Borden. Who is he? What do you need me to do with him?"

"We'll get to that when you're done with Simons."

"Then we should straighten one matter right now. I'm no killer."

Greeley's fist slammed down on top of his desk so hard that the impact was probably heard throughout all three of the *Delta Jack*'s decks. "You're in no position to dictate anything to me! You wanna know what a killer is? Look behind you, Mr. Mason. That there is one of *my* killers and he may not be able to get to Simons, but he can damn sure get to you."

Mason didn't need to look behind him to know the overman was there. He could feel the gunman's stare boring holes through the back of his head.

"You still owe me more than ten thousand dollars," Greeley continued, "and I've killed men for a lot less than that. You wanna know why I don't send more men after Simons or why I don't go after him myself or why I don't pay one of them crooked lawmen to do the job for me? I don't owe you answers to *any* of them questions. I own your hide, Mason, and if I decide I want you to dance across the Atlantic Ocean to pay off that debt, then by God that's what you'll do. Understand?"

"Yes," Mason said evenly.

"Good. Now you can stop looking at the other names on that list. We're docked here and staying put because this ain't too far away from the town where Simons is holed up. You'll get off here, go into town, find a quick way to bury Simons, and then come back onto this boat in no less than two days." Greeley jabbed a bony finger at Mason and added, "I better not have to tell you what a bad idea it would be to try and ride away without doing your part here. Simons may be dug in, but you're not. My boys will find you no matter where you go."

"You don't have to tell me that, Mr. Greeley," Mason said. "They already found me when even I didn't know where I was going."

"Good. Then we understand each other."

"We most certainly do."

"Then collect your guns and get the hell out of my office."

Chapter 20

When Mason got back to his cabin, he was so light-headed that he thought he might have dreamed his entire conversation with Greeley. He put the odds of that happening at less than twenty percent, which was being generous. The notion that so much bad news hadn't been dropped onto him at once was simply too appealing to turn away. But a man in his line of work didn't get anywhere but the poorhouse by betting everything on a long shot simply because he wanted it to win. There had to be other factors to swing a bet in that direction, and there were none to swing this one.

He was in the muck up to his eyes and there wasn't any good way to get out of it. Not yet anyway.

"Damn it," he sighed when he saw the small box sitting next to his washbasin.

Reluctantly Mason went over to the box. It was about a quarter the size of the washbasin itself and wasn't sealed. Using one finger to move one of the top flaps aside, he looked in to see several rounds of .44-caliber ammunition and approximately twenty dollars in cash. The money was wrapped in a piece of paper that read: *For the job and expenses—G.*

As was the case most of the time, the long shot proved to be a loser. The conversation had happened. The muck was just as deep as it had ever been.

His cabin's door creaked slightly as it was opened by someone from the hallway. Mason pivoted toward it while making a grab for his Remington.

"It's just me," Maggie said as she stopped half in and half out of the cabin. "Can I come in?"

Mason took his hand away from the sawed-off pistol tucked under his belt. "Sure. Why not?"

She stepped into the room, shut the door behind her, and stood with her back pressed against it. Reluctant to take another step toward him, she said, "I take it this conversation with Greeley went as well as the last one."

Looking down, Mason saw that his jacket had snagged on the shoulder holster. Both Remingtons were exposed, so he straightened his jacket to cover them once again. "You should leave."

"Why?"

"Because I've got to go somewhere and you shouldn't . . . you can't go with me."

Maggie approached him and reached out to place one hand on his chest. She already knew where to touch him, so it didn't hurt as she asked, "What did Greeley tell you?"

"We set up an arrangement," he said. "To settle that debt of mine."

"This can't just be about a debt."

"Why not?"

Her brow furrowed with concern. "Because this isn't the first big debt that someone's owed Greeley. Lord knows he wouldn't make this big a fuss every time it happened."

"Well, he's making a fuss now and I'm in the middle

of it," Mason snapped. "If it's the first time or last time really doesn't matter, now, does it?"

"It does," she replied. "It matters a lot." Maggie's features softened, but only for a moment before they regained the subtle edge that was as much a part of her as the nose on her face. "Any other time and Greeley would have dumped you over the side, dragged you alongside this boat, or tossed you into the paddlewheel."

"You know about all that, do you?"

"Of course I do. There's a lot of talk around here about those sorts of things. How have you not heard it?"

Mason chuckled. It was more of a way to let off some steam instead of expressing anything he found even slightly humorous. "I guess I have heard it. When I'm at the table, I'm usually thinking of other matters."

"Well, instead of trying to figure every angle before it happens, you should take more time to soak up the world around you." When she saw the surprise on his face, Maggie added, "I've figured out a lot about you while we were sitting at that card game. I could see the wheels turning behind those pretty eyes of yours then, just like I can see them now."

Grinning, Mason said, "If I'm that easy to read, it's no wonder I'm in so much debt."

"You're not easy to read," she assured him. "I suppose I was just paying closer attention to you than most."

"Should I be flattered by that?"

Maggie leaned even closer to him and placed a gentle kiss on his lower lip. "Yes," she whispered.

Mason couldn't have stopped his hands from encircling her waist if he'd wanted to. Fortunately he didn't want to. "You've been a surprise, Maggie. A good one. What happened at that game was a surprise as well."

"Which, I'm guessing, wasn't a very good one."

"Not even close."

"It happens to all of us," she said. "You get a read on someone, you think you have a hand completely figured out, and then the hammer drops. Sometimes it's because something was fixed in the game, and sometimes you're just . . . wrong."

Mason shook his head. "I've thought about that hand plenty. Part of me hasn't stopped thinking about it."

"Yet another thing that makes you similar to every other gambler in the world. Most of the hands we win get chalked up to a day's work and forgotten. The couple we lose stick with us. We remember every little thing." Straightening his tie, she added, "Isn't that why we all drink so much whiskey?"

"Greeley wasn't cheating," he said. "If he was cheating, he's better and smoother at it than me or anyone else I've ever known. No. He played that hand straight."

"You mean he outplayed you." When Mason looked at her with a pained wince, she rubbed his cheek and said, "You were wrong. That's the possibility that hurts the most. Believe me. I know. It's so much easier to know you were cheated. You might feel stupid for being tricked or falling for a lie, but at least there's someone else to blame. When you're wrong . . . it's just you."

"How long have you been on the circuit?" Mason asked.

Without needing to think about it, she replied, "Six years."

"Ever been cheated?"

"The only players who don't cheat a little bit at some point or another are the ones who line the pockets of people like us. To answer your question, though, yes. I've been cheated. It stung like hell, but I got over it."

Mason took more comfort from just standing there holding Maggie in his arms than from all the whiskey that had ever been distilled. "Ever been wrong?" he asked.

She didn't bat an eye before saying, "Of course not. Do you think I'm some kind of idiot?"

Mason was stunned for a second, but quickly started to laugh. Once he started, he couldn't stop. Eventually he wound up on the bed with her. He and Maggie didn't lie down or even embrace. He simply had to get off his feet and she sat beside him with one hand resting on his knee.

"Any chance you know a quick way to get to Europe without anyone knowing about it?" he asked.

"I've got a few good routes to Mexico or Canada."

Mason shook his head. "I'll need to get farther than that."

"To avoid Greeley? He barely ever leaves this boat. Just put a few days' ride between you and the Mississippi River and you should be fine."

"He's committed himself to this even more than I have. If he lets me get away, it makes him look bad. A man like him can't afford to look bad."

"Who gives a damn what he wants or likes?" she asked.

"He's got deep pockets," Mason said. "And there's always plenty of men out there who'll do dirty work for someone like that. Besides, I've never been the sort of man who runs. Even if it's good for him."

Maggie rubbed his leg and placed her other hand on his cheek. Drawing him in with the slightest of movements, she kissed him gently and said, "I'm liking you more and more."

"Too bad. I may not be around for much longer." Mason gave her a kiss and stood up. He picked up the box that had been left for him and set it in his carpetbag.

"What is it that Greeley wants from you anyway?"

"He wants me to kill a man."

"But you're no killer."

Gathering up the few personal things he had lying about, Mason put them in the bag and said, "That's what I told him. He wants me to do it to work off what I owe."

"So you're to become one of those men doing dirty work for a man with deep pockets?"

Mason stopped what he was doing so he could think for a moment and then let out a tired laugh. "I suppose so. Irony is a cruel, twisted thing."

"There's no need to go along with it, you know."

"How would you suggest I avoid it?"

"Simple," she said. "Don't go along with it."

"It's not that easy."

When Mason started to turn away so he could finish packing his bag, Maggie stopped him. She placed her lips so close to his ear that he could feel the heat from her breath as she said, "People like us know that the best plans are often pretty simple. Getting away with them is the tricky part."

"Yeah, especially when my life's on the line."

She shrugged. "Killing this man won't be easy, I take it."

"Not hardly."

"Could you get shot while doing this job?"

"If the man I'm after is overly fond of breathing, he may fight to keep doing it," Mason said.

"Then your life is on the line whether you go along with this or not, right?"

"Pretty much."

"What's the worst Greeley can do to you? Get you

killed twice instead of just once? Seems to me a man of your talents should be able to read this angle if you'd just take a moment to think it over. And for a man who bogs himself down with so much thinking," she added, "I'd say that's fairly ironic."

Chapter 21

Mason wished he could take more time with Maggie, but there simply wasn't any to spare. If he was going to figure a way out of the pickle he was in, he couldn't afford to waste a single moment. The gears in his head were turning to try to put himself as many steps ahead of the game as possible.

She'd been right about some very important things, especially when she'd told him that Greeley couldn't do much worse to him than what he was already facing. Putting a man in a corner with his life hanging by a thread no matter what his options were was a tactical mistake. Once Mason followed her advice and calmed himself enough to see that particular angle above all else, a weight lifted from his shoulders. It was a classic case of not seeing the forest through the trees.

The weight on his shoulders, the anxiousness, the lack of appetite, the exhaustion were all more than products of a rough couple of days. Once he'd accepted the fact that each choice presented by Greeley was potentially just as dangerous as the others, they essentially canceled themselves out. For a man who lived by figuring odds, having two sets of facts and figures wipe each other away like that was a blessing as well as a chance to take a breath and regroup.

Now only two choices remained. He could either do what Greeley wanted or not. Since the first choice guaranteed certain disaster, he was left with no choice at all. The only thing left was to figure out the best way to defy a greedy outlaw with a gang of loyal killers at his disposal. Rather than spin his wheels any longer, he finished up his preparations and made his way off the *Delta Jack*.

Two overmen were waiting on the dock, and when Mason stepped off the boat, one of them approached to keep him from going any farther.

"Wait here," the overman said. "Mr. Greeley wants another word with you."

"I thought he might." Turning toward the second overman, who was already boarding the *Jack*, Mason added, "Tell him in advance that I could use another drink."

When the second overman returned with Greeley, there were no drinks to be found. A third overman approached the dock on a horse, which he dismounted and led by the reins to the point where the dock met the shore.

"That horse is for you," Greeley said. "At least, for as long as you need it to put Simons in the ground."

"Any thoughts on how I'll find him or am I on my own for that as well?" Mason asked.

"When you get there," the overman with the horse said, "look for a saloon called the Bistro."

"Sounds fancy," Mason said.

"It wants to be. Apart from a group of French ladies doing the cancan every other night, there ain't nothing different there than in any other saloon. Simons usually sits at a table in the middle of the place."

"What's he look like?"

"Like a little man trying to be king. You won't miss him."

Since he doubted he'd get much more than that from the gunman, Mason took the reins from him and let the matter rest.

"You get that package that was left in your room?" Greeley asked.

"I did," Mason replied. He peeled back his jacket to show his holster as he said, "I'm loaded and ready to hunt."

Not only did his display fail to impress any of the men around him, but it caused all three overmen to slap their hands against their own holstered pistols in preparation for a draw. The trio tensed like bowstrings, making it plenty clear to Mason that if he wanted to take a shot at any of them, he'd be dead before his nose picked up the scent of burned gunpowder.

Calmly covering his holster again with his jacket, Mason eased his hand away and laughed nervously. There were a few passengers watching from the upper decks, and most of them lost interest when they saw there wasn't going to be any bloodshed.

"I take it the town I need to ride to is that way," Mason said while pointing in the direction from which the overman had come with the horse.

"That's right," the overman standing near the animal replied. "It's called Sedrich. Just take this road for a couple miles and there it is."

"Sounds simple enough."

Greeley wore one of his expensive suits but had left his jacket on the boat. Hooking his thumbs beneath his suspenders, he squinted into the afternoon sun. "You're really gonna do this?"

"What choice do I have?" Mason asked.

"None that end well for you."

"There you go, then. So I find Simons and kill him. Anything else? Anyone need something while I'm in town? Some flour? Maybe a few bags of sugar?"

"Keep makin' jokes and you'll catch a bullet," Greeley warned. "Simons may be a weasel, but he'll shoot a man without blinking. And if he don't pull the trigger, one of his kin will."

"You'll have to excuse me. This is my first time as a hired gun. I'm not familiar with the etiquette."

The gnarled expression on Greeley's face made it clear that he hadn't understood at least one of the words Mason had just spoken. Quickly becoming annoyed by that, he went back to what he knew and jabbed a bony finger at Mason. "You just do what we discussed."

"I will," Mason assured him.

"I'll need proof when the job's done."

"Won't one of your men be following me?"

Instead of confirming or denying that, Greeley said, "He wears a ring on his little finger. It's gold but ain't worth a fortune or anything. By the looks of it, I'd say he can't pull it off his fat hand, so it remains there. To get it off, it'll need to be cut off."

"You want the ring?" Mason asked.

Greeley nodded. "And the finger it's on."

"And . . . the finger?"

"Yeah. That should be enough proof."

"Isn't that a bit . . . gruesome?"

"So's killing a man," Greeley pointed out, "but you're willing to do that much."

Mason couldn't help squirming at the prospect in front of him. "Yes, but . . . how does one . . . remove a finger?"

"It's not as hard as you might think," one of the overmen on the dock said. "Just put his hand on a table and cut it like you're cutting an old sausage. Lean your weight down into it. The quicker the better."

"All right," Mason said quickly. "I'm sorry I asked."

"For a man who wears two guns," the overman said, "you seem awfully squirrelly."

"I'm not squirrelly. I'm just not a butcher."

Greeley and all three overmen broke into laughter.

"What's so funny?" Mason asked.

When he caught his breath, Greeley said, "We've spoken to Willowby."

"You mean Winslow?" Mason snapped.

"Yeah. That's the one. We spoke to him and he told us about what you did to get away from him when my boys found the two of you near their rowboat."

"That was different," Mason explained. "That was—"

"Cold is what that was," the overman closest to Mason said. "You shot his leg, gave him a bit of time to get doctored up, and then stuck a sharp stick into the bullet wound. If that ain't cold, I don't know what is!"

One of the overmen standing at the edge of the plank leading back onto the boat mused, "I'll have to use that one myself sometime."

"And don't forget the part about punching the poor bastard in the face," Greeley added.

"I'm leaving now," Mason said while climbing onto the horse he'd been given. "The lot of you enjoy yourselves."

"Go get him, Butcher!" an overman called out. Since Mason had already decided to ignore them, he wasn't sure which overman had made the comment. All of the men on the dock found it amusing enough to parrot the comment, however, while more laughter spread among them like a brush fire.

Mason sighed. After his horse had taken a few steps, he felt compelled to look over his shoulder at the *Delta Jack*. Greeley and his men were already walking aboard and having a grand old time along the way. Of the few passengers who'd continued to watch from above, only one remained.

Maggie looked down at him from the third deck. Both of her hands were on the railing, and her eyes were locked on him as if she were still close enough to whisper into his ear. She raised one hand and smiled in a way that made Mason feel as if they were the only two people on the face of the earth. He'd heard others say things like that and written them off as either fools, drunks, or drunken fools. Mason might very well have joined one of those categories, but he was feeling too good to care.

He snapped his reins, rode away from the *Delta Jack*, and headed into his first day as a hired killer.

Chapter 22

The town of Sedrich was exactly as advertised: small and impossible to miss. In fact, anyone using the road that led to the dock where the *Delta Jack* was waiting would have been forced to pass through the town on their way to just about anywhere else. Sedrich was like many other towns that had sprung up out of opportunity instead of necessity. Storefronts and saloons lined the road on both sides with smaller streets branching out here and there at irregular intervals. It catered to travelers, gamblers, and river folk. Anyone with money in their pockets and a hankering to spend it as quickly as possible was welcome in Sedrich. Mason felt at home almost immediately.

Upon entering town, Mason let his professional instincts guide him to the closest saloon. As a man working the gambler's circuit, he earned his living being able to sniff out big games or fertile hunting grounds. For someone in his line of work, saloons were the best hunting grounds available, and the louder they were, the better. Quiet saloons were filled with men who thought before they acted or sat back to watch for signs of trouble. Noise, on the other hand, meant liquor was flowing and customers were letting down their guard. There were no grounds more fertile than those for any gambler.

Mason's gut instinct pulled him toward a little place called the River Rat. It had the look of a saloon frequented by locals, which was low-hanging fruit for a man of Mason's talents. He wasn't in Sedrich on regular business, however, and shifted his sights a bit farther down the street.

The Bistro was bigger than the River Rat, but not by much. A bouncy tune being played on a piano drifted through the air from that place. Every so often, some uproarious cheers would erupt. It had been a while since Mason had seen cancan dancers, and taking in a show seemed like a pleasant enough way to start his visit. First, he tied his horse to a post outside the Bistro and made sure there was a good amount of water in the trough. He then anxiously stepped inside the saloon and allowed his senses to soak everything up.

A stage at the back of the room was positioned so someone passing by the Bistro's door or front window would get a glimpse of the show without seeing too much. Although there was enough room for at least ten girls on the slightly elevated platform, only four were dancing at the moment. Whatever dance they were doing wasn't the cancan, but Mason enjoyed it all the same. The girls were dressed in matching dresses made from wispy material that almost wasn't there at all. They spun, twirled, and waved to the audience while giving the men seated throughout the place an occasional glimpse of long legs and pale skin beneath their skirts. Mason cheered along with the others when the girls all bowed and strutted offstage.

He fell into his normal routine like an old wagon

wheel settling into a rut in the road. Whenever he went to a new saloon for the first time, Mason looked around the room, made his way to the bar, and struck up a conversation with whoever served him his drink. The Bistro's barkeep was a fellow with a large round face and dark, olive-colored skin. After ordering a beer, Mason asked him about the saloon's specialties and any recommendations he might have for what to order next. That got the man talking in an animated fashion while Mason nodded and took another look around.

Now that the bartender was friendly with him, the rest of the customers figured he was just there for a drink. Essentially Mason would go unnoticed for a while until he made a move that would set him apart from any other man with a thirst. Mason preferred to watch folks when they thought they weren't being watched. Little habits would make themselves known, and Mason could get an idea for which men were on bad terms or which might be working together. Every saloon had a flow that could eventually be discerned by anyone who knew what to look for. As far as the Bistro went, almost every current in the place flowed to a table that was just to the left of the room's center.

Five men sat around that table. At first glance, it looked as if a deck of cards had been spilled onto the table by someone who'd tripped over their own feet. Mason sighed and grumbled to himself, "Damn seven-card stud."

While Mason appreciated the seven-card variation of stud poker, he didn't particularly enjoy it. There were plenty of opportunities to bet, but far too many chances for an overeager player to get lucky. Being too anxious was supposed to be a gambler's downfall. If they had more than five cards to make a hand, such players were given chances for a reprieve. One thing that Mason admired most about poker was its brutality. Adding more cards to the mix beyond the regular five as God had intended was pulling some of the teeth from the game.

Mason only had to watch this table for a short while to realize there were only two men worth his attention. One was a fair-haired gentleman with a long face, and the other was balding and had a laugh like that of a hyena being rolled over by a slowly moving wagon. Part hacking cough and part cackle, the laugh came at the expense of everyone else at that table as he raked in a pot.

"Real nice call there, Wade!" the balding man said, jeering. "A couple more like that and I can afford a new horse!"

One of the quieter men at the table, presumably Wade, shook his head and took a drink from his beer.

Everything about the balding man rubbed Mason the wrong way. From the way he gnawed on his cigar to the sloppy manner in which he heaped his chips in front of him spoke of someone who'd been raised by wolves. "I'm dealing next hand," the balding man announced as if the entire world were interested. "Threes are wild."

Mason ground his teeth together. Wild cards in a poker game were for children who didn't want to learn how to play but still wanted to win. Many a heated argument had been sparked at card tables throughout the Dakotas when Mason was foolish enough to give those opinions a voice. After that, he'd learned to keep his mouth shut and teach those overgrown children how to play real poker through trial and error. Mostly, their error.

Deciding to remain at the bar, Mason nursed his drink in the hopes that the next man to get the deal would change the game. Otherwise he would just have to plaster a smile onto his face and pretend he enjoyed children's games so he could get a seat at that table. As it turned out, the hand swung in Wade's favor as he showed he could give as good as he got.

"Looks like you won't be able to buy that new horse after all, huh, Randy?" he chided after winning the hand.

Like most spoiled children, the balding man could dish out the insults but had a thin skin when they were fired back at him. "Shut up, Wade," he snarled.

"Shouldn't have made them threes wild. That's how I wound up with four of a kind!"

"I said shut up!"

Wade must have been taking a ribbing for a while before Mason had arrived, because he wasn't about to let up now that it was his turn. "How about you settle up with some of that jewelry? Or were you trying to pass yourself off as some sort of dandy?"

Randy's sudden burst of thrashing movement might have been an attempt to flip the table over. All he wound up doing was tilting it just enough to spill some of the other men's drinks. Annoyed by the laughter his tantrum had caused, he got up from his seat and stomped over to Wade's. It wasn't until that moment that Mason realized exactly what Greeley had meant when he said the man he was after would act like a little king. The king part had been obvious enough. Now that the balding man was on his own two feet, the little part became clearer. When Randy stood up, he was eye to eye with Wade, who'd remained in his seat.

"You think you're funny or something?" Randy asked.

"No, Randy. Just go back to your seat and settle down."

Randy reached for the gun at his side, using one of the sloppiest draws Mason had ever witnessed. Considering the number of drunks he saw on a daily basis, that was saying something. After two or three attempts, he finally got his fat little fingers around the grip of his pistol. He drew the gun and smiled victoriously while jamming its barrel into Wade's side.

Throughout the process of Randy's draw, anyone in the saloon could have skinned their own weapon and put the stout fellow down. They might have too, if not for the two other armed men sitting nearby. Mason watched the scene unfold in front of him and noticed that the other men at that table all looked to at least one of those others as if they feared them more than the little fuming man confronting Wade.

"You still think you're funny?" Randy snarled.

Wade looked to the neighboring table where a skinny man wearing an old Army model Colt leaned back in his chair so his hand could dangle within inches of his holster. Looking back to Randy, he said, "No. It wasn't funny."

"That's right. You got anything else to say?"

"Sorry, Randy."

Randy placed a finger to his ear and leaned in a little closer. "I didn't catch that. What did you say?"

"Don't push this any further than it needs to go," Wade said. "I'm not about to grovel for you."

"What was that?" Randy straightened up, which put him at just slightly higher than Wade's eye level. "You getting your hackles up on me?"

"He said he was sorry," one of the other players said. "That's the end of it. Let's play some more cards. I'll buy the next round of drinks."

"No," Randy said. Poking Wade in the chest, he added, "*He's* buying."

"Fine," Randy sighed. "I'll buy. I'll just use your money to pay for them drinks anyway."

Randy's eye twitched. "Get up," he said.

Wade was more than happy to stand. He pushed his chair back, got to his feet, and glowered down at the shorter man. "What now, Randy?" he asked.

Without a moment's hesitation, Randy balled up a fist and delivered a straight punch below Wade's belt. When Wade doubled over, Randy swung at his jaw. Even though his knuckles landed more or less on target, he simply didn't have enough muscle behind them to do much more than turn Wade's head.

"You stinkin' little—" was all Wade got a chance to say before he was roughly shoved back down into his chair.

Mason had been watching the confrontation along with the rest of the saloon, and he'd barely noticed the man with the Army Colt leave his table until he was within arm's reach of Wade.

If Wade had been ready to start a tussle with Randy, he was nowhere near as ready to get into anything with the fellow who'd put him back in his seat. In fact, Wade seemed downright timid when he said, "This isn't anything serious."

The man with the Colt looked over to Randy and got a nod from the smaller man. He then knocked Wade's hat from his head, grabbed a handful of hair, and dropped a fist onto Wade's face like driving a railroad spike into the ground.

Mason hadn't seen anything so crude and viciously callous as that in a fistfight. Usually fighters tried to take swings at each other or aim for various pieces of anatomy. Whoever this man was, he smashed Wade's head as if he weren't hitting another living thing at all. It was barbaric in every sense of the word.

At first, when Wade leaned back in his chair, Mason was certain he was out like a snuffed candle. Eventually Wade pulled himself up and pressed his hands to his face. From there, he slumped forward and trembled. "I'll pay the money back," he said through his hands.

Randy couldn't have been more satisfied with himself if he'd been the one to get his hands dirty. "What money?"

"The money I won. Take it back."

"Nah," Randy said as he patted Wade on the shoulder. "You won it fair and square. It's yours. You should just be a little more courteous, is all."

"I'm sorry, Randy."

"See? This time, I believe you." Turning toward the stage, Randy hollered, "Where are them dancing girls?"

The men who played the music were nowhere to be found, but the girls who'd been on the stage earlier stuck their heads out to greet the crowd. They didn't have anything to dance to, so they walked out to wander from table to table instead. None of the men in the Bistro seemed to mind one bit.

Randy was on his way to the bar when he found one of the girls, a dancer with a slender frame and thick, curly hair. He made a few lewd comments to her, put his hand on her hip, and showed her a smile that was scummier than the back end of a swamp rat. To her credit, the dancing girl made a real good show of not being disgusted until she convinced him to let her go. By the time Randy made his way to the bar, Mason was already standing there.

"Gimme a beer," Randy said as he stood on the brass rail in front of the spittoons and slapped the top of the bar.

The entire place was back to the state of merriment it had been in when Mason first arrived. Randy nodded and gazed about in self-satisfaction as if he were the cause of all the smiles on his fellow men instead of the beautiful women making their rounds. As soon as a beer was set down in front of Randy, Mason said, "I'll pay for that drink."

Randy looked over at him and raised his mug. "Obliged, mister. Do I know you?"

"Not yet."

"Then . . . why pay for my beer?"

"You're the man who brought them girls out from where they were hiding, aren't you?"

"You saw it for yourself," Randy said.

"That seems like a good enough reason for celebration to me."

"Ha! You got that right! I didn't catch your name."

"Because I never tossed it," Mason replied, using a joke that usually went over well with obnoxious men.

Randy ate it up as if it were coated in syrup. "Randal Simons, but everyone calls me Randy."

Mason pulled one of his aliases from the back of his mind a whole lot faster than he could have drawn his Remington. "William Abner," he said. "Pleased to meet you."

Simons stuck out his chubby hand. It was the one with a gold ring wrapped around one finger so tight that it looked to be permanently wedged within his flesh. The instant Mason shook that hand, he knew what he was going to do to cross Simons's name off Greeley's list.

Chapter 23

Mason ignored his personal preferences and sidled up to the card table to play a few hands of seven-card stud. Granted, that was after having a few beers with Simons, but that small amount of bitter brew wasn't nearly enough to cushion the blow of tossing in an ante for that dreadful game. Once he reminded himself he was playing with Greeley's expense money, Mason felt a whole lot better.

That night wasn't about gambling as far as Mason was concerned. He won a few hands and lost a whole lot more. Considering the low caliber of competition at that table, losing without looking as though he'd meant to lose was a feat in itself. Every moment he spent in the Bistro that night was directed at getting a feel for Simons and any of the men working for him.

The girls were soon back onstage, but only one of them was on her feet. The other two sat with their feet dangling over the side while having conversations with customers. A blonde stood in the middle of the platform, singing along to the tired strumming of a man with a guitar. It was well past midnight, and though Mason wouldn't normally be ready for bed, he was very short on sleep.

"I think that's enough!" Simons announced as he stood up from his chair. "I'll win more of your money tomorrow."

Players scattered throughout the room said their good-byes to the short man who'd bought so many rounds of drinks. The few who remained silent were armed and watched the people around them like hunters picking out the ducks they meant to knock from the sky. Mason wasn't sure if they were deputies, bounty hunters, or just frightening members of the Simons family. He was certain they were looking out for Randy's interests, though. During the entire night, when Simons had been angry, those men perched at the edges of their seats and didn't relax until Simons did. When Simons had been happy, those men sank into their chairs and took advantage of the lull preceding another squall.

That was more than enough for Mason to believe those men were the threats Greeley had described. If he was a gunman himself, he would have spent more time sizing those men up. He would possibly have gauged their proficiency at killing by the guns they wore or where they sat. As a gambler, Mason knew which players to challenge and which to give a wide berth. While those armed men definitely fell into the latter category, only one of them seemed at all interested in leaving that saloon. While that struck Mason as odd, he wasn't about to turn his nose up at one of the rare bits of good fortune he'd had recently.

Simons left the Bistro and staggered down the street. The gunman who followed him was the man carrying the Army Colt. After giving them a slight head start, Mason followed as well and had no trouble spotting them on the mostly empty street. Simons and his escort walked down one street and turned a corner to continue on until they reached the end of the part of town illuminated by torches. Apart from those two, several locals were staggering to their own destinations. Some working girls tried to tempt every man they saw. One of the men they didn't try to snag was a vagrant with a filthy, yet familiar face who shadowed Mason from several paces behind. Mason quickly became certain of two things: That man was one of Greeley's overmen and he was being very careful not to get too close to Simons or any of the armed men nearby.

Mason's first thought was that if an overman could get this close, why couldn't he just take a shot at Simons and be done with it? All he needed to do to answer that question was remind himself of how tightly wound those gunmen had been at the Bistro and how quickly they would respond to a shot being fired at Simons. Obviously the overmen weren't so deeply devoted to the whims of their employer that they were willing to walk into a cross fire for him.

Following Simons and the gunman around another corner and down an alley, Mason watched the two men swap a few parting words. The gunman wandered away. Simons unlocked the door to a narrow building with two floors and as many windows and went inside.

Mason stood in a shadow for a while, waiting to see how long it would take for either the same gunman or another one to come along. Surely they patrolled the area to keep watch on Simons. When no patrol came along, Mason broadened the scope of his search to include the vagrant or anyone else who might be there to watch him instead of Simons. Once again, he came up empty.

"Perhaps I should be a hired gun after all," Mason

said under his breath. "Seems like an easier job than I thought. Let's just put that to the test, then, shall we?"

While Mason wasn't much of a quick-draw artist, he placed his hand on his holstered Remington as if he were. Nobody came at him from some hidden spot, so he took a few cautious steps toward the door.

Still . . . nobody.

He approached the door and got close enough to reach out for the handle. His blood raced through his veins, and his heart skipped several beats when a dog somewhere else in town started barking wildly at something that had caught its eye. Once he was able to draw a breath, Mason realized he was still alone in that alley. He even touched the handle and gingerly tested it to find the door was locked.

Taking his hand away, Mason looked around and saw there was still nobody who took any interest in who he was or what he was doing. He put his ear to the door and listened without being disturbed, which told him the security around Simons wasn't nearly as heavy as Greeley had believed. The only sounds he heard within the building were the shuffle of tired feet and the occasional cough from Simons. Mason quietly stuffed his hands into his jacket pockets and walked away so Simons could drop his guard even further.

Mason returned less than two hours later. While there were still signs of life throughout Sedrich, things had quieted down considerably. He took a different route through town to see if he attracted any more attention than he had before. As far as he could tell, even the overman he'd spotted had called it a night and found a bed somewhere.

When he returned to the door he'd tried earlier, Mason could hear nothing from the other side. The door was still locked, but that didn't mean much so long as he had the proper tool for the job. He reached under his jacket to draw the dagger secreted at the small of his back. The blade came out and his finger found one of the rings at the top of the handle. Fitting the scratched tip of the blade into the lock near the door's handle, Mason closed his eyes and felt for what scraped against the sharpened metal. He found the sweet spot without much trouble and got the door open on his second try. Just before the lock gave way, he heard a metallic snap. Some part of the lock's mechanism had been broken by his forced entry. Under most circumstances, that would have been a bad thing. This time around, Mason figured he could use it to further his own purposes.

Once inside, he eased the door shut. The room was so dark that he couldn't make out all the walls. After his eyes adjusted, Mason could tell he was in a kitchen. There were cabinets on one side, a large water basin in a corner, and a small wood-burning stove in the other. Judging by the stink of rotten potatoes and mold, Simons wasn't much of a cook. There was a dim light source coming from the next room, so Mason stepped carefully in that direction.

Mason had snuck out of enough places in the middle of the night for his feet to be almost as sensitive in looking for imperfections in the floor as his hands were in looking for weaknesses in a lock. When his boot scraped against a board that was raised just a bit above the rest, he stepped over it and didn't come down with all of his weight until he'd tested for squeaks. It was a tedious process, but he inched his way into the next room without making a sound.

Simons was asleep in that room. His drunken snoring rolled through the air, marking his location in the dimly lit space even better than the pair of lanterns hanging nearby. As Mason approached the undersized figure, he reconsidered his options as far as getting the ring was concerned.

The men who were supposed to be guarding him might have been watching the saloons for Greeley's boys, but they weren't nearly as big a threat as Mason had anticipated. Then again, those men could still be about and were well armed. One curious set of eyes would become a nasty thorn in Mason's side. There were at least a dozen ways he could meet his end just by being careless. If he got sloppy, even if he managed to get the ring from Simons, there was no guarantee he'd make it out of Sedrich alive.

Even if he could get the ring away from Simons while the little man snored in a deep drunken sleep, Mason knew he wouldn't survive a fight against overwhelming numbers on his way out of town. So he decided to stick to his original plan.

Maggie was right. Sometimes he just thought too damn much.

Simons sat in a chair surrounded by shelves and a small square table. Even in the sparse amount of light coming from the lanterns hanging near the front door, Mason could see there was an abundance of clutter in that room. The closest lantern's wick crackled and fought to stay lit but didn't have much longer before it went out. Mason crossed the room to a darkened hallway that extended for less than a yard before leading to a set of precariously narrow stairs.

Keeping his boots to the edges of each step, Mason climbed to the second floor and found a perfectly good bedroom. A quick search of the room told him it was not only empty, but hadn't been used in quite some time. Simons was probably too drunk most nights to bother climbing the stairs, and if his familiarity with the girls at the Bistro was any indication, he most likely spent the remaining nights in another bed entirely. Mason headed back downstairs, comfortable enough in what he'd learned to be able to hasten his movements at the expense of making a bit more noise. Simons was sleeping so deeply that Mason could have ridden his horse in through the front door without disturbing him.

He approached Simons with dagger in hand. How easy it would have been to simply cut the little man's throat and then separate a finger from his hand. But that wouldn't have satisfied the questions that had been nagging at Mason from the moment he started following Simons to this shabby little dwelling. It was from that point onward that Greeley's story had come off the tracks.

This was too easy.

Something wasn't right.

Every instinct inside Mason told him to fold this hand, so he went straight for the one hand that truly mattered. He got ahold of Simons's ring and pulled, but the damn thing wouldn't budge. It was wedged tightly in place and to make things worse, Simons opened his eyes.

Chapter 24

"Wh-what . . ."

In the time it took Simons to form those two croaking syllables, Mason had cracked the blunt end of his dagger against his temple to put him right back to sleep.

Simons awoke sometime later. He was groggy at first and when he tried to roll over, he couldn't move. His next attempt was to reach for his head, but his arms were tied even tighter than his body. The only thing he could move freely was his head, and when he did that, he saw Mason sitting perched on the edge of a chair next to him.

"Are you all right?" Mason asked.

Blinking furiously, Simons wriggled and squirmed. "William? What the hell are you doing here?"

"I came by to check on you," Mason said while looking at him with wide, concerned eyes. "I thought there might have been some trouble after that scuffle you had with Wade and—"

"Why am I tied up?" Simons roared.

Flinching at the other man's angry tone, Mason said, "I just got here. I knocked, but nobody answered. The lock was broken, so maybe someone forced their way in."

"Cut me loose!"

"Oh, of course."

This time, it was Simons who flinched when he saw Mason draw the dagger from the scabbard hidden behind his back. Knotted linens had been used to tie Simons to the chair, and it was a simple matter for the sharpened blade to slice through them. When he was free, Simons hopped up from the chair and rubbed his wrists as if he'd been held captive for days instead of hours. "What's going on here?" he asked.

"Like I said, the lock on your door was broken. When I knocked, the door opened. I heard something suspicious, so I came in. You were tied to this chair and someone was here with you."

"Who?"

Mason shrugged before putting the knife away. "I don't know. I barely got a look at him, but he was a muscular fellow dressed in rags. He was carrying a club." When he reached for the scabbard again, Mason shifted so his jacket opened to reveal the Remington holstered under his arm. As soon as the blade was sheathed, he straightened his jacket to cover the weapon. Judging by the nervous expression on Simons's face, that brief glimpse of the .44 had been received just as Mason had hoped.

"You said you came in here to . . . check on me?" Simons asked.

Pulling up the chair he'd been sitting in while waiting for Simons to wake up, Mason said, "I didn't think you'd buy that."

"Of course I didn't. I'm not stupid."

In Mason's experience, one thing that was certain

about stupid people was that they were always anxious to say they were otherwise. He played into that by nodding as if conceding a defeat. "Actually I was sent to kill you."

Simons tensed.

Mason knew the other man didn't have any weapons, because he'd already taken them from him while he was knocked unconscious. The instant Simons's features betrayed his intention to lunge or make some other aggressive move, Mason brought his hand up to the holstered .44. Although most any man could touch a holster with impressive speed, drawing a gun from it and firing with any degree of accuracy was another matter entirely. Bluffing at such a skill was a dangerous play to make, but Mason thought he might be able to get away with it in his present company.

Slowly, carefully, Simons opened his hands and held them up. "All right. You got me," he whispered.

"If I wanted to kill you, I would have done it already," Mason said.

"Then what do you want? Money?"

"Have a seat, Randy."

Simons took a seat, placed his hands on his knees, and then rocked back and forth while awaiting Mason's next words.

This was the first time Mason had ever conducted an interrogation, but he guessed it would have a similar flow to a poker game. An opening move of aggression followed by a well-placed bluff. Then the pot was made juicier before the final blow was struck. Mason couldn't help grinning at the similarities, the sight of which made Simons even more nervous.

"You've made some folks real upset," Mason said.

"Comes with the territory."

"One of those folks is Cam Greeley."

The color drained from Simons's face. "Oh Lord," he moaned. "I knew he'd come after me sooner or later."

"Why is he after you?"

"You . . . don't know?"

"Actually I was just sent to do a job. When I got to town, things didn't line up to match what Greeley told me, so I got curious. Tell me how you know him."

Leaning forward, Simons spoke at a frantic pace. Each word had the urgency of a man grasping at a dwindling length of rope before falling over the side of a sheer drop. "I brokered a few jobs for him. Nothing much really. He was looking for some help and I steered a few men in his direction. With my family . . . I know plenty of men in that line of work."

"Which is?"

"They're gun hands," Simons said. Scowling, he asked, "You didn't know?"

"I was told to kill someone and I came to do it," Mason said in a tone that was bereft of any of the brighter emotions. He was actually doing his best to mimic what he'd heard from the overmen. "That usually doesn't require me to ask many questions." Although the tough act seemed to be holding up, he didn't want to push it. In keeping with his poker mentality, now was the time to goose the pot a bit with a small strategic retreat. "I went to the Bistro to get a look at you and figure the best time to finish you off. But I could tell you weren't the animal Greeley described. Furthermore, you seemed like a fairly decent man."

"What did Greeley tell you?"

"That you surrounded yourself with crooked lawmen

and bounty hunters," Mason said. "You paid men to gun down any of Greeley's overmen that might track you to Sedrich."

Simons expelled a tired laugh and rubbed his head where Mason had hit him. "Overmen. Are they still tossing folks into the paddlewheel of that boat?"

"Last time I checked."

"You're not one of them. An overman, I mean. I can tell. It's in the eyes," Simons said while swiping his finger between his own eyes. Wincing, he brought that hand back to his temple, where a nasty mark had already formed. "I swear . . . it was you that hit me."

Mason furrowed his brow as if he were trying to imagine such a strange possibility.

Watching Mason carefully, Simons eventually chuckled. "It was just a glimpse, really, but I swear it was a glimpse of you. I suppose getting cracked in the skull will make you see things."

"It's been known to happen. That man who I saw before is likely to come back. The only reason he's not here already is probably that he figured I'd do the job I was sent to do."

"Yeah," Simons sighed. "Greeley doesn't like to get his hands dirty. Just do me a favor, huh?"

"What's that?"

"Make it quick."

"I already told you I'm not going to kill you," Mason insisted.

"I know how this goes. You get me to relax so I don't make a sound or put up a fight and then you shoot me. I've seen it plenty of times."

Drawing from his considerable experience in reading people, Mason doubted that very much. Simons had heard about it, perhaps, but not seen. "So, what have you been doing here?" Mason asked. "And why would Greeley want you dead?"

Simons was sweating profusely. His hands swiped at his face and neck to clear some of the larger rivulets tracing down into his shirt as he said, "I don't know! This ain't the first time he's tried, though."

"There's got to be a reason."

"Like I told you, I was doing work for him. Greeley wanted to hire on some enforcers for his new business venture."

"You mean the *Delta Jack*?"

"This was before he got the boat. Back when he owned a saloon or two in Louisiana. He wanted to expand into other venues and needed men he could trust to be his enforcers. I guess he had some trouble with the local gunmen or maybe he just thought my kin could do a better job. A few of my cousins did jobs like that for him a few months earlier."

"Did Greeley have your cousins kill for him?" Mason asked.

Simons started to answer that but quickly stopped himself and grimaced like a man who'd been caught in a lie. Or perhaps caught just before the lie. "My cousins are bad men. They'd tell you the same. I didn't ask what they did for Greeley, but let's just say men like them don't get paid as well as they were for just saying nasty words to people. Know what I mean?"

"Yes."

"My cousins were always in trouble for something or other. They were always on the run. Always hiding. Always wanted in some territory for this and set to hang somewhere else for that. They kept in touch with their kin, though. I could get word to them and tell them where to find more work. They gave me a cut and told me they'd protect me if anyone came to try and get to them through me."

"Sounds like a good arrangement," Mason said.

"It was. It really was."

"You want a drink?"

Simons waved that off. "Nah." He took a deep breath and then said, "I don't know how a man like Greeley got his hands on a whole boat, but he sure as hell did. When he got the *Jack*, he wanted men to be there to do whatever needed to be done. Some of my cousins jumped at the chance and were signed on. My kin ain't exactly the kind to settle much of anywhere for long, though, and they started jumping ship. When they come back," he added while leaning forward, "they told me stories about things they saw . . . things they done. Things Greeley was doing."

Resisting the urge to lean forward as well, Mason asked, "What sort of things?"

"Killings, but not the sort them cousins of mine were used to. These were gruesome. Real bloody. Bloody enough to make bad men cringe. You know what I mean?"

Mason didn't even want to pretend to know something like that. Keeping his face unreadable, he said, "Go on."

"Well, it wasn't long after my cousins jumped ship that men started coming around looking for them. Found a few of them, too."

"Your cousins were killed?"

"Not all of 'em." After taking less than a few seconds to reflect on that, Simons grunted and then wiped his nose with a pudgy finger on the same hand that bore his tarnished gold ring. "Eh, they would've been killed sooner or later. They knew it. The whole family knew it. Only thing is that Greeley started coming after me next. Ran me out of four towns in as many counties until I wound up here. As to why . . . I don't know for certain. Could be on account of me being able to get word to the rest of my kin." Simons grinned. "There's still a few rotten apples in the ol' family tree. Couldn't blame Greeley for wanting to make sure nobody puts them onto his scent. Even with them overmen he's got on his payroll, he'd be in for a hell of a fight."

That explanation didn't set well with Mason, but he would have bet that Simons was being straightforward with him. "Is there anything else you're not telling me?"

"What do you want to know?"

Mason smirked and leaned back until his spine was flush against the chair. "I'd like to know why you're so willing to have this talk with me, for one."

Simons shook his head and prodded his temple some more. "If Greeley did send you to kill me, you probably already know all this. Not like it's a big secret between me and him."

"And if I'm not in Greeley's pocket?"

"Then I'd want to help in any way I could to cause him grief. I'm through with that son of a bitch."

"Is that why you're in a town that is so close to the river?"

"I don't know. Maybe. I ain't even really thought of it. Being near or far from the Mississippi never made much difference before, and this place is mighty comfortable. Whatever's gonna happen is gonna happen. I'm done running from Cam Greeley." Simons put on a convincingly aloof facade. He even had Mason fooled until he cowered a bit and asked, "What is gonna happen anyway?"

"That depends."

"On what?"

"On if I can count on you to get out of this town and stay hidden for a while."

"I can get out," Simons said. "Staying alive after I do is another matter."

"I have a place you can go to that will be safe," Mason said. "Greeley doesn't know about it. Not many people do, actually."

Unable to contain his enthusiasm, Simons practically sprang to the edge of his seat. "Really? Where is it?"

"First let's get you out of Sedrich."

"That's the easy part!"

Mason stood up and walked to the window that gave him a view of the darkened street. In a matter of seconds, he'd found what he was looking for. "Those men that were with you at the saloon," he said. "The ones with the guns. Were they your cousins?"

"One was an uncle. Another was a cousin. Gunmen in my family are runnin' in short supply as of late."

"Any chance you could get a few of them over here?"

"I doubt it," Simons said. "Turns out they've been more than happy to watch my back when I was in a saloon. Apart from that, they tend to keep their heads down. It's what they're best at. Even if I could get word to either of 'em, they'd be useless until they slept off all the liquor they swallowed."

"That's a shame," Mason said. "We could've used them."

"Why?"

Mason stepped away from the window so Simons could take a look.

After peering through the glass, Simons spotted the man in tattered clothes. "Oh yeah," he said. "That's one of Greeley's boys. Garza is his name. Joseph Garza. I suppose that's the one you saw when you first come in here?"

"Yes," Mason lied.

Simons stepped straight back from the window and said, "I can make a run for it."

Now was the time for Mason to make the play that would allow him to sweep the pot off the table. He shook his head gravely and said, "I doubt you'd make it. There's bound to be others. The overmen tend to run in packs."

"You're right about that," Simons said. Panic grew in his eyes like a flame that was being fed a steady trickle of kerosene. "They probably got this place surrounded. Maybe my kin's already dead. Aw, no! This is it. This is when that bastard Greeley finally makes his play. Damn it!"

Mason went to the other window, eased aside the shabby curtain hanging in front of it, and took a look out. Even though he saw nothing but shadows and a pair of half-starved cats out there, he quickly pulled the curtain back and said, "That way's no good either."

"More of 'em?"

Mason nodded.

"I shoulda run further away," Simons groaned. "What was I thinkin'?"

"When I came here," Mason said, "I thought this might happen."

"You did?"

"Yes. I've done other work for Greeley, you see, and

he almost always sent his hired guns to watch over me to make sure things got done right. If I just let you go, there's a real good chance they'll come sniffing around to double-check that the job's really finished."

Before Mason could stop him, Simons went to one of the small tables situated against the wall. He reached under it and pulled a .32-caliber pistol from where it had been stashed. "Guess that don't leave no choice."

Hiding the fact that he'd missed that gun when he searched the room earlier, Mason said, "Wait. You want to shoot your way out?"

"You gonna try and stop me?"

"If that's the way you want to go out," Mason said, "I could just put an end to you right now."

Suddenly Simons squinted at him and asked the question Mason thought would have come a while ago. "Why would you want to help me anyways?"

"Because I don't like being lied to," Mason said. "Greeley told me you were a bloodthirsty killer and that you were planning to take the fight to him. Since I took a look around and had a word with you instead of walking up and killing you straightaway, I see that's not the way it is."

"My kin may be crazy," Simons said, "but they ain't crazy enough to go after someone like Greeley. They ain't even any good when I need 'em now!"

"Greeley and I are about to part ways," Mason continued. "He just doesn't know it yet. When I decide to make that happen, it'll do us all some good to make certain there are a few less overmen to worry about. There's the men that are here as well as some on that boat. Now, I don't believe I can take out all of them, but getting in close enough to Greeley to do some damage will go a long way to giving me a head start in putting him and the *Delta Jack* behind me."

"You mean . . . behind us?"

"That's right. If I play this right, I should be able to give Greeley enough to worry about that he won't be able to come after anyone for a while. You'll be rid of him once and for all."

There was a mix of fear and admiration on Simons's face when he said, "You've really got this all worked out."

"A man should always have an escape route planned. I'm sure your cousins know about that sort of thing."

"They know a lot about making a run for it. Least they did until they started getting themselves killed."

Mason looked out the window where there was only a cat to look back at him. "You'll need to leave this town and get somewhere far away from where Greeley might find you. I can help in that regard, but you're going to have to help me in return."

"Anything."

"First we need to get you out of here, and the best way to do that is for us to get Greeley to stop looking for you."

"How do you propose we do that?" Simons asked. "Come to him with hat in hand and say pretty please?"

"I was thinking more along the lines of making him think you're dead."

All the hope that had appeared on Simons's face quickly faded away. "How do you intend to do that?"

"When I was sent here," Mason explained, "Greeley gave me specific instructions to bring back proof that you were killed."

"Boy, he sure don't trust you, does he?"

"He only needs to trust me for a short while. To accomplish that, I'll have to show him the proof he needs."

Simons nodded expectantly. "We can do that. Shouldn't we take care of them fellas outside, though?"

"If I get what Greeley wants, we should be able to send those overmen away without a fight."

"Fine, but as you can see, I don't got much for you to take."

Nodding down toward the smaller man's hand, Mason said, "You've got that ring."

Grabbing his finger, Simons pulled as if he meant to yank his entire hand clean off the end of his arm. Even with all that force, however, the ring didn't budge. "Just give me a minute," he grunted. "I can . . . get it off. Used to wear this when . . . when there was less of me. Know what I mean?"

"Yeah," Mason said as he drew the knife from his scabbard. "I know what you mean."

"What's that for?"

"Greeley didn't want just the ring."

Simons was still tugging at the ring. When he looked down, his eyes widened. "No, no! He wants you to cut off my hand?"

"The finger will do just fine."

Even though it was a step up from killing him, Simons didn't seem much happier about it. He glanced toward the window and slumped into his chair. "Think I'm gonna need that drink after all."

Chapter 25

Mason wasn't about to switch professions to doctoring, but his first time performing surgery went better than expected. Thanks to the advice he'd gotten beforehand along with liberal doses of whiskey to prepare his patient, Mason got what he needed from Simons in no time at all. When it was done, he drew the Remington and cocked back the hammer.

"Wait, wait!" Simons wailed as he held up his bandaged hand. "I thought you did this so you wouldn't have to shoot me!"

"I'm not going to shoot you," Mason said. "But there's still someone outside waiting for something to happen. They need to hear a gunshot or two."

"Oh, so you'll just . . ."

"I'll fire a few shots into the ceiling."

"Um . . . could you make it the floor?"

"What the hell difference does it make?" Mason asked.

"I've got some personal items upstairs that I wouldn't want to get damaged if the bullet happened to . . ." Getting a real good look at the scowl on Mason's face, Simons shook his head while tucking his injured hand under his other arm. "You know what? Shoot wherever you like. I'm gonna be leaving this place soon, right?"

"That's right. Unless you'd like to be left here with your precious things upstairs?"

"No, not at all. Go ahead." With that, Simons made himself even smaller than normal by hunching down and covering his ears with his hands.

Mason fired a shot into the floor, kicked himself for bending to such an idiotic request, and then fired a round over his head. Despite being told his life was in immediate danger, agreeing to pull up stakes and even losing a finger, Simons actually looked up at that hole above him with genuine heartache. Whatever was up there must have been good.

"You ready to go?" Mason asked.

"Let me go pack a bag. Is that all right?"

"Just do it quietly. From this point on, you're supposed to be dead. Act like it. In fact," Mason added, "find somewhere to hide until I get those overmen away from here."

"I will. And, William . . . thanks."

Mason had almost forgotten the false name he'd given upon first meeting Simons. "Don't mention it," he said while removing the two empty bullet casings from his cylinder so he could reload. Once Simons had scampered up the stairs, Mason opened the front door and walked outside. By the time he reached the step leading down to the street running in front of the shabby building, the man who'd been following Mason stepped from an alley to meet him.

"Took you long enough," the man said.

"And who might you be?" Mason asked.

"As if you didn't know." To emphasize his point, he pulled aside his tattered coat to show the club hanging from his belt.

"Ah," Mason said. "You'll have to excuse me. The lot of you start to resemble one another after a while. It's Garza, right?"

The overman's expression barely shifted, which was a triumph in itself. "Did you do what you were supposed to do?" he asked.

"Of course I did."

"Let's see it."

"See what?" Mason said.

"Make me ask you again and I'll put this club to use by cracking your head open."

Mason sighed. Every second he stalled bought some time for Simons to get away. Of course, that would only be possible if there was a clear path for the other man to get out of his home and to a horse. Digging into his pocket, Mason said, "It occurs to me, since you made it into Sedrich without much trouble, that you could've just done this job yourself."

"Mr. Greeley wanted you to do it. That the ring?"

Holding a small bundle wrapped in an old rag he'd found on Simons's floor, Mason said, "It is."

"Did you do it like I told you to?"

Straining to make out more of the other man's face in the darkness, Mason said, "Oh yes. It worked just like you said it would. Nice and quick, leaning down on it, simple."

Garza took the bundle and unwrapped it. Not only did he seem unaffected by its contents, but he appeared to be genuinely amused when he said, "I heard the little guy yelping in there. I thought for certain you'd wait until he was dead before cutting this off."

"Guess I'm full of surprises. I did just shoot a man in there, so let's not stand right outside his door talking about it, all right?"

"Don't worry about the law or anyone else for that matter. I've hardly seen a soul in this part of town."

"If it's all the same to you," Mason said, "I'd still rather not stand in the open like this."

"Sure," the overman replied. "You go on and I'll have a look inside."

"What are you going inside for?" Mason asked.

"To see the body."

"Isn't what you're holding proof enough?"

"It's not curiosity. I'm to clean up the mess you left behind. That is, unless you want to do it for me?"

Mason had never been more ungrateful for another man's work ethic. "That can wait," he said.

Garza had already pocketed the blood-soaked rag and walked past Mason to the building's front door. Stopping before opening that door, he turned to face Mason and asked, "Wait for what?"

"You asked what took me so long to pull the trigger," Mason said as his mind raced to come up with what he should say next. "I was questioning him."

"About what?"

"About where to find those bounty hunters he used to watch his back. I know where they are."

Garza chuckled at what he must have thought was a private joke. "Don't worry about them," he said.

"He's got armed men to protect him," Mason insisted. "They may not be here at the moment, but they're close."

"I told you we don't have to worry about them. If anyone comes around, they won't make it back."

Mason was on a roll and kept rolling for the sake of buying as much time as possible for Simons to get away. He'd told Simons where to go after leaving town, and now he just had to get him there. "Why take that chance?" he said. "Let's take care of them now before they get suspicious. At this time of night, they'll most likely be out of sorts and won't put up as much of a fight as they would if they were fresh."

Narrowing his eyes, the overman asked, "What did you mean by that?"

"I mean they'll most likely be tired if we get them now instead of—"

"No. What did you mean when you said Simons has got armed men to protect him?"

Mason knew where this was headed, but he passed it off as if there were nothing at all to suspect. "Mr. Greeley told me about the men Simons surrounded himself with in this town. I saw them myself. If you were paying attention while you were here, you must've seen them too."

"You said he's got armed men," the overman pointed out. "As if he's still got them. Not *had* them."

"What's the difference? As far as those men know, they're still working for him, right?"

Shaking his head slowly, Garza said, "Seeing as how you're the man who killed him, you'd know better than anyone that Simons don't *have* anything anymore. Should still be fresh in your mind. There's no way in hell you'd make that mistake while the blood on your hands is still wet. I should know. Any man who's killed another man would know."

"It's late," Mason sighed. "I'm tired. I said the wrong word. You want to go in and stare at a corpse, then be my guest. I'm finding a room for the night so I can get to the boat bright and early."

Garza placed one hand on the door and the other on the pistol tucked under his belt. Before pushing the door open, he asked, "Where's the body?"

Since he'd fired the Remington in the front room where the flash from the barrel would surely have been seen through the window, Mason only had one way to answer that question. "Front sitting room," he said, knowing full well that he'd slipped up by not going upstairs to fire the shot.

Mason's thoughts were flooded with all the different lies he could tell to explain why there was no body on the floor near the front window. He'd even selected the best of the bunch when Garza opened the door to find the man who should have been lying on the floor creeping down the stairs instead.

Simons froze on the staircase as if that would keep him from being seen.

Mason felt a wave of icy cold wash over him as the one thing he'd wanted to avoid above all others came to pass.

Garza stood in the doorway and snarled, "I knew it."

Chapter 26

Simons was dead.

That was all Mason could think when it became clear that his deception had been discovered. Simons was dead and so was he.

Unwilling to surrender to the inevitable, Mason reached for the .44 under his left arm. It was a foregone conclusion that an overman would be able to draw his own weapon first, and the man in the tattered coat did not disappoint in that regard. Mason hadn't seen where Garza's pistol had been holstered, but it cleared leather in a smoothly practiced motion and spat its round through the air.

One drawback to a well-practiced set of motions was that they were difficult to change on short notice. The overman was intent on putting his round through Simons's head, and when his target reflexively ducked, Simons's small frame allowed him to drop down just a bit faster than a man of average height. The bullet punched into the wall behind the little man to rain plaster down onto his neck.

After that first shot went off, Mason figured he had enough time to fire one of his own. Seeing as how he was behind the overman, he thought he could even take a moment or two to aim so he could get the job done right. Mason was wrong on both counts.

Without even needing to look over his shoulder, Garza raised his left arm so he could bring his right across the front of his body and point his pistol behind him. He fired a quick shot that didn't draw Mason's blood but came close enough to tear through his jacket. Mason hopped backward and pulled his trigger, coming closer to hitting Simons than his true target.

"Stop!" Simons wailed. "I give up. I give up!"

But it was too late for surrender. The overman had a job to do and wouldn't be swayed by words. Rather than waste another bullet, Garza twisted around to face Mason and line up a clean shot. By the time his shoulders were squared to the front of the room, Mason was no longer in sight. There weren't many places for someone to hide in that room, but the front door was now mostly shut where it had been fully open a moment earlier. Garza sent a round through the door to flush Mason out. As Mason raced past the window next to the door, Garza fired again.

If Mason hadn't anticipated that shot, he would have caught a piece of hot lead through his eye. Instead he stopped suddenly while covering his face to avoid the bits of flying glass that sprayed in the bullet's wake several inches in front of him.

"Gonna kill you!"

Those words stood out to Mason even more than the gunshots, mostly because they'd been completely unexpected. It was Simons who shouted them as he launched himself over the banister of the staircase to fly at the overman like a giant bat. Mason would never have guessed the little guy had it in him to pounce like that instead of seeking shelter somewhere upstairs. For that matter, he didn't even know how Simons made it over the banister.

Mason watched through the broken window as Simons wrapped his arms around Garza's neck and held on with every ounce of strength he had. Knowing Simons wouldn't last very long in that spot, Mason hurried back through the door to lend him a hand.

Despite all Simons's snarling and thrashing, Garza didn't show any concern toward the little man trying to choke the life out of him. He even went so far as to clamp one hand over both of Simons's to keep his passenger locked in place as he aimed his pistol at the front door. The moment Mason stuck his head into sight, the overman took his shot.

Splinters exploded from the doorframe less than an inch away from Mason's head. That bullet had come so close to ending him that Mason swore he could see it hissing through the air as it passed him by.

"Toss that gun or I'll wring your damn neck!" Simons said.

Still gripping Simons by the wrists, the overman threw himself backward against the banister to crush the smaller man between it and him. That took the breath from Simons's lungs, but Garza slammed him one more time just to make absolutely certain. When the overman let him go, Simons dropped like a sack of dirt.

Mason had been preparing to fire but held off so as not to hit Simons. Now that he had a clear shot, he pulled his trigger. Garza turned to one side and then wheeled around to face him. Mason fired again but was unable to stop the other man from charging straight at him. He would have pulled his trigger a third time if the Remington hadn't been knocked from his hand. That same hand darted toward the sawed-off pistol tucked against his belly, but the overman got to it first.

The rusty stench of blood filled Mason's nose, combined with the odor of burned gunpowder. There was no time to find the source of the blood, however. Mason was too busy trying to keep from getting shot by his own weapon. Garza had already snatched the .44 from where it had been hidden, so all Mason could do was grab hold of the other man's wrist and force the Remington in another direction.

Knowing all too well how perfectly suited the shorter pistol was for close engagements, Mason strained every muscle to its limit to push it away. The overman was quickly asserting himself and when Mason felt the blunted iron brush against his torso, he grabbed the back end of the pistol so its hammer dropped on the meaty portion of his left hand instead of the next bullet's firing cap.

Pain spiked through Mason's hand to lance all the way up his shoulder. He kept his hand in place until Garza tore the pistol away with one brutal, bloody pull. Since Mason was still only inches away from him, the overman swung the Remington back in an attempt to knock Mason's head from his shoulders. Mason ducked down while stepping back. As the pistol sailed over his head, he drew the knife from its scabbard at the small of his back. Mason waited until Garza's arm was extended as far as it could go before lunging forward to press his blade against the larger man's throat.

"Drop the gun," Mason said.

The overman kept his arm in place but didn't relax his

grip. "You kill me," he snarled, "and you're still dead. Greeley and the rest will come after you."

"Not if they think everything went according to plan here tonight."

"You gonna cut my throat? 'Cause that's what it's gonna take to keep me from putting you down."

Pushing the blade against Garza's neck hard enough to draw a few drops of blood, Mason said, "Tell me what's really going on here. I know Simons isn't just someone who refuses to pay a debt."

The overman shook his head, not caring how his flesh dragged against the edge of Mason's blade in the process. "I don't know what you're talking about."

"Kill him!" Simons said from the relative safety of another room. "Do it and be done with it!"

"The little fella's got a point," Garza said

"No man's ready to throw his life away over something like this," Mason said. "This is just a job to you."

"That's right. And I didn't get paid to answer questions from a swindling cheat like you."

When the fight had started, Mason needed to defend himself. The odds of that overman sparing his life were so long that they weren't even worth considering. When he'd drawn the dagger and placed it to Garza's throat, Mason knew what needed to be done. Now that the fire in his blood had cooled a bit and he'd gotten a moment to catch his breath, the certainty he'd felt not too long ago was fading.

The overman's cold eyes studied Mason carefully. Most likely, he'd seen the change within him as well. "All right, Mason. It's over."

"Drop the pistol."

Holding his arm out to one side, Garza opened his fist

and allowed the Remington to hit the floor. "Now what?" he asked.

That was the very question that was plaguing Mason. If he only had an extra moment or two to think it over . . .

"Kill him!" Simons shouted. "He's gonna do the same to you. Just kill him before he gets the chance!"

Garza had his hands in front of him and held at waist level. Even though he was the one in the most immediate danger at the moment, he was also the most relaxed. He glanced in the direction of Simons's voice but was unable to pin down exactly where the small man had crawled off to.

Mason shifted on his feet and stepped on some of the knotted linens he'd used to tie up Simons. He kicked them toward the next room and said, "Simons, get in here and tie this man's arms and legs."

Simons poked his head out of the shadows from that room. "You can do it yourself."

"Get over here now!"

"I can barely walk. I think my back was broke when I hit that banister."

"Your back is *not* broken!" Mason roared. And then he committed a critical mistake by allowing his eyes to dart toward Simons. As soon as that happened, Garza took advantage by shoving Mason away. Now that he had some room to maneuver, the overman pivoted toward the gun he'd dropped to scoop it up with one hand.

Mason didn't have to think about what to do next. He took a quick step backward while flipping the knife around in his hand. The instant he felt the flat part of the blade slap against his fingers, he cocked his arm back and sent the dagger flying. It turned once in the air before sticking solidly into Garza's chest.

The .44 was in the overman's hand, but he'd lost the strength to move it any farther. His finger clenched around the trigger, sending a bullet into the wall several feet to Mason's left. When he looked at Mason, Garza was clearly surprised by something. Whether he was surprised that Mason had actually stricken the killing blow or just taken aback by whatever he was seeing as he gave up the ghost would remain unknown. Garza dropped to all fours, rolled onto his side, and was still.

Mason slowly walked forward. Every muscle in his body was just as tense as when the fight was at its peak. The Remington was only a few inches away from Garza's outstretched hand. Mason reached out tentatively at first and then snatched up the pistol as quickly as he could. At the first hint of movement, he thumbed the hammer back.

Simons froze after stepping from the darkened room. "Just me," he said.

Mason stood to his full height, pointing the .44 down at the fallen man while using one foot to push him onto his back. Garza let out half a breath. Some pink foam bubbled at one corner of his mouth and his eyes stared up into nothingness.

Approaching to stand near the staircase, Simons looked over at the grisly remains. "Looks like you got him good," he said.

"Shut up."

Simons backed up so quickly that he once again slammed into the banister.

It took a moment for Mason to realize what had spooked the little man. Then he realized he'd raised the .44 to point it at Simons. He lowered the pistol while looking down at the body. "We're going to bury him."

Simons shook his head. "I'm not about to go through so much trouble for a damn killer."

Mason reached down and pulled the knife from Garza's chest as if he were taking it from a thick cut of steak. For the moment, at least, he wasn't feeling anxious or much of anything else. That numbness must have shone through, because Simons quickly changed his tune.

"All right," the little fellow said. "I'll get the shovel."

Chapter 27

Mason wasn't normally of a mind to ride when he couldn't see more than a few yards in front of him, but he wanted to get out of Sedrich and didn't care how he did it. After he and Simons had dealt with Garza's body and parted ways, dawn was swiftly approaching. By the time Mason had ridden halfway along the road that would take him back to the river, streaks of dark orange and purple began to show in the sky.

As soon as there was enough light to see a better portion of the road in front of him, Mason snapped his reins to get moving even faster. He arrived at the *Delta Jack* and was greeted at the dock by a single overman who stepped off the boat to take the horse's reins.

"You alone?" the overman asked.

"Yes."

"You sure about that?"

"If you're referring to the man Greeley sent to spy on me," Mason replied, "I don't know where he is. Last I saw of him, he was staring down some of the men who were trying to guard that little fellow."

"And where is he now?"

Mason climbed down from the saddle and had to

shove past him to board the *Jack*. "I didn't even know he was supposed to be there! If I was supposed to be his wet nurse, then someone should have told me." Handing the bloody little bundle of rags over, he said, "Here. That's for Mr. Greeley." Then Mason continued walking onto the riverboat and didn't much care if anyone tried to stop him. Nobody attempted to get in Mason's way during the entire walk back to his cabin. Once there, he dropped onto his bed and closed his eyes.

Mason didn't know how long he slept, but a knock on his door rudely woke him. The light streaming in through his cabin's window was much brighter than it had been when he arrived. It took a moment for him to shake off the disorientation that came in the first seconds of opening his eyes, and as he gathered his wits about him, another knock rattled his door on its hinges. Mason had barely heard the first series of knocks and was about to ignore these when he decided to get up and see who was out there before they came back a minute or two later.

When he opened the door, Mason saw nothing. He leaned out a ways and spotted a familiar, shapely backside. "Maggie?"

She was already walking away when she heard his voice, turned around, and ran toward him. Mason was almost knocked to the floor by her enthusiastic embrace. Although he managed to put a little distance between them just so he could get a look at her, she quickly took his face in her hands and planted a kiss on his lips that curled the toes within his boots.

"I thought you were dead," she said.

Mason stepped backward into his cabin, which

brought her along as well. After closing the door, he said, "I wasn't gone that long."

"Yes, but there was always the chance that you would be killed before you even got to that man on your list."

"I still think if Greeley wanted me killed, he could do it at his leisure and he wouldn't need to leave the comfort of his boat."

She kissed him again. The hair hanging loosely about her face smelled of clean air and cool river water. "Let's not talk about that. You're here now and that's all that matters."

"Agreed."

Stepping up close to him, Maggie smiled while allowing her hands to wander along his shoulders and down over his chest. She didn't make it to his waist before stopping and saying, "I thought you'd like me to give you a proper welcome."

"I appreciate it, Maggie. I'm just tired, is all."

"Would you prefer it if I left you alone?"

"No."

She smiled warmly and led him to the bed. Maggie sat at one end of the mattress with her back resting against the cabin's wall and her legs tucked beneath her. Before Mason could say another word, she pulled him down so he was lying with his head resting in her arms. There wasn't much space for the two of them on that bed, but neither seemed to mind.

"There," she said quietly while running her fingers through his hair. "How's that?"

"That," Mason sighed, "makes me believe there is a heaven."

"Good. We don't have to talk about anything. We just sit here and let the world pass by for a while."

Mason was inclined to take her up on that offer. In fact, the idea of letting the world pass by for more than just a while seemed very appealing. He closed his eyes, enjoyed the feeling of being so close to her, and listened to everything around them. Between the sounds of the boat itself and its passengers on all three decks, there was plenty to choose from. Eventually the creaking of the timber that formed the *Delta Jack*'s hull held his attention.

As if sensing exactly what he needed, Maggie placed her other hand on his chest and gently rubbed. Just then the entire boat came to life as the engines began to turn the paddlewheel.

"Sounds like we're casting off," Maggie said.

"Good. The sooner we get away from here, the better."

"I'm curious about what happened while you were away. But if you'd rather not tell me . . . I understand."

"It went fine," he sighed. "Just fine."

"Now, that's a bald-faced lie," Maggie said as she continued to soothe him with her touch. "Any man in your condition after the night you've had would not be just fine."

"I'm looking bruised again?"

"And you smell like gunpowder."

Mason started to get up but was held in place by the hand on his chest. He wasn't about to fight to get away from her, so he leaned back again. "Greeley isn't telling me all of what's going on here," he said.

"Now, there's a surprise." Maggie chuckled. "A man like that is actually lying to you?"

"I know it's strange, but it made more sense when he told me he wanted Simons dead because of a gambling debt. I mean, he was about to kill me for the same reason and I don't even know how many others he's killed before me."

"It's just a bluff with a good amount of groundwork laid down ahead of time. Nothing new there."

"I know that now," Mason said. "But after I got past the bluff, I still don't see what the purpose of it was."

"He had to tell you something to get you to go on that job."

"Not really. I do owe him a hell of a lot of money and I still don't think he forced me into that predicament."

"But he must not have wanted you poking around into what was truly going on," she said. "He gave you a story that wouldn't be hard to swallow so you'd just go off and do the job you were given. Speaking of which . . . did you?"

"Did I what?" Mason asked.

"Did you do the job?"

"Yes."

Maggie sat up so quickly that she nearly threw Mason onto the floor. "What did you just say?"

"That I did the job," Mason replied.

"You killed a man in cold blood?"

"It wasn't cold blood. It was the job I was given."

"Isn't that cold blood?" she said.

Mason blinked and furrowed his brow in thought. "I don't . . . think so."

He let her hang for a few more seconds before letting her off the hook. "I didn't kill him, Maggie."

"I knew it," she sighed. "You couldn't fool me."

As they both leaned back into their original positions, Mason waited until she was relaxed once again before saying, "I did cut his finger off, though."

She patted his chest and replied, "Sure you did."

Now that the tension had been relieved somewhat, Mason felt more like talking. After giving her a quick retelling of what had happened in Sedrich up to the last hour or two, he said, "Simons had a lot to say about his history with Greeley."

"And do you think you can believe him?"

"Yes."

Being no stranger to gut instinct, Maggie accepted that. "What did he tell you?"

"That he helped Greeley hire enough gunmen to get his business ventures going."

"And why would Greeley want him dead?"

Mason thought back to his conversation with Simons. Eventually he had to admit, "We never really came up with an answer to that."

"There're other names on the list, right?"

"Yes. Two more of them. You think one of those other men will know why Greeley hates Simons so much?" Mason asked.

He could feel Maggie shrug behind him. "Maybe. Maybe not. I was just thinking that you might get a better idea about what the whole picture is once you got a look at more than one piece of it."

"You're probably right."

"So, what happened to Simons anyway?"

"He's headed east," Mason said. "I've got a small place in New York City that I'm loaning him for a short while. I got the impression that he was just as happy to get away from his cousins as he was to get away from Greeley."

"Family is always trouble. I never had much luck with mine."

"I think his family is a bit more than just trouble. At least some of them are killers."

After a slight pause, Maggie said, "My aunt Irene is a real piece of work. If I introduced her to Simons, perhaps he'd run as far as the Alaska coast."

Mason laughed a bit but found himself distracted. More than anything, he wanted to simply lie there and enjoy as much silence as he could get before Greeley summoned him. Something was bothering him, though, and had been for a while. Like the proverbial burr under a saddle, the matter became more painful the longer it was allowed to sink in. Finally he said, "I killed a man."

Maggie's hand came to an abrupt stop over his heart. "What was that?"

"I said I had to kill a man. While I was in Sedrich."

"Who was it?"

"One of the overmen," he said.

"Good Lord. Was one of them following you?"

It was at that moment that Mason realized he hadn't mentioned the overman when he told her about what had happened in Sedrich. Mason started talking again, retelling parts of his account only with all the key participants in place.

When he got close to the end, he said, "I put my knife to his throat just to end the fight. If I'd killed him in that instant, I think it would have been easier."

"He meant to kill you."

"No doubt about that."

"And he would have killed you if you'd let him go, right?"

Mason thought about that, but not for long. "Probably. I'd say he was there to put me down if I didn't play along like I was supposed to. Then again, if I'd done the job like I'd agreed . . ."

Shifting on the bed, Maggie situated herself so she

could face him. "If you'd done the job like Greeley wanted, you would have killed an innocent man."

"Simons wasn't exactly innocent."

"Neither are we, in case you haven't noticed. That doesn't mean we deserve to be executed."

"Depends on which judge you ask," Mason said. When he saw the scolding expression on Maggie's face, he added, "But I do see your point."

"That man was there to kill you. I don't see your problem. Haven't you ever had to defend yourself before?"

"I have. Usually you can feel a fight brewing," Mason said. "You can tell it's coming, and by the time it does, you know why it happened and where it's headed."

"You really do think that much about every little thing," Maggie said as though she'd only then taken that as truth. "I'm surprised your head hasn't torn itself apart yet."

"You've been on the circuit. It's like you just said. We're not innocents. We both have bent the rules or broken them outright to get where we needed to go. Sometimes it's justified and sometimes it's just convenient. But when we get caught and there's trouble headed our way . . ."

Maggie nodded and put her hand on his knee. Since Mason was getting flustered, she said, "When there's trouble, we know we've got it coming."

He met her eyes. "Yeah. With what happened in Sedrich . . . I knew it might happen. Even so, it just seemed so . . . cold. Does that make sense?"

Laughing just a little, she said, "You didn't deserve the trouble that you got. That's what's different. You're not used to being the innocent one in a fight. Even if it is just partly innocent."

"I hadn't thought about that, but I suppose you're right."

"You shouldn't feel bad about what happened or what you had to do. It sounds to me like things turned out as best they could."

Mason shook his head and sighed. "I didn't even dislike him."

"The man you killed?"

"He was there doing a job . . . just like me. If a man is going to put another one off this earth, it makes things a whole lot easier if he can at least hate him."

Maggie gave him a kiss. "You're a good man in a bad spot. That's all."

"Stupid man is more like it," he groaned.

"How do you figure?"

"Making that bet on a straight to the eight. Damn, that was stupid."

Holding him tight, she said, "Yes, it sure was."

Chapter 28

For someone who bluffed so much and spent most of his days with folks doing their best to bluff him, it was refreshing for Mason to be with someone who told him everything, whether it was good to hear or not. By the time one of Greeley's men came along to collect him, Mason was feeling almost as good as if he'd gotten some sleep. The young man who'd knocked on the door of Mason's cabin was tall and dressed in black pants and a white shirt. If that didn't make it clear he was one of the waiters in the largest of the *Jack*'s dining rooms, the small red apron tied around his waist sealed the deal.

When they went to the fore of the riverboat's third deck, Mason said, "This isn't the way to Mr. Grecley's office."

"No, sir. It isn't."

"Where are we going?"

"Mr. Greeley wanted to meet with you. He's having breakfast right over there."

They were in an elegantly furnished restaurant looking out to the Mississippi. The sun's rays reflected off the swaying waters, and the entire front wall of the room consisted of large windows for people to take it all in.

Food was brought in from a kitchen located elsewhere, freeing up all the space within the bright room for wrought-iron tables and polished wooden chairs. A light green carpet completed the illusion that passengers were dining on the terrace of a mansion instead of floating down a river. Greeley sat at the table closest to the window so he could look straight out at the water while his ever-present armed escorts kept other folks a good distance away.

As soon as he saw Mason, Greeley stood up and waved him over. The young waiter came as well, plastering a smile onto his face as soon as he got close enough to be heard without shouting. "What can I get for you gentlemen?" he asked.

"I'll have some more of these crepes," Greeley said.

When he heard Greeley request the fancy little pancakes, Mason couldn't help thinking of an old phrase about putting a dress on a pig but not being able to make it dance. "Coffee for me," he said.

"You must be hungry. Order whatever you like," Greeley insisted.

"Fine. I'll have some biscuits and gravy."

"Good choice," Greeley said while shooing the waiter away. "Now have a seat. We got some things to discuss."

Mason sat across from Greeley. He tried to get comfortable but finally had to concede the fact that the chair had been made as more of a display piece than anything that might make a man feel grateful for being off his feet.

"So," Greeley said, "tell me about Sedrich."

"I would have thought your spy had told you all about it."

"Oh, come, now. You must have guessed I'd send someone to keep an eye on you."

"Yeah," he said. "I suppose I did. I take it he came back on his own?"

Greeley didn't respond to that. He showed no emotion whatsoever. Mason took that as a sign that he wasn't a suspect in Garza's disappearance and was more than happy to move along to other matters.

"So," Greeley asked, "what happened?"

"I rode to the Bistro and found him just like you said I would."

"Simons is hard to miss, ain't he?"

Now that he thought the hook was sunk in nice and deep with Mason, Greeley had taken a more familiar manner with him. While it made for easier conversations, Mason already missed the terse threats of bodily harm. Having Greeley treat him like an old friend made Mason want to vomit.

"He sure is," Mason replied through a smile that he wore like a cheap coat of paint.

Greeley was so wrapped up in his own smugness that he barely seemed to notice. "What about the bounty hunters? Did they give you any trouble?"

"The men I saw were armed, but they looked more like rowdies than assassins. And there weren't too many of them."

The expression on Greeley's face showed no sign of suspicion, which meant he almost certainly already knew what he'd just been told. He nodded, anxiously awaiting the next part of the story.

"I sat down at Simons's table and played poker for a few hours," Mason continued. "Got him good and drunk and then followed him to his home. Once he was there, I went in and killed him."

Naturally that was the moment when the waiter returned with coffee. He refilled the cup that Greeley had already been working on, set another cup in front of Mason, filled that, and did all that without showing that he'd just overheard a conversation involving murder. "Your food will be ready in a short while," he said.

"Much obliged," Greeley said. After the waiter left, Greeley stirred some sugar into his coffee and said, "That man's served me breakfast and lunch more times than I can count and I couldn't tell you his name. So, how'd you do it?"

"Do what?"

"Kill Simons. I had to deal with that obnoxious little turd on more than one occasion and would have liked to kill him myself. I wanna know how he finally met his end."

"I shot him," Mason replied.

"Before or after you took his finger?"

"What does that matter?"

Somehow Greeley managed to handle his coffee cup like a truly civilized dandy when he said, "It's a matter of how much screaming was involved."

Unable to contain himself any longer, Mason said, "I'm not going to dredge up such matters for you or anyone else's amusement. If you want to tack a fine onto my debt, then go right ahead."

Greeley laughed once and sipped his coffee. "Don't try to look down at me from some high horse. That may have suited you when you were just some gambler who made a bad call. Soon as you brought me that finger wrapped in a bloody rag, you showed your colors well enough."

"Colors? You didn't leave me any choice."

"But you performed your duty, ugly as it was, real well. Ain't that right, Abner?"

"Yeah."

"I would've laid good money on you coming back here with just the ring. Maybe some blood on it for appearances, but just the ring." Not only did Greeley's eyes take on the steely chill of which Mason had become so familiar, but they looked across that table as if expecting to find similar dead orbs in Mason's face. "So, tell me. I know you remember. Did that little weasel scream?"

"Yeah," Mason replied as he thought of all the carrying on Simons had done from the next room during the fight with Garza. "He screamed."

"I knew it." Greeley leaned back in his chair as the breakfast plates were brought to the table. The waiter set them down along with silverware and hurried off. Picking up his fork, Greeley used it to point at Mason and said, "You're gonna work out better than I expected."

"Thanks, Mr. Greeley."

"Call me Cam." After using the fork to take a small piece of crepe to his mouth, Greeley pointed it once more at Mason, but a little lower than the last time he'd done so. "How's your hand?"

Mason had completely forgotten about catching his hand beneath the hammer of his own Remington. When he and Simons had taken Garza out of the house to be buried in the closest patch of ground, Mason grabbed the cleanest towel he could find and shredded it to be wrapped around his hand. The wound hurt, but no more than any other number of aches, pains, cuts, and bruises he'd collected of late. For Greeley, he summed it up with "It's fine."

"What happened to it?"

"There was a scuffle at Simons's house."

"Scuffle?"

"I'm sure you can imagine," Mason said. "I was, after all, there to kill him. Most folks don't take too kindly to that sort of thing."

"Why were you so much more pleasant when we were playing cards?"

"Because that's my element."

"Does this sort of work truly put you out of your element?" Greeley asked. "Or might you be confused about what your element truly is?"

"This place, these dainty tables, these expensive plates," Mason said while motioning to each of those things in turn, "aren't even my element. I'm a cardplayer. A gambler. While I do enjoy civilized niceties, I've come to realize that I don't enjoy what comes along with them."

"And what's that?"

Mason had done exactly what he hadn't wanted to do. He'd spoken out of turn and out of the character he was trying to portray. Once again, it seemed, Greeley had outplayed him. Before too many awkward seconds ticked by, Mason salvaged his misstep by putting on a smile and tapping his coffee cup. "Civilized folk don't drink whiskey for breakfast. That is something I simply cannot abide."

Back when Mason was new to the *Delta Jack* and its owner, he would have been certain that the smile he saw on Greeley's face was genuine. Now he wasn't so sure. Instead of sitting and pondering the matter, Mason simply dug into the biscuits and gravy as if there weren't anything else in the world requiring his attention.

"Civilized folk don't do a lot of things," Greeley said. With a wink, he added, "That's why I don't allow them on my boat."

"Hear, hear!"

"So, when was the last time you saw the man I sent to keep an eye on you?"

"You mean the spy?" Mason asked.

"As you like."

"He was dealing with some of Simons's men."

"That's right. And how did you know he was there in the first place?"

Mason took a bite of biscuit before replying, "I got lucky."

Greeley didn't take long to digest that response. It seemed to fit in with what he'd expected, so he took another bite of food.

"I want to talk about Virgil Slake for a second," Mason said.

"Who?"

"Virgil Slake. The man with the loaded dice. Surely you must have had a look inside his cabin after his partner and I took our unexpected departure from this boat."

"Oh, right!" Greeley said. "You two did leave quite a mess. I nearly forgot about him."

"Well, I didn't. I sniffed him out when he could have been soaking your craps games for a good while longer than he already had."

"And I let you apply the money you took to your debt."

"He would have taken more from you," Mason insisted. "At least another couple thousand over the course of a week or two."

"And?"

"And I want to apply the money you didn't lose . . . money you still have because of me . . . to my debt as well."

Greeley took another bite and gnawed on it as if he was also trying to eat the tines from his fork. "That's crazy."

"Why?"

"Because you might as well say I'm saving money because you're not sittin' at any of my card tables winning hands that might have gone to me."

Raising an eyebrow, Mason said, "I hadn't thought of that. But that's different than what I'm asking for."

"How?"

"Because I wasn't cheating," Mason said. "Virgil Slake had a real good system going. More than likely it would have kept going because of someone on your payroll. After all, those dice had to get switched out somehow. Having it happen once or twice is possible. Having it happen consistently enough to make a man set up shop in his cabin is something else."

"Tell you what. If you find how them dice were gettin' switched or if any of my people were in on it, then I'll see about shaving off some more of that debt."

"All right, then." Mason breathed a little easier and took a bit of breakfast that he was actually able to enjoy. Now that he'd shown some confidence along with a liberal dose of greed, Mason was fairly certain he'd regained some of Greeley's trust. They were once again two snakes in the same patch of grass. "So, who's next on the list?"

"You don't recall? I thought any man that's been on the gamblers' circuit would have a sharp memory for names and faces."

"I didn't see any faces on that list. Second, it's a list. It was written down. If it's written down, I don't have to recall it."

Greeley shook his head. "That's just plain laziness."

"Fine, then. Keep your job and we'll call it square."

"Just because I'm giving you some credit for what you done to Simons, don't think that entitles you to give me lip," Greeley warned.

Mason nodded and used the hunk of biscuit on his fork to sop up as much gravy as he could. Now that he'd started eating, his stomach was reminding him of how long it had been since it was properly filled.

"Maggie," Greeley said.

"She's not on that list," Mason replied. "I would've remembered that."

"No, she ain't on the list. I hear you've been spending a lot of time with her."

"That's right."

"May not be such a good idea," Greeley said. "I hear she's also been spending time with Jervis Crane."

"That twitchy fellow from our game?"

"One and the same. Could be she's making the rounds to get something on some of the better players here. Women gamblers do that sort of thing to get an edge."

"Do you really think you need to tell me something like that?" Mason asked.

"Just making sure you're not blinded in a way that every man can become blind."

"All right, you delivered your warning. What about the next name?"

"The next one on the list is Seth Borden," Greeley said.

"I suppose you've got something in mind for me to bring back after I kill him?"

"Don't need to kill him." Greeley took a bite of his

crepes and washed it down with some coffee. "You're to bring him a message."

"No mementos?" Mason chided. "This should be easy."

"Come to think of it, I would like something else. His wife and daughter."

Chapter 29

A short time later, Mason was seated at a table in one of the smaller card rooms on the third deck. Up near the top of the ship, the breezes were always just a little warmer and somewhat more fragrant. This room was more of a parlor and outfitted with simple furnishings that didn't steal one's gaze from the large windows filling two of four walls. Older gentlemen seemed to prefer this room for their games of backgammon, chess, and rummy. The table where Mason sat was one of the smaller square ones. He was alone there for the first hour or so, dealing hands of solitaire while barely going through the motions of playing. His eyes rarely left the single spot upon which he'd been focusing since he first sat down.

A low murmur went through the room, moving through the air like a ripple upon tranquil waters. Mason looked up and watched as Maggie crossed the room carrying a tall glass in each hand. Along the way, the old-timers greeted her with polite words and flowery compliments. She accepted every flirtation as though it were the first she'd ever gotten, but she walked straight to Mason's table and sat down.

"Sorry I couldn't get here sooner," she said. "When

you came to get me, I thought that game was drying up. I was wrong."

"You did well?" he asked.

"Let's just say these drinks and any other drinks in the foreseeable future are my treat."

Mason picked up the glass and sipped what turned out to be a mint julep. It was made by one of the bartenders who'd honed his skills down to a science, but all Mason could muster was a nod and a grunt to acknowledge the effort.

After sipping her own drink, Maggie said, "Do I even need to ask how your talk with Greeley went?"

"I believe you just did."

"If you'd prefer to be cross, I can come back some other time. I'm sure plenty of these men would like to trade unpleasantries with you. Like that one, for example," she said as she raised a finger to point at one of the tables on the other side of the room. An old man with a pinched face sat there, nursing his coffee and wearing a frown that made him look as if he wanted to chew the cup in his hand.

Even from a distance, the old man noticed Maggie's gaze and responded with the closest thing to a smile his glum features could manage. She brightened his day even further by waggling her fingers in a dainty wave.

Mason couldn't help being amused by the exchange between her and the old men in that room. Even though none of those fellows were going to be completely drawn in by her with just a wave and a few well-placed smiles, she would undoubtedly have some ammunition to use if any of them sat across from her in a game with some real stakes. "It's good you took your time in getting out of that game downstairs," he said. "I would have been even worse company earlier."

"I'm guessing you and Greeley discussed that list of his?"

"Yes, we did," Mason said while slapping a red eight on top of a black nine. "The next name is Seth Borden. Ever hear of him?"

Maggie thought about that for a few moments and then tapped on the ten of hearts. Once Mason had moved the column headed by the black nine over there, she said, "I don't believe so."

"What about his wife and child?"

"No." Her eyes widened and she dropped her voice to a harsh whisper. "Does Greeley want you to kill a woman and child?"

"No. Just kidnap them."

She took another drink. Clearly, it wasn't strong enough to suit her purposes, so she set it down. "Are you going to do it?"

"I've been sitting here trying to think of how I can avoid it. So far, the best plan I've come up with is to find some other people to stand in for Borden's family."

"And do what?" she asked. "Kidnap them instead?"

"That's where the plan falls apart."

"You haven't come up with anything else? Considering how much pondering you do, I highly doubt that."

"Well . . . I have come up with another course of action."

Maggie leaned forward and looked at him anxiously. "Yes?"

Looking up from his cards, Mason said, "I could go through with the original plan."

"You mean Greeley's original plan?"

Mason nodded.

"If you wanted to do that, then you should have just gone ahead and put a bullet through that first man's head," she said.

"This is different," Mason said. "This is . . ." Suddenly he became very aware of how quiet it was in that room. Just raising their voices to a normal conversational level would send their words through the entire space whether they wanted them to or not. "I need some air," he said as he gathered up his cards.

Maggie picked up her glass and stood up. "I think we both do."

Outside, the two of them walked along a path that would take them around the *Delta Jack*'s entire perimeter. The day was turning out to be a mix of gloom and light as scattered clouds rolled across the slate blue sky. At the moment, the sun's rays were clawing at the edge of a small patch of fluff while the riverboat steamed ever northward.

"How could you even possibly think about kidnapping someone?" Maggie asked. "That could wind up being worse than shooting them."

"How do you figure?"

"Because at least someone's pain is ended with a bullet. Delivering someone to the likes of Greeley and those damn overmen could be condemning them to something much worse."

Mason couldn't help asking the question that sprang to his mind. "Are you talking from experience?"

She lowered her head. "I've never been kidnapped."

"But . . ."

"But . . . I know some people who have. I was spending time in San Francisco, working the fan-tan parlors in Chinatown. There was a man who owned half a dozen parlors along with twice that number of opium dens throughout the city. When a gambler owed him enough money or if he crossed him in some manner, he would snatch away someone close to him."

Mason let out a slow breath. "You're talking about Pieces Hobart."

Snapping her eyes to him, Maggie asked, "You've heard of him?"

The chuckle Mason let out had no humor in it whatsoever. "Anyone who's gambled in San Francisco has heard of him. A horror story passed around all the tables in between hands. 'Watch yourself in Chinatown,' they'd say. 'If Pieces gets his hands on you, that's all that's gonna be left.' " Mason wanted something to wash away that particular memory, but the sweetness of the drink in his hand wasn't going to do the trick. He set it on the next table they passed. "Been a while since I thought about that story."

"It's more than just a story to frighten superstitious gamblers," Maggie said. "Some friends of mine got on Hobart's bad side."

"How?"

"I never got a chance to ask. The first pieces that were sent back to their families were their feet. Weeks later, it was their heads. A family doesn't exactly come back from something like that. They were destroyed. Lord only knows what those people went through that were captured." After the chill had worked its way through her, Maggie looked to him and said, "You can't become something like one of those kidnappers. What if you don't come back from it either?"

Mason held his tongue as they walked past a table occupied by two men playing dominoes. Once they were out of earshot, he said, "If I had more time to work with, I'd do something different. I was lucky to get away with crossing Greeley once, and it's only a matter of time before he discovers that overman I killed won't be coming back."

"Then skip this kidnapping job and go to the next name on the list."

"That was the first thing I tried to do. Greeley wouldn't have it."

"Who gives a damn what Greeley wants?" Maggie snapped. "What's stopping you from just getting off this boat and putting it and him behind you? Do you honestly think he can find you no matter where you go? That's just another story passed by superstitious men!"

"So was Pieces Hobart," Mason reminded her. "That one turned out to have at least some foundation on truth." He drew a breath and wrapped his arm around hers so they would look like just another couple out for a stroll. It was also a way to keep her from storming off, which Mason's read on her told him she was very close to doing. "Look, Maggie. I know we haven't been acquainted with each other for long, but you've got to know I'm not some fool who takes Greeley's word as gospel."

"I used to think so." Almost immediately she winced and added, "I still do. It's just a surprise to hear you've decided to go along with him."

"If I don't, someone else will. Greeley's obviously working on something that I haven't seen yet, which means these jobs and that list are important to him. If I refuse, whether we get away or if I'm killed and dumped in the river, he'll find some other way to get those jobs done."

"What's wrong with him finding someone else to do his dirty work?" she asked. "It's not like you can stop every wicked deed Greeley might do."

"No, but maybe I can stop these particular ones. What would you say the odds are that the next man Greeley finds will have aspirations like that?"

Judging by the look on Maggie's face, her thoughts in that regard weren't particularly inspiring. "But if you're just going to follow through on what Greeley wants, how will you be stopping anything?"

He held on to her arm a bit tighter as his slow walk took a more leisurely quality. "That's the good part. If I'm the one to get to this Borden gentleman, then I can get a better idea of what it is Greeley is after with this whole list business."

"And what about Borden's family?"

"Something tells me that Greeley truly does want to just hold them here. At least they'll be accounted for while I figure out what's to be done next. Then, at my earliest opportunity, I can set them free."

"There's a lot that could happen to those poor folks while they're held captive on this boat," Maggie pointed out. "Would you want your loved ones at the mercy of someone who's so quick to slice off another man's finger before having him executed?"

Mason nodded. "No. Which is why that's the last resort. My intention is to do everything possible to keep it from getting that far. I don't have all the parts to this story yet, so in the meantime I've got to make this up as I go."

Patting his arm, Maggie said, "You'll come up with something. I know it. If there's anything you need from me . . . just ask."

"Are you sure? I'd hate to get you wrapped up in this more than you already are."

"This isn't my first trip down the Mississippi on this particular boat, you know. And there are plenty of stories going round about Greeley. Considering how brazen his overmen have become, one doesn't even need to rely on hearsay in that regard. My point is that I know what sort of man Greeley is and still I've been putting money in his pockets by coming here, playing his games, and buying his liquor. That makes me responsible, even in a small way, for where Greeley is now."

"I suppose you could look at it that way, but . . ."

"Also," she quickly added, "he's a murdering kidnapper and I don't like kidnappers."

"It could be dangerous," Mason said. "And I'm not even sure if I can end this directly after the kidnapping. There's one more name on the list after Borden's, you know."

"I know. I'd like to do this. And when it's done, you'll owe me a rather large favor."

He leaned over and kissed her. "I certainly will."

They walked for another several paces, enjoying playing the part of two carefree souls enjoying a pleasant day. As they approached the bow, Maggie smiled brightly.

"What's gotten you so happy?" Mason asked.

"We."

"What?"

"Before . . . when you were talking about getting off this boat, you said *we* would escape instead of *you* would escape."

"A slip of the tongue," Mason said.

She held on to him a little tighter and rested her head on his shoulder while continuing the rest of their stroll.

Chapter 30

Although Borden was next on the list, it would be a little while before the *Delta Jack* arrived at a spot where Mason could easily get to him. He was given some time to himself, and Mason's first thought was to get some sleep. His only regret was that he wasn't able to enjoy the sensation of lying there under his covers with his eyes closed for a spell before drifting off to sleep. Instead, seconds after his head hit the pillow, Mason was out cold.

Sometime later, he was woken by a not-so-gentle tussle of his hair. He sighed at first, thinking he was dreaming. Once he opened his eyes and realized someone was in his room, he sat bolt upright and started to dive for the holster slung over a nearby hook in the wall.

"What in the . . . ?" he groaned. "Maggie?"

"Who else would it be?" she said. "It's not as if you've made many other friends on this boat."

"What are you doing here?"

"Giving you what you need the most after sleep." When she saw the wry grin drift onto his face, she added, "Besides that."

"What, then?"

Someone knocked on the door and Maggie immediately answered it. After having a few brief words with the people in the hall, she turned back to Mason and said, "A bath!" She then stepped aside so the people from the hall could drag in a narrow tub that was half-full of water. It was placed in his room and the young men who'd brought it inside quickly left.

"I've got other things to worry about," Mason said.

"And you can worry about them while cleaning yourself up. Trust me," Maggie said, "you'll feel better once you feel more like your old self."

"You barely know what my old self is!"

"Then we'll both feel better once you don't smell so bad."

Knowing he wasn't about to dissuade her, and realizing that a bath didn't sound half-bad, Mason began unbuttoning the cuffs of his shirt. "Will you be joining me?" he asked Maggie.

She grinned and replied, "That would only distract you. Don't forget there's work to be done."

As she stepped out of his room, the two who'd brought in the tub returned with pitchers of steaming water. After two more trips, the tub was filled and steaming as well. Mason closed his door, locked it, and stripped down so he could slip into the inviting water.

Maggie was right. He felt better almost immediately.

The rest of the day passed into early evening. He was cleaned up, ate lunch, and found himself involved in a poker tournament organized by a small group of passengers. Mason played through dinner, working his way up the ladder to become a true contender for first place. When he got a low straight after drawing two cards during one of the pivotal hands, he thought it was a bad omen. This time, however, the straight held and he took the pot. Several hands later, he was busted by a greenhorn from Philadelphia who managed to stumble into a full house. Since second place paid a hundred dollars, Mason was satisfied with the outcome.

He and Maggie had dinner followed by dessert in the moonlight. And still, there was no sign of Greeley. The only time Mason caught sight of an overman was when a drunk got a bit too loud at the roulette wheel in the main room. He was dragged out, kicking and screaming, to be taken somewhere he wouldn't be a nuisance to the rest of the passengers.

"Say what you will about Greeley," Maggie said. "But he does run a fine riverboat."

Mason nodded. "Even with that taken into consideration, I'd say his faults far outweigh his virtues."

She snaked an arm around his waist as they turned back toward the door that would lead them inside where seats at the poker tables were quickly becoming scarce. "You're getting quiet. That means you're thinking too hard again."

"I don't rightly know what to do until I know where I'm going or when I'm supposed to leave or any number of other details."

"That's right. We don't know, but you can't drive yourself out of your mind while waiting. That's no way to live. You'll come up with something and it will be fine. One thing's for certain, no matter what you decide, Greeley's not going to like it, and that makes me feel pretty good about the whole thing. Until then," she added, "shouldn't I send you off properly?"

Mason allowed himself to be steered in the direction of the stairs that would take them to the second deck.

From there, he would allow her to take him to his cabin, and once inside . . .

"No," he said, and then winced as if he'd stubbed his toe on a rock.

"What do you mean, no?"

"I mean . . . we probably shouldn't. Or . . . I shouldn't . . ."

"You don't sound sure of yourself," she said.

Still wincing, Mason replied, "I'm not."

"Then let's go with our instincts. My instinct is telling me to put one more smile on your face."

"You know what mine says?"

"Something tells me I don't want to know," Maggie sighed.

"My instinct," he continued despite her protests, "tells me that when we're in the middle of . . . being indisposed . . . that's when Greeley will send one of his gorillas to fetch me."

"That's just expecting the worst."

"Greeley wants to rake me over the coals for that bet I placed," Mason said, "and there's no better way than that to torture a man." Somehow he found the strength to peel himself away from her. "Besides, there are still some preparations I need to make."

Maggie let out a labored breath. "Fine. If you insist. Are you sure I can't change your mind?"

"I'm positive you can change my mind," he said. "That's why we should say our farewells right now."

Although she was unhappy with his decision, she respected it. Of course, that didn't mean she wasn't about to torture him a little before they parted ways. She pressed herself against him and gave Mason a lingering kiss that he would feel for the next couple of days. Leaning back just far enough for their lips to stop touching, she said, "I'm going back in there to find a game."

"Good luck."

"You too. And be careful."

Mason let her start to turn away from him and then pulled her back fiercely. She barely had enough time to be surprised by that before being wrapped in his arms and given a kiss that would linger just as long as the one she'd given to him. Judging by the stunned expression on her face when he left her, it might even last a bit longer.

Once he was in his cabin, Mason picked up his carpetbag and checked it over. As far as he could tell, it hadn't been tampered with since the first time.

He'd already cleaned and prepared his weapons, so Mason set those on the bed.

The next thing he took was from the very bottom of the carpetbag. It was a polished mahogany case with an interior that was divided into three rows of two compartments each. The two compartments on the left and the two on the right were of equal size, containing markers of various size carved from polished sandstone that were used as betting chips or playing pieces in several different games of chance. Many sporting men carried markers made of more exotic or expensive material, but these were the first markers Mason had ever had. More than that, they'd been given to him by his father. On a whim, he took one of the markers out and tucked it into a vest pocket. The two compartments in the middle of the case were split so the lower one was larger than the upper. Dark blue poker chips were packed into the upper compartment. Tucked within the lower was a deck of cards, two pairs of dice, and a .22-caliber derringer.

Mason removed the derringer from the case and looked it over. It had two barrels, each holding one round. Not only was the pistol light and compact, but it was also narrow, which made it well suited for several different purposes. Just to be safe, he disassembled the pistol, checked to make sure each vital part was in good working order, and then put it back together again. He set the pistol on the bed before searching through the narrow markers within the third compartment. The one he was after looked similar to all the others, but with one crucial difference. When he pressed it between his thumb and forefinger, he was able to slide the marker into two slender halves.

One half was thinner than the other and its top edge had two raised notches. Mason ran that edge along the interior corner of the box lid until he found a set of corresponding slots hidden by the grain of the wood. Once the notches were fitted inside the slots, he could lever open the panel, which created a false top in the case. Having unlocked the panel, Mason slid the marker shut again and fit it back in with the others.

Secreted between the panel and the genuine top of the case were components of a device that looked more like random bits of junk taken from a tinkerer's workshop. There was a canvas band with straps and buckles stitched to it, a set of flat zigzagging metal sticks connected to what looked like a hollow metal clamshell, and a few thin bands of rubber. A set of small screwdrivers were attached to the back of the panel, and Mason took those out so he could get to work.

Assembling the device had taken quite a lot of practice. It wasn't an overly complicated mechanism, but if it didn't work perfectly, it could very easily get a man killed. Mason went through each step with extra care to make sure he got every last thing right. He attached the interlocking metal sticks to the top of the canvas strap, oiled the screws holding them together, and then put a rubber band in place. One end looped around the strap mechanism and the other hooked around a post midway up the diagonal rows of sticks.

"There we go," he said. "Now to make sure I still have the touch."

Mason rolled up his left sleeve so he could buckle the strap around his elbow. The metal pieces rested on his forearm with the clamshell several inches below his wrist. When he bent his elbow, the metal sticks extended like an accordion to move the clamshell toward the bottom of his palm. Straightening that arm again allowed the band of rubber to pull the accordion bank in so the clamshell slid down along his arm once again.

"Perfection in motion," Mason said proudly.

Such devices were called holdouts and they were used for delivering stashed cards when they were needed most. They weren't uncommon among gamblers. Illegal, most definitely, but not uncommon. Mason's holdout was a quality model, although not one of the most impressive ones. Among some cheats, designing a holdout specific to their needs was something of an art form. Mason preferred simplicity and reliability.

The idea for the modifications he now attempted had only just occurred to him; otherwise he would have started much sooner. He considered going to ask Greeley when they would be arriving at the next port of call or at least asking where the port was. Doing so would only have used up more precious time, and Greeley seemed intent on preserving an air of mystery on the subject. Mason was inclined to let the man have his mystery. He didn't think he would need much time to make the modifications to his holdout anyway.

Reaching for the deck of cards in the mahogany box, he pulled out one card and slipped it into the metal clamshell. That card lay flat against his forearm until he bent his elbow to deliver the card into his hand. Keeping it extended, Mason took hold of the card using his free hand and waggled it back and forth to test the grip of the clamshell that was holding it.

"This should be easier than I thought," he muttered under his breath.

Operating a holdout device took a good amount of practice. Simply having the mechanism buckled onto his arm caused Mason's muscles to grow anxious. He straightened and bent his elbow a few more times, delivering the card to his hand and plucking it from the clamshell with greater ease every time. Once the card was out, he prodded the clamshell with his fingers to get a feel for how it was constructed.

"Only one way to see if this'll work, I suppose."

Before Mason continued with his modifications, he turned over the card that he'd plucked randomly from the deck. It wasn't just an eight, but an eight of the same suit as the one he'd used to make what he thought was going to be a winning straight.

"Funny," he said to God or the Fates or whatever deity might be in charge of toying with gamblers. "Very funny indeed."

Chapter 31

As it turned out, Mason had plenty of time to make his modifications. Nobody came to his door until dusk the following day, which also gave him the opportunity to do a bit of sewing. Mason had never been much of one to work with needle and thread, but necessity had made it prudent for him to do some of his own alterations from time to time. Mainly, the use of a sleeve holdout like the clamshell device of his required a looser cuff to accommodate the draw. Rather than tip his hand by using a tailor, Mason did his own work. In fact, he'd gotten quite good at it and was finished well before an overman came to fetch him.

When the knock rattled his door, Mason was more than ready. He answered wearing his newly stitched shirt beneath a black suit and a vest chosen specifically for this occasion. "Yes?" Mason said to the large man in the hallway.

"Mr. Greeley wants to see you," the overman grunted.

"Of course."

"I'll take your weapons."

Mason held his jacket open and allowed the overman to take his pistols. Using rough, pawlike hands, the gunman turned Mason around and then plucked the knife from the scabbard at the small of his back.

"Happy?" Mason asked.

The overman answered that by quickly examining Mason's pockets. Only when that was finished did he say, "Now I'm happy. Move."

Although Mason had seen this overman several times by now, he didn't know the gunman's name. He was beginning to suspect that Greeley forced his highly paid guards to give up their Christian names altogether as part of their entry fee into calling the *Delta Jack* their permanent home.

Mason was taken down to the lowest deck and along the perimeter. Greeley and two other big men in pearl gray suits stood clustered together at a spot that was gated off from the normal flow of foot traffic. It was one of the few spots on the *Jack* that Mason hadn't visited yet.

The engines had stopped, allowing the roar of voices from other parts of the boat to roll through the air like rumblings of distant thunder. Music drifted from several rooms as well, making the night feel strangely festive. Mason looked toward the shoreline and asked, "Why is the boat stopped?"

"This is where you get off," Greeley said.

Mason looked toward the shore one more time, only to see the very same thing as before. "But there's no dock."

"That's right."

"You want me to swim?"

"You'll be taking the rowboat."

Sure enough, the little boat that had been beached when the overmen came to take care of Winslow was bobbing in the water alongside the *Jack*'s hull. It was so small that Mason had all but lost it in the fading traces of daylight.

"Do I have any particular destination in mind, or should I get in and just start rowing?" Mason asked.

"Look farther up along the shore," Greeley said. "There's a dock. Row to it and get out, and you'll see a house. That's Seth Borden's place. Bring his wife and daughter out to the dock in two hours and we'll meet you there."

"Don't you think a man will try to defend his family?"

"Probably."

"And you want me to just walk in there and take that family from him?"

"I didn't say it was gonna be easy," Greeley replied. "You may get yourself killed, but that's why I'm having you do it instead of risking one of my boys. Do you know how much I've got invested in these men? More than your sorry hide is worth, I can tell you that much."

"You seem rather cross this evening, Cam," Mason said.

Stabbing his finger at him, Greeley snapped, "I had to step away from one hell of a game to see you off like this, and my streak ain't gonna warm up for at least another hour or two. You hear them sounds? That's every soul on this boat gambling away every dime to his name, and I wanna get my piece of it."

"Don't let me stand in your way," Mason said. "If I get this done quickly enough, perhaps I can sit in on a game or two myself."

"It should be a walk in the park. Even for you. Borden isn't known to have much in the way of firearms. If you can get them two outside and to the dock, you shouldn't have much trouble."

"Should I be wearing a mask or something?" Mason asked. "Isn't that what outlaws do?"

"Don't be stupid. Just go and do your part."

"How much of my credit will this clear?"

Greeley had already started walking away from the small group. He stopped and wheeled around to say, "Don't you worry about that. When I tell you to do something, you just do it!"

Mason shook his head. "This is all about that debt of mine. If I'm not chipping away at that, I've got no reason to do this at all."

"Half," Greeley said.

Studying the other man's face for a hint that he was lying, Mason replied, "That would have sounded good at the start, but I've already cleared half. You saying this will square me up?"

"No. I'm saying this'll clear half of what's left of your debt. You got one more job after this, and that will square things between you and me."

"All right, then. That's better." Looking to the overmen, Mason asked, "Which of you men is going to help me row?"

Greeley might not have been in very good spirits that evening, but the overmen in attendance got a good chuckle out of that. By the time Mason had climbed into the boat and gotten settled, two of the three overmen had gone. The one who was left reached over the railing to hand Mason's guns back to him.

After holstering both Remingtons, Mason asked, "What about the knife?"

The overman produced the blade from beneath his

jacket, but held on to it just a bit too tightly. "Think I may hold on to this."

"Why? You'll hand me back my guns, but keep the knife?" He checked the sawed-off .44 quickly to find that it was indeed loaded.

"I just like this," the overman said as Mason checked the .44 under his arm. "You can get another one."

"The hell I will. Give that back or I don't go." After a few seconds, Mason added, "You really want to tell your employer why I refused to paddle away from here?"

Even the feared enforcers weren't quick to annoy Greeley that night. With a snap of his wrist, the overmen sent the knife spinning through the air to stick in the rowboat near one of the brackets holding an oar. "Damn gamblers and yer good luck trinkets."

After sheathing the blade, Mason asked, "What should I be expecting when I get to that house? Or is Greeley just sending me off to get killed?"

"You shouldn't have any trouble."

"Have you met this Borden fellow?"

The overman nodded. "A stiff wind could knock him over."

"And a job like that will wipe away so much of my debt?" Mason asked.

"I don't make the decisions. I just see they get carried out. You'd best get going. Otherwise I'm supposed to knock you around some."

Having been knocked around more than enough already, Mason untied the rowboat from the hull and pushed away using one oar. He started rowing and took a look at the *Delta Jack* as he slipped away from her. He thought he saw Maggie on the third deck looking down at him, but it was just one of the other women on board.

He wasn't surprised that she hadn't guessed when he was leaving or where he would make his departure. In fact, Mason hoped she was having better fortune than he was.

Considering how things had been for him lately, that wasn't really saying much.

Chapter 32

Before he'd been collected by the overman from his cabin, Mason changed the dressing on his wounded left hand. The shredded skin between his thumb and forefinger looked a lot worse than it felt. It hadn't been much of a trial for him to use it to modify the holdout apparatus. The only reason it sprang to mind now was that it hurt like hell every time he leaned back to drag the oars through muddy river waters. Mason winced the first several times he'd rowed, but that had quickly become a grimace as he repeatedly aggravated the wounded hand.

The dock was between a quarter of a mile and half a mile north of where the *Jack* had dropped anchor. While that wasn't very far to go, Mason started looking toward the shore for alternative routes. He wasn't about to leave the rowboat so far away from his destination, but the clear stretch of riverbank brought a relieved smile to his face. He steered toward shore, climbed out, and trudged through the muck until he reached dry land.

"Damn it all," he grumbled. "I just had these boots polished."

The current was weak enough that Mason was able to kick the rowboat out a bit and drag it along using the mooring rope. Every so often, he would have to stop and kick it again or drag it over a sandbar, but the exercise did him plenty of good. Once he got over the initial shock of getting his feet dirty and his suit wet, the rest was much easier to stomach. He wrote that clothing off as a loss and kept moving along the river.

Once he got a good pace going, Mason was fairly sure he made better time than if he'd kept struggling to row that damn boat. After a while, he could see the dock protruding into the water farther upstream. Soon after that, he could make out the shape of a large house beyond some trees. Mason hefted the rope over one shoulder, pulled the boat ashore, and made certain it wasn't going anywhere. On the chance that someone was watching him from the *Delta Jack*, he waited until he'd made it into the trees before going through his final preparations.

He put his back to a particularly thick trunk, dropped to one knee, and pulled up his right pants leg. Two pairs of socks made that leg much heavier than normal, and when he rolled them down, he could finally get to the holdout device strapped around that calf. The arm of the holdout ran along the inner part of his leg with the canvas strap buckled around his ankle. The other end of the arm was tied just below his knee by a thin piece of twine. Thanks to the double layer of wool he'd worn on that leg, the overman hadn't noticed the device when he quickly patted Mason down outside his cabin. It wouldn't have held up to a more thorough search, but the overman was sufficiently convinced that Mason was too cowed to try anything worth worrying about. Such was the benefit of laying groundwork before making a big play.

Leaning back against the tree, Mason pulled off his shoe and reached inside for the two halves of the clamshell secreted there. The easiest thing for him to smuggle was the rubber band, which lay at the bottom of his pocket. After his modifications and a liberal amount of practice while waiting to be summoned from his cabin, Mason was able to assemble the holdout in no time at all and then strap it onto his arm where it belonged. He was grateful for the removal of the metal arm scraping against his leg, but found he missed the added arch support he'd gotten by walking on the metal clamshell pieces. The last item he'd smuggled was the derringer. That was wedged against his side beneath a thick wrapping of cotton bandages. Even though he'd been allowed to bring his pistols on the job, he didn't want to take a chance on losing the smaller gun. He tucked it away and got his clothing situated again.

Mason had to make up some ground in a hurry. He broke into a run through the trees, nearly tripping several times over rotten logs and stones that were becoming increasingly hard to see in the fading light of dusk. Almost completely out of breath after so much exertion, he broke through the tree line to find not one house, but two. The larger of them was the only one with any light behind its windows as well as a woman in a rocker on the porch. The smaller house was well maintained and completely dark.

Since he had to figure the woman on the porch wasn't blind, Mason put on a friendly smile and walked straight to the house. There was only about twenty yards of open ground to cover before reaching the porch, but with that woman staring at him, it was a very long twenty yards.

Before he reached the house, the woman stood up and opened the front door so she could say something to someone inside. She remained on the porch, however, and put on a nervous smile to greet him. "Hello?" she said.

Mason held his hands in front of him and said, "I am so lost! I don't suppose this is Atlanta?"

The woman was somewhere in her early thirties and had a simple elegance to her features. Her clothing was plain and she held on to the shawl wrapped around her shoulders as if it were a suit of armor. Thanks to the warmer smile she had after Mason's awkward joke, that armor wasn't as tightly buckled as it had been a moment ago. "Atlanta?" she chuckled. "I don't think so."

Mason approached the porch but stopped short of mounting the first step. His proximity clearly rattled her, since the small bit of friendliness he'd managed to spark in her was immediately wiped away. "I'm not some wild man from the woods, I assure you," he said. "I wonder if I can have a moment of your time, though?"

Remaining in her spot in front of the rocker, she nodded uneasily. Her hair was tied back into a bun and held in place by a lace bonnet, giving her a somewhat matronly appearance. Even so, her blue eyes and soft lips made her naturally striking. Now that he was a bit closer, Mason could see the hunting rifle propped behind the rocker. She remained within reach of the rifle as she said, "All right. What do you need?"

"First of all, could you tell me if this is the Borden home?"

The front door swung open and a slender man with sunken facial features stepped outside. What little remained of his hair was thinning and bright white. A pair of wire spectacles sat perched on the bridge of his nose and he carried a shotgun in his hands. "Who are you?" he asked in a dry, snarling voice.

"My name's Abner Mason. Might you be Seth Borden?"

"That's right. Do I know you?"

"Not as such. Is there any chance we might continue this inside?"

"No," Seth replied as he tightened his grip on the shotgun. "You'll state your business where you are. In fact, why don't you back up a few steps?"

"I understand your nervousness, but—"

"Papa," the woman said quickly. "He's wearing a gun under his jacket."

"Two of them, if I'm to be completely frank with you," Mason said.

Seth brought the shotgun to his shoulder and lined up his sights. "Get off my property!"

"Let me at least have a word with you. Please."

Reaching out to place one hand gingerly on the side of the shotgun, the woman moved it aside.

"What do you think you're doing, Allison?" the old man asked.

"Can we just hear him out?" she said.

Although he'd been trying to maintain his composure, Mason was quickly becoming more anxious than both of them combined. "I'd really appreciate it if we could get inside."

"Why are you so insistent on getting into my home?" Seth asked. Although he tried to move the shotgun back around to point it at Mason, he was either unwilling to shove the younger woman aside or too frail to do so. Considering the fact that he looked to have less muscle on him than a scarecrow, either explanation was just as likely.

The woman was obviously willing to listen to him, so

Mason looked at her when he said, "You can take my guns if you like. I really need to have a word with you and it's got to be right away."

"Please," she said. "Just tell us what this is about and then we'll see about going into the house."

Mason shifted his eyes to Seth. "Mr. Borden, you and your family are in danger."

"What kind of danger?" he asked.

"Do you know a man named Cam Greeley?"

"Yes."

"He sent me here to kidnap your wife and child. I'm not going to do that, but there are most likely men following behind me who won't be so charitable." Seeing that he'd sufficiently shaken the two people on the porch, Mason added, "Can we take this inside now?"

Chapter 33

Seth didn't only take Mason's guns, but he did a better job of searching Mason than the last overman who'd been given the task. All of Mason's weapons as well as the holdout apparatus lay on the polished surface of a dining room table within the house. Mason's sleeve had been torn in the process of removing the device, and now that they'd come this far, the three of them all sat around that table staring at one another.

"Allison," Seth said, "put those guns somewhere safe."

She gathered them up as if she were afraid one of the Remingtons might bite her hand. After she had taken them, the derringer, and the knife into the kitchen, Seth relaxed a bit. The shotgun was still in the old man's hands, however, and ready to be used.

"All right," Seth said. "You're inside. Start talking."

"How do you know Cam Greeley?" Mason asked.

"He stole my boat."

"Your boat?"

Seth nodded. "I own a riverboat named the *Allie Girl*."

"Alley girl?" Mason asked. "As in . . . a girl who works the alleys?"

"No!" Seth barked. "As in Allie. Short for Allison. *My* little girl!"

Allison stepped out of the kitchen carrying a pitcher of water. "I told you that name sounded bad, Papa."

Seth angrily waved off what was an argument they'd apparently been having for a while. "No matter what the damn boat was called, that bastard Cam Greeley stole it from me!"

Setting the pitcher down, Allison nodded her agreement and asked, "Does everyone want something to drink?"

"That would be good," Mason replied.

Seth grunted a quick "Yes" before easing back into his chair.

"I'll get some glasses," Allison said as she went back into the kitchen.

"How did Greeley steal your boat?" Mason asked.

"No, no," Seth said. "You're the one sitting in my house on my property. You'll answer my questions first. What's all this about Greeley wanting to kidnap my family?"

"He sent me here to do just that, but I assure you that's not my intention."

"You're one of his men?"

"I've incurred quite a debt," Mason replied. "My back got put against a wall and I was to be either killed in a most unpleasant way or forced to work off what I owed doing some unpleasant things."

"Oh," Seth grunted distastefully. "A gambler, huh?"

This not being the first time he was on the receiving end of that particular look, Mason said, "That's right, but I'm no kidnapper. In fact, my hope is to turn the tables on Mr. Greeley very soon."

"And how do you propose to do that?"

"By making him think he won, waiting for the right moment, and then snatching that victory away. He's nearby and he's got a good number of hired guns with him. If he wanted to take your family by force, I'm betting he could do just that. Our best chance of putting an end to this is by delivering one or two good sucker punches when he's least expecting them and before he can swing back."

As he listened, Seth ground his teeth together hard enough to make the muscles in his jaw stand out. He responded to the enthusiasm on Mason's face by saying, "That's just a whole lot of double talk that barely goes anywhere. You're no gunman, are you?"

"No, sir."

"I can tell that by the belly gun you had with you. That's the weapon of someone who ain't looking to win a straight fight. That's a gun meant to be fired under a table or so close to the man in front of him that he barely saw it coming."

Mason nodded. "Right! A sucker punch. Just like I was saying."

When Seth laughed, he let out only one choppy breath that could just as easily have been a burp. "I've dealt with plenty of gamblers in my days," he said. "It's refreshing to have one be so honest about what he is."

"Thank you, sir."

"Even if what he is ain't exactly something to be proud of."

Mason's grin waned somewhat. "Um . . . yes. I suppose so."

Allison came from the kitchen carrying water glasses for all of them. "You'll have to excuse my father's way of paying backhanded compliments. It becomes part of his charm once you get used to it." Staring at the old man, she said, "After twenty or so years."

"Let me remind you, girl," Seth grunted, "that this stranger is still the same man who told us he'd come along to kidnap you and your ma."

"But he hasn't taken any steps to do so. In fact, I'd say the only thing that makes any sense is what he's told us so far."

"Thank you for that, Allison," Mason said.

Seth reached for a glass with one hand and held it out for his daughter to fill. "Mister, why don't you keep your eyes on me and keep talking? I'm not quite convinced of why I shouldn't blow your head off just yet."

"The last man I visited," Mason explained, "was named Randal Simons. Does that ring any bells for you?"

After a moment to think, Seth shook his head. "Who is he?"

"One of Greeley's more unsavory associates. I didn't think you'd recognize him. What about Oscar Lazenby?"

"I know him all right."

Contrary to what he might have said to Greeley, Mason did recall the last name on his list. The more ignorant Greeley thought he was, the better position Mason would find himself in when the smoke cleared.

"What's Greeley got planned for him?" Seth asked.

"I don't know exactly, but I can guarantee it won't be good. Who is he?"

"He works for the government."

"Doing what?" Mason asked.

"Inspecting river trade and transport, issuing permits for trade to be conducted, and reporting transgressions."

"You certainly do know a lot about this man."

Seth shrugged. "I used to have to deal with him quite a lot back when I was in the business of selling boats and such."

"You sold boats?"

Chuckling, Seth said, "You really don't know much, do you?"

"Not about this sort of thing. Like I told you, I was tossed into this without a lot of warning."

"And for the first time since you mentioned it, I'm starting to believe you." Seth reached for the water he'd been poured and took a drink. "I've sold everything that can float from this here spot for the better part of twenty years. Conducted all my business in the house right next to this one and brought all the boats to the dock I got outside. Most were small merchant craft as well as a few passenger boats. It was more of a side business, really. Made most of my money selling horses and wagons. Used to have one of the biggest stables in the—"

"I don't think he wants to hear all about that," Allison said.

" 'Course he does! That's why he asked. Right?"

Mason didn't want to encourage him with a nod and he didn't want to insult him with a shake of his head. Before he could decide how to respond, the old man picked right up again on his own.

"I sold three deluxe carriages to a man named Edward Bartholomew," Seth continued. "That man was trying to unload a riverboat he'd come into some way or another and I managed to get it away from him."

"How?" Mason asked.

"Traded him my horse and carriage business. That boat of his needed work, but I got it into prime shape in no time."

Allison sat in one of the chairs close to her father. "It took five years," she said. "Five years of looking outside my window at that thing."

"And five years of permits to allow it to stay here while I worked on it. Damn government and their permits."

"And Oscar Lazenby was the man who issued the permits," Mason said.

Seth nodded as if he was thinking about an old enemy that had given him the slip. "I think that man enjoyed coming over here every month to wring whatever he could out of an honest workingman. He was crooked too."

"Was he?"

"Good Lord, yes. Did you know gambling is illegal on a riverboat?"

Of all the things that had happened and everything he'd seen since this mess started, this one surprised Mason the most. "What? That can't be!"

Seth grudgingly amended his claim by saying, "It sure is frowned upon. Actually it depends on where a boat is and where it wants to pull in to port. Whatever the case is, there is a whole mess of paperwork to sift through in order to get a riverboat up and running the way I wanted it to run. She was gonna be the best! The fanciest! Lord Almighty, she was going to be stupendous."

"And Greeley got ahold of her?" Mason asked.

"Greeley got ahold of Ed Bartholomew, is my suspicion."

Allison cleared her throat to politely insert herself into the conversation. "He must have worked with Mr. Lazenby as well, because that eyesore of a boat was taken away on a legal dispute over its ownership."

"Stolen!" Seth said as he pounded his fist against the table. "My *Allie Girl* was stolen from me, plain and simple!"

"It wasn't exactly a robbery," she explained, "but the law did come around with Mr. Lazenby to issue a warrant for my father's arrest."

"Damn government said I stole that boat," Seth grumbled. "Nobody in the government would know their ass from their elbow."

"Be that as it may," Allison said, "the boat was seized. Thankfully my father was not."

"How did Greeley get his hands on the boat?" Mason asked.

Allison shrugged. "I honestly don't know. I'm just glad to be able to see the water when I sit on my porch instead of having to look at the side of that monster of a boat. I'm sick of all boats, actually. The folks who bought horses and carriages were good, honest people. Most of everyone who wanted one of those boats was either a gambler or a smuggler."

"Or both, most likely," Mason said.

"Yes," she replied with a shy smile.

Once again, Seth pounded his fist on the table. The sound would have been more jarring if he'd had more muscle behind it. "Selling boats put food on our table, young lady!"

"I know, Papa, you've told us that for years."

"Then why do you keep forgetting it?"

"I hate to interrupt," Mason interrupted, "but there really is the matter of a kidnapping here."

"What? Oh, right," Seth said. "Why can't you just leave here without kidnapping anyone?"

Before Mason could open the same can of worms he'd

already emptied in his discussion with Maggie, Allison said, "Because if Greeley wants to do us harm and this man doesn't do it, he could very well hire someone else to do it."

"Well, if he wants a shot at Oscar Lazenby any time soon, he'd have to find a replacement pretty damn quick," Seth grumbled.

"What was that?" Mason asked.

Seth furrowed his brow and looked at Mason as if the gambler had just sprouted horns. "Lazenby is here."

Pointing to the floor beneath his feet, Mason asked, "Here?"

Allison shook her head. "Not here as in this house or this land. He's not on this land, is he, Papa?"

"No, don't be silly," Seth said. "This is the time of month when Oscar comes around to inspect river merchants and tradesmen and otherwise bother good, honest men looking to ply an honest trade on the muddy banks of the beautiful Mississippi."

"Where can he be found?" Mason asked.

"There's a government office about three miles northwest of here," Seth replied. "Take the road that goes past my front door and follow the stench of bureaucracy."

When Mason looked over to her, Allison nodded. "It's about three miles away," she said. "There's no stench."

"If Greeley's after Lazenby," Seth said, "I can tell you what he wants."

"Yes?"

"When I was working on getting the *Allie Girl* ready to become the finest craft in the river," the old man said fondly, "that stinkin' bureaucrat went on and on about his permits and licenses and fees . . ."

Mason let out a tired sigh. "So you've mentioned," he groaned as he let his head hang forward.

"And," Seth said as he raised a finger as if he were instructing an orchestra to hold a high note, "he couldn't stop talking about corruption in organized gambling."

Grateful to be back on track, Mason leaned forward to try to keep the old man from drifting into another rant. "What did he have to say on the subject of corruption, Mr. Borden?"

"That there was plenty of it among the men who run games on riverboats. That outlaws and thieves couldn't be allowed to have free rein in such a lucrative and far-reaching marketplace like the Mississippi River. That such a thing would be like a cancer where common card cheats might grow into . . . into . . ."

"A disease," Allison said.

Seth snapped his fingers. "Yes! That's what he called them. A disease."

"What did he intend to do about it?" Mason asked.

"What any government pea brain would do. Make his inspections, thump his damn law books, levy his fines."

"Make arrests?"

Seth scowled and then shrugged. "I suppose so."

Mason felt a chill work through his body as all the pieces fell together. Judging by the look on Allison's face, even if she didn't have as many pieces as he did, she saw enough to get awfully nervous.

Chapter 34

Allison excused herself from the table to get some more water. Mason stood up to join her under the auspices of getting a breath of fresh air, and Seth didn't have a problem with it. The old-timer warned he would be watching through the kitchen window with shotgun at the ready, which was just fine with both of them. Outside, Allison took the pitcher to a pump and started working the handle.

"You're going to snap that off if you keep it up," Mason pointed out.

That didn't convince her to ease off in the least. "He's trouble," she said. "I always knew that."

"Who are you talking about? Greeley?"

"Greeley, Oscar Lazenby, my father, take your pick. Why can't they all just enjoy what they have and be done with it? Why do they all want more? It's not like they need it. I mean, how much money does a person need? We're not rich, but we're comfortable. There are some men who don't live far from here who are much better off and they seem just as comfortable. When is anyone just going to slow down and live instead of spending every waking moment grabbing for more?"

Mason stuck his hands in his pockets, looked over to the kitchen window, and nodded at the armed man staring back at him. "Money keeps the wheels greased and turning. Always will, I believe."

"Why would I expect you to understand?" she sighed. "You're a gunman."

"No, I'm not. I'm a sporting man."

"Right. And that's so much better."

"Pardon me, ma'am, but I'm not the one who started any of this," Mason pointed out. "I am trying to fix it, however, and there isn't a lot of time to do that."

"I suppose there are real gunmen on their way so they can turn this house into a battlefield?"

"They'd be coming either way, as you already explained to your father in there. Considering the fact that Oscar Lazenby is only here a short time, I'd have to imagine the timing of a visit to this place from someone or other would also have been the same. At least I came to warn you and have a talk instead of kicking your door down and taking prisoners."

The pitcher in Allison's hand had overflowed several seconds ago, but she just now seemed to notice. She poured a little bit out, set it down on the step leading to the kitchen door, and dried her wet hands. "You're right. It's just that I don't . . . not that I'm not . . . it's just . . ."

Mason smiled at her. "You don't know if you can trust me. Part of you wants to, but the other part is nervous that your father and his shotgun are in there instead of out here."

Suddenly Allison's hands appeared to have frozen in place. When she was able to move them again, she said, "Yes. That's exactly what I was thinking."

"It's a miracle." Mason tugged his lapel in what he

thought was a very stately manner. "I am quite the wonder."

"Or a lucky guesser."

He dropped the stately act and said, "You're a very nice woman and that just seemed to be something you might be thinking, which you would also have trouble saying to a man's face. Also . . . why would you trust a complete stranger who brings such peculiar news?"

She winced, looked to the kitchen window, and showed Seth a very tired smile. "When he decided to sell off a perfectly good stable and carriage shop for that riverboat, I thought about putting him in an asylum. Soon the rats came out of the woodwork, asking for any number of favors from him. They were looking for money, offering bribes, trying to set up their games in the boat's casino, demanding percentages from my father's profits. It was a nightmare."

"Sounds like it."

"And after I thought it was over . . . here it comes again."

"As a duly appointed representative of that nightmare," Mason said, "I sincerely apologize."

"Thank you. At least someone doesn't think that riverboat was the best thing that's ever come along."

Mason removed a handkerchief from his breast pocket, took it to the pump, and dampened it. He then handed it over to Allison. "I believe we can put an end to this business with Greeley."

She took the handkerchief and used it to dab at her brow. "Do you?"

"Yes."

"Will it be ended quietly and without anyone getting hurt?" she asked.

Wincing, Mason said, "My intention was to do my best to—"

"That means no," she snapped. "After living with my father for this long, I know mindless double talk when I hear it." Allison glanced toward the house like a little girl who was afraid of being caught with a boy in the hayloft. Lowering her voice, she said, "He's really not crazy."

"I don't believe I was the one who mentioned putting him in an asylum," Mason said.

Grinning sheepishly, Allison handed back the handkerchief and said, "You seem like a good person, Mr. Mason, and I appreciate you trying to fix this instead of blindly following Greeley's orders. Do you know my mother is in a bed upstairs and can't be moved?"

"No."

"Of course you don't," she said quickly. "Why would you? She is, though. That's why I can't have anything like this happen here."

"I suppose you already know what I have in mind?"

"Whatever it is, it's not likely to end up good for us and it could go especially bad for a woman who is too sick to stand up or get out of this house if need be. After all, that is the way men like Greeley and you deal with things, isn't it?"

On one hand, Mason wanted to flatly deny he was the sort to deal with anything in a way that might get the wrong people hurt. On the other, he had to remind himself that there was a whole mess of guns and a knife inside that had been brought to that house on his person. While he struggled to pick the right words, Allison jumped right back in with some of her own.

"The road you want is right there," she said while pointing to a wide path that dipped in close to the house before angling back out again. "Follow it for those few miles that we told you about and that's where you'll find Oscar Lazenby's office. Give him our regards and that's that."

"No," Mason said, "it isn't. Now, I've been polite so far because I could use your help, but we're only going to get one chance at making a move against Cam Greeley."

"You're the one making a move," she said. "My family and I are simply out here living our lives."

"This feud or whatever you want to call it involving Greeley, your father, and whoever else was going before I knew anything about it. Come to think of it, I'm the one who's being trampled by this whole thing and I didn't have anything at all to do with it."

Allison stepped up to him and stared defiantly into his eyes. "And what is it you want me to do about it?"

"I'd appreciate some modicum of courtesy or possibly a hint of gratitude for being the one to deliver you out of this mess instead of delivering you into the waiting arms of Cam Greeley."

"So you keep reminding me!"

"Only because you don't seem to remember it," Mason fired back.

"I'll tell you what I do remember," Allison said. "This land belongs to me and my family and we would be well within our rights to shoot anyone caught trespassing on it! We posted a sign if you'd bother reading it."

Mason laughed. "You posted a sign? Then why don't I just go back to my own business and we'll see how your next visitors feel about your sign?"

The kitchen door swung open and Seth came out with shotgun in hand. "There a problem here?" he asked.

"No, Papa," Allison said. "Go back inside."

"Looked to me like you two were having words."

Mason did his best to keep his voice level when he said, "It was just a misunderstanding. That's all."

Keeping his eyes on his daughter, Seth asked, "That all it was?"

Allison rubbed her water-cooled hands against her temples before nodding. "Yes. That's all it was."

"Even so," Seth said as he fixed his eyes upon Mason, "perhaps you'd best leave before we have ourselves another misunderstanding."

"Fine," Mason snapped. "If you want me to go, I'll go."

"You do that."

"Have it your way," Mason said in exasperation. "When Greeley and his men come calling, you can ask them what they want. I just hope you've got it."

"I can tell you what Greeley wants," Seth said.

Both Mason and Allison looked at him, half expecting some tirade or other bit of nonsense to come out of his mouth. "What is it?" Mason asked.

"The original ownership papers for the *Allie Girl*."

"You've got those?" Allison asked.

The old man nodded. "Why the hell do you think I keep calling it *my* boat?"

Chapter 35

"It looks legal to me," Mason said as he flipped through the papers that Seth had brought him.

The three of them were sitting at the dining room table once again. Only this time, they were on the same side so they could all get a look at those papers.

"Do you even know what you're looking at?" Allison asked.

Mason held up each page so he could examine them up close. "I've been in more than a few card games where a man has nothing left to bet besides deeds to some piece of land, a mining claim, or any number of things that require legal documents. While I'm no lawyer, let's just say it's in my best interest to be able to spot a forgery. This seal, the stamps here by the signatures, it all looks proper to me."

"Of course it's proper!" Seth barked. "I said it was, didn't I?"

"Yes, but . . ." Instead of insulting his host, Mason stopped short and pretended to have his interest captured by some speck on the page in front of him.

Allison, on the other hand, wasn't as concerned about

putting the old man's nose out of joint. "You say a lot of things, Papa," she said to Seth while rubbing his arm.

"I suppose so," Seth replied. "But I'd like to hear what Greeley has to say when he gets called out by Lazenby."

"Called out for what?" Allison asked.

"He must have been dodging inspections somehow or other if that boat is still on the water with him as its owner," the old man said. "There's no shortage of crooked government men, to be certain, but if what this fella here says is true, then Greeley's got to be nearby. Lazenby is here also and he's been on a real tear!"

Mason looked up from the ownership papers. "How so?"

"Oscar Lazenby's been like a man possessed," Seth said. "I still talk to plenty of men who used to do business with me when I was selling boats and such, and they've been grousing to high heaven about that man and the bureau that pays him. Business ain't like it used to be when a man could get away with an infraction or two here or there. Now boats are all getting inspected and heavy fines are being levied."

"It's true," Allison said. "Over the last week, I've seen boats forced to drop anchor for hours or even days while they're inspected. Their captain or some of the crew come here because we're still friendly with a lot of those men."

"And they say things with Lazenby have gotten bad?" Mason asked.

"Sounds to me like the man's just doing his job, but—"

"But nothin'!" Seth said. "Free trade is what this country was built upon, and nobody owns the damn river!"

"I think some men in Washington would have something to say about that, Papa."

"And I think I know exactly what's been going on here!" Mason said. "I've been thinking it over, but still had some kinks to iron out. Now it all makes sense. Allison, where's your mother?"

"She's upstairs in bed."

"Can she be moved?"

"No one's moving my wife!" Seth bellowed.

Calming her father with a touch from a gentle hand, Allison told Mason, "She's too sick to go anywhere."

"Then what about the room she's in?" Mason asked. "Can the door be locked so the two of you can remain safe inside?"

Allison nodded.

Scowling at Mason, Seth said, "I don't want no bloodshed in my home."

"I know, sir, and it wasn't my intention to bring any trouble to you. That may be unavoidable, though."

"Papa, if there's to be trouble anyway, I'd rather take a stand here than just wait for the next man to come along. We both knew Greeley would come back someday."

Seth's face twisted into a distasteful grimace. "You feed a mangy dog once and it'll always come skulking back around for scraps. I just don't like the notion of making a stand so close to my kin."

"That's why I'd hoped to move the women from here," Mason said. "Is there anyone else in the house besides the four of us?"

"No."

"Then it seems this is how . . . Wait. What about the house next door?"

"That's where I used to run my businesses," Seth said. "Ain't had much use for it lately."

"That'll be the spot, then."

"How do you plan on getting Greeley or anyone else to show up there?" Allison asked.

"Greeley is after something, and this," Mason said while holding up the ownership papers, "has got to be it. He won't be happy about it, but he'll come if it means getting what he wants."

"I don't give a damn about whether that thieving snake is happy about anything," Seth said. "But if he's got gunmen working for him, he'll probably bring them along."

"Which is why you're going to go to Oscar Lazenby and bring him here," Mason said. "He's probably got some deputies or someone like that working with him, right?"

Seth had to think about it for a few seconds, but he eventually nodded. "I suppose he always did bring some young fellas with him whenever he boarded a vessel to make an inspection."

"He does," Allison added. "I've seen him with the marshal when they've been stopping those boats here lately."

"Good," Mason said with building excitement. "Seth can tell Lazenby what's going on and bring as much help as he can back here. Allison, you lock yourself in your mother's room where you'll both be safe. Try to keep quiet. We'll pass it off as if the two of you got away. There's no reason Greeley would know about your mother being bedridden."

"Not unless he or one of his men comes upstairs to have a look for themselves," Allison said nervously.

"I'm not about to let that happen," Mason said. "I know this isn't ideal and I hate to put good folks like you in the line of fire, but— "

"But nothin'," Seth said with much less venom than the last time he'd used those words. "Greeley already knows where I am, so it ain't like we was hiding in the first place. Besides, I've been itching to have a word with that snake ever since he floated away in my boat. Maybe I should stay here with you to greet him."

"No," Mason said sternly. "We'll stick to the plan. If this has any chance of working, we'll need reinforcements, and Oscar Lazenby is just the man for that job."

Reluctantly Seth agreed.

"All right, then," Mason said. "It's settled. Allison, you take that shotgun to use in case anyone makes it upstairs to get to you or your mother. Are there any other weapons in the house?"

"I've got a hunting rifle," she said.

Remembering the rifle propped behind her rocker on the porch, Mason nodded. "Good. Anything else?"

"No."

"That'll have to do."

"And what if you get yourself killed?" Allison asked.

Mason shrugged and simply replied, "I won't."

"This is how it's gotta be," the old man said as if he'd been the one to come up with the plan in the first place. He handed her the shotgun. "Just let the men do their work and this'll all be over soon."

Mason stood at the end of the dock protruding from Seth Borden's property, watching a plume of smoke work its way above the trees to inch toward the Borden place. It stopped before rounding the bend, bringing the *Jack* most of the way to the spot of the pickup. He checked his watch yet again and snapped it shut to wait for the promised meeting. Finally, and only slightly behind schedule, another one of the *Jack*'s rowboats came along. There were two men in pearl gray suits in the small craft, and thanks to the muscle behind the oars, they arrived at the little dock in no time at all.

"You were supposed to bring two women along," the first overman in the boat said. "Where are they?"

"They're in the small house," Mason replied.

"Go get them."

"How about you go back and get Mr. Greeley instead?"

"You really want to start giving orders? Just because you've got those guns on you doesn't give you any sort of edge. You even twitch toward them pistols and we'll burn you down."

"I realize that," Mason said.

"And if you make any other moves we don't much like, your lady friend waiting for you on the *Jack* will have a real bad night."

Mason's eyes narrowed. "What did you say?"

"You heard me. Mr. Greeley isn't stupid. He knows you and Maggie have been keeping company and can get to her anytime he wants. She'll be left alone so long as we've got them two women you were supposed to get."

"I know what this is about. I can save Greeley some time if he comes back here himself. Tell him that's the only way he's getting his hands on the papers he's after."

"What papers?" the overman asked.

Mason shook his head. "I did my part. All I'm changing is the spot where those ladies are being kept. I'll explain myself further but only to Greeley."

"You don't give orders around here."

"And you don't know where I put those papers. Kill me and you're going to be the one to row back to Greeley and tell him he'll just have to take his chances on his own with those government men. Don't try to tell me you don't know what I'm talking about, because I can already see in your eyes that you do."

That struck a nerve with the overmen. One looked to the other and then said, "Fine. I'm staying here with you and he'll go get Greeley. It ain't like he's got far to go."

"That's the spirit," Mason said.

The first overman climbed out of the boat and onto the dock. As soon as his boots hit the wooden slats, the second gunman started rowing away. There wasn't much of a current and it moved in the overman's favor. The rowboat made swift progress going downstream.

"Which house is it?" the remaining overman asked.

"The smaller one," Mason said while pointing in that direction. The larger house was darkened now and the smaller structure had a few lanterns burning inside its first-floor rooms. When he turned around, Mason was being held at gunpoint. He hadn't even heard the overman draw.

"Drop the guns," the overman said. "Slowly."

Having already gone through the motions several times by now, Mason went through them again and disarmed himself quickly. Both Remingtons hit the dirt near his feet, followed by the knife.

"Move," the overman demanded. As soon as Mason turned and walked toward the smaller house, the overman scooped up the pistols and kicked the knife into the grass away from the dock.

It was a short walk to the small house, and when they got there, the overman stepped to one side so he wasn't in line with the door or windows. "You got anyone waiting in there and you die first," he warned.

"I just want to get this over with as quickly as possible," Mason replied.

"Then you should've brought them hostages to the dock like you were supposed to."

"One of them is bedridden," Mason explained. "And Seth Borden himself made arrangements to send those papers to the law if he didn't check in with his attorney every so often. Anything happens to him and we all go to jail."

"Yeah," the overman said. "We'll see about that."

Mason was afraid of this. Getting Greeley to step foot off the *Jack* was a long shot, but it was worth a try. When he saw the deadly confidence on the overman's face combined with the tone of his voice, Mason knew that rowboat was coming back with reinforcements and Cam Greeley wouldn't be among them.

Approaching the front door of the smaller house, Mason looked over to the man beside him and asked, "What's your name?"

"Huh?"

"Your name. You know my name and I know Greeley's name. All I know about you men in the gray suits is that you're overmen."

"What more do you need?"

Mason opened the door. "Just being sociable."

"Pete," he grunted.

"There. That was easy."

Mason stepped inside first, followed by Pete. The lanterns that had cast their light upon the windows were placed on small tables here and there. Apart from those tables and a few chairs covered in sheets, there were no other furnishings to be found.

"Where are they?" Pete asked.

"In the kitchen. Tied to the stove."

Pete held his pistol at hip level and used it to motion in that direction. "Go on, then."

Mason strode through the house and was about to push open the kitchen door when Pete said, "Stop right there."

"Yes?"

"You got anything hidden in there," Pete warned, "and you'll get a bullet through the knee."

"You've got nothing to worry about," Mason said.

"So open the door!"

Mason pushed the door open halfway. He must not have been moving fast enough, because Pete lunged forward and kicked him in the stomach. When Mason let out a grunting breath, he was shoved against the wall next to the door. His back hit and his feet slipped out from under him, causing him to land heavily on his rump.

Moving cautiously past him, Pete shoved the door the rest of the way open while keeping his gun aimed at Mason. "What kind of fool do you take me for?" he snarled after looking into the kitchen. "There's nobody in there."

"Really?"

"And lookee here," Pete said as he found the hunting rifle that Mason had propped against a table.

When Pete leaned in to grab the rifle, Mason bent his left arm sharply. The holdout device buckled to that arm extended smoothly, but instead of a high card, the clamshell was clamped around his two-shot derringer. Although the modifications Mason had made to the device allowed it to hide the gun up his sleeve, he hadn't had enough time to perfect it. As soon as the metallic arm was fully extended, the derringer slipped from the clamshell and clattered to the floor.

The overman turned around, but couldn't move as smoothly as he normally would since he was wedged halfway between the kitchen door and its frame. Pete still had his pistol aimed in Mason's direction and he fired a quick shot. Because Mason needed to duck down to pick up the derringer, the bullet punched into the wall above him.

Mason's hand found the derringer and he flopped onto his side to present an even smaller target. Before Pete could fire again, however, Mason pulled his trigger. The derringer popped once, hitting Pete in the right shoulder and causing him to stagger away from the door. Mason took better aim and sent his second round into Pete's chest.

The overman hacked up a breath and leaned against a wall for support. He tried to lift his pistol, but his strength was fading thanks to the two small-caliber rounds lodged in him.

Mason jumped to his feet and hurried past the overman to grab the hunting rifle. "You can sit there and wait for someone to get you some medical attention," he said, "or you can do something stupid."

Pete hacked up one more breath before using his last bit of strength to lift his pistol and point it at Mason. The hunting rifle spat its round into him long before Pete could take his shot. The rifle had much more kick than the derringer and dropped Pete to the floor.

Mason set the rifle down and took the dead overman's pistol. The next thing he did was pull up his sleeve and remove the holdout device. If Pete had searched him any differently than the overmen usually did, he might have found the device strapped to Mason's arm. In fact, many factors could have spelled disaster for him, but luck had nothing to do with it. Observation, planning, and patience were the keys. Now those familiar allies just had to stay with him a little while longer.

He pulled off his boot and reached inside for one last weapon he'd smuggled off the *Delta Jack*. Mason tucked that weapon into his pocket, pulled on his boot, and went outside to collect his guns. Only then was he prepared for the final hand to be dealt.

Chapter 36

Mason charged into the main house with the hunting rifle in his hands. He stomped inside and kicked the door shut behind him before yelling, "It's only me, Allison."

From upstairs, Allison shouted, "I heard shooting next door."

"Yeah. It turned out all right. Stay in that room, though. I'll let you know when it's safe."

"All right," she said.

Mason picked a spot in the front room where his back was to a wall and he had a clear line of sight to the front door as well as to the bottom of the staircase. He took a knee, held his rifle in the closest semblance to a firing stance that he could manage, and waited.

It wasn't long before he heard voices outside but couldn't tell if they were coming from the road or the river. Mason quickly realized it was both, since the voices rose into shouts with gunshots quickly following.

"All right," he whispered. "Here we go."

Most of the gunfire sounded like pistol shots, but Mason wasn't absolutely certain. When the shooting waned, the shouting flared up. And when firing commenced again, the shots came quicker and closer together.

More shouting.

Fierce shooting.

Enraged, desperate voices.

The gunshots ripped back and forth until Mason thought they simply wouldn't stop.

Finally something heavy battered against the back door of the house. Mason shifted to point the rifle in that direction to see who might be coming.

Footsteps thumped against the floor as a familiar voice drifted through the air. It was one of Greeley's men and he rushed toward the stairs.

Mason pulled his trigger and put the man down.

Outside, the shooting had stopped.

The front door swung open and Seth Borden walked inside.

"Sir," someone shouted from the porch. "Let me go inside first. I heard a shot."

"I know!" Seth said. "I heard it too and my family's in here!"

Mason stood up with the rifle held in a loose grip across his body. "What happened out there?"

"Oscar Lazenby brought a few men with him as deputies. Men fresh out of the army, mostly. I brought 'em all here and when we showed up, a group of them gun hands in gray suits were coming out of the trees. I imagine you heard the rest."

"Any of those gunmen left?" Mason asked.

"One or two. They're being trussed up so they can be brought to the local law. How about you tell me what happened in here?"

"This one came in, probably looking for the papers or someone to use as a hostage. He didn't find either."

"That's not Greeley."

"I know."

A few other men walked inside behind Seth. One was a tall, gangly fellow with a trimmed beard and a few strands of dark hair hanging from beneath his bowler hat. Seth hooked a thumb toward him and said, "That's Oscar Lazenby."

Lazenby tipped his hat. "I don't suppose you'd know where we can find Cameron Greeley?" he asked in a smooth British accent.

"Yes," Mason replied. "I believe I do."

The *Delta Jack* was sitting less than a quarter of a mile from Seth's dock. When Mason, Lazenby, and a few of the federal deputies boarded her, there were only a couple of overmen to be found. Since the hired guns weren't idiots, they surrendered to the superior numbers without a fight. Mason himself went straight to the main theater and headed for the office in the back. Just for his own amusement, he knocked on the door before entering.

"Come in," Greeley said casually from the next room.

Mason opened the door and stepped inside. "Hello, Cam."

"Where's them hostages?" Greeley asked as he got up and walked around his little desk.

"You really don't know, do you?"

"Know what? That you're gonna get your teeth knocked out before I toss you over the side of this boat? Oh, I know that real well."

Smiling, Mason said, "Do you see any gray suits around me? That's because there aren't any left. They're either dead or under arrest. Now come on out and get what's coming to you before things get even worse."

Greeley scowled and flipped his jacket open to uncover the pistol hanging at his side.

"Give it a rest," Mason said. "If you were any good with that thing, you wouldn't have so many gunmen around to keep you from getting those soft hands dirty."

"What did you just say to me?"

"I'm saying I've played this game long enough to have you figured front to back. You're a sniveling little coward who isn't even good enough to be called an outlaw. At least most outlaws have some sand to them. You can't even stand up to a mercantile inspector, let alone steal a boat properly." Mason wasn't worried about speed when he drew the Remington from his shoulder holster. His read on the man in front of him was spot-on, since Greeley didn't so much as twitch toward the gun he'd so proudly displayed. "Lose that pistol," Mason said.

"You don't know what you're talking about," Greeley said rather unconvincingly as he gingerly removed his firearm and threw it into a corner.

Mason reached into an inner pocket and pulled out a bundle of folded papers. Slapping the papers onto the desk, he said, "There's the legal documents you were after. How did you even get your hands on this boat anyway? Actually, forget I asked. Even if you stood there and explained it all to me, I don't care. All those men on your precious list are alive and well, which means you had a good run but it's over now."

Greeley walked right over to him and sneered. "You're real tough right now on account of those guns you're wearing."

"You're afraid."

"Of you? Hardly."

Mason removed his shoulder holster and tossed it into the corner where Greeley's pistol had landed. As he removed the sawed-off Remington and tossed it there as well, he said, "You're afraid of losing what you've got. Any gambler worth his salt will tell you that's a fatal weakness."

"Close that door and we'll see who walks out of here."

"You're also afraid of witnesses," Mason said while walking to stand in the doorway. "That's why you wanted Simons dead. Because he knew all about you hiring murderers and sending them off to have good men killed just to suit your needs. He also knew who, exactly, your first overmen were. He had names and I'm sure at least a few of them have a bone to pick with you. What'd you do? Cheat them on their pay? Hang some of them out to dry when they got caught by the law while on one of your filthy errands? Any one of those sounds about right, coming from you. At the very least, Simons could connect you to known murderers, and that's something you simply cannot abide."

"You're dead."

Mason reached into the pocket where he'd stashed the last weapon smuggled from his cabin. "I knew you would say something like that, just like I know you're not going to make a reach for any of those guns. You rely on hired muscle too much. They're good, but once they're gone you're vulnerable."

"You've got nothing but a lot of talk on your side," Greeley said. "Whatever you've done to distract my men, it won't last forever."

"You think I was bluffing about your men? Damn, how the hell did I lose that hand to you?" Mason slipped the knuckle-duster onto his right hand and closed his fingers around the curved iron brace. He looked down at the dented strip crossing his knuckles and then to the little sharpened spike emerging from his fist. "I am really going to enjoy this."

Greeley stood tall and confident that he could not possibly be harmed while on the holy ground of his precious *Delta Jack*. Mason convinced him otherwise by slamming a reinforced fist into Greeley's stomach.

Greeley straightened up and took a swing at Mason in return. He missed his first attempt but connected on the second, which was a strong left hook. "You misread me again, Abner," he said as he drove a quick uppercut into Mason's midsection. "That's why you'll always be a loser."

Even though Mason was surprised at how well Greeley took that first punch, he didn't let that prevent him from delivering a few more. The first two were jabs to Greeley's chest. The next two went to the ribs. When wearing a knuckle-duster, picking the proper targets was essential if a man wanted to keep his opponent awake or alive.

"You wanted me to be the one seen going after Simons," Mason said while continuing to pepper Greeley with punches. "And you wanted me to be seen leaving Sedrich just like you wanted me to be seen going after Seth Borden. That way, I could take the blame for whatever happened to them."

Greeley pulled in a labored breath. When he tried to stand upright, he didn't quite make it. "You weren't supposed to make it out of Sedrich alive, but you did and you ruined the sweetest deal any men like us could hope to get. After how you carried yourself through this, I was thinking about cutting you in on the profits from this gold mine. Now you'll get nothing!"

Thanks to the difficulty Greeley had in drawing breath, Mason could see the next punch coming at him from a mile away. He stepped out of its path and pounded the knuckle-duster into Greeley's face. That dropped Greeley to one knee, where he spat some blood onto the expensive carpet.

"I'm getting my reward right now," Mason said.

"Lazenby will hurt all of us," Greeley wheezed. "Damn near everyone on this boat has cheated and we all got things to hide. That inspector woulda found out about me and my overmen, but he woulda found out about you too! I was protecting *all of us*!"

The fight had taken them into the theater. There was nobody onstage at the moment, but most of the tables were filled by people who couldn't believe what they were seeing and were unwilling to look away. "None of us is putting our necks on the block for you or those bloodthirsty animals on your payroll," Mason declared. "Isn't that right?"

Nobody in that room was about to disagree.

Gritting his teeth, Greeley reached down to expose one boot so he could pull out the .32 holstered there. He stopped before drawing the weapon when he felt the knuckle-duster's short blade pressed against the side of his neck.

"If I so much as twitch right now," Mason warned, "this part of your neck gets opened up and you bleed out like a stuck pig in less than a minute. You really want to take a shot at me that bad?"

Greeley eased his hand away from the holster and let

out a tired sigh when Oscar Lazenby and his deputies walked in through the theater's main entrance.

"I would've paid my debt," Mason said. "But you wanted more than that. You wanted to run me into the ground, step on me to get what you wanted, and then bury me just because it suited you. Well, since you got so greedy, you won't get anything you were after. I didn't kill Simons, but I also got him stashed somewhere safe so when you're put in front of a judge and witnesses are needed to prove you guilty, Simons will provide them. Seth Borden and his family are alive, so the old man will get his boat back. He'll name it after his girl and Mr. Lazenby will surely help him get his permits. You'll be the one hung up and left dangling, Cam. All because you got greedy."

"I'm gonna—"

"Enough idle threats," Mason said. "You see all these folks here? They spend their days and nights sitting at card tables, swapping stories, and right now I'm giving them a good one to tell. They'll spread the word about how your big, bad overmen were swept away and you were dragged out of your office to be beaten down for all to see."

Greeley looked up at him and said, "I'm not down yet. You don't have the—"

Mason hit Greeley with all he had, square in the jaw. Greeley flopped back, bounced off the leg of the closest table, and fell facedown on the floor.

"That was impressive," Maggie said as she approached them.

Mason straightened up, removed the knuckle-duster, and wrapped an arm around Maggie's waist. "I suggest we do ourselves a favor and leave," he said.

"Why?" she asked while Lazenby and his men swarmed around Greeley.

"This boat is about to change ownership and I doubt it'll bode well for the atmosphere around here. Greeley may have been a slimy bastard," Mason said with a tired grin, "but he ran a damn good casino."

Read on for an excerpt from

SHOTGUN CHARLIE

A Ralph Compton Novel by Matthew P. Mayo
Available now from Signet in
paperback and e-book.

The dove's throaty growls had startled him at first, made him jump right off the bed. Surely she was in pain, some sort of trouble. A bad dream at best. Then it had occurred to Charlie that no, this was a natural sound. And this was as close as he'd ever come to hearing it.

Through a thin lath-and-plaster wall mostly covered with paper, still pretty but not nearly so vivid as he was sure it had been a long time since, with tiny pink flowers—roses, he thought they might be—surrounded by even tinier green leaves, Charlie finally knew the sounds for what they were. They were the sounds of a man and a woman doing what he was still a stranger to. Would be forever, he guessed.

And so, big ol' Charlie Chilton, barely fifteen years old, spent the first night he had ever spent in a town, the first night he'd ever spent in a hotel, the first night he'd ever spent in a bed—an honest-to-goodness spring bed under a cotton-ticking mattress and all—and he spent it mostly awake.

He wondered as he was roused again and again from a neck-snapping slumber, if he should rap on the wall. He didn't want to invite trouble, but he needed sleep. He felt sure when he'd checked in that he was about to receive the finest night's sleep a body could get.

That the hotel was in the habit of renting out unoccupied rooms for short-term trysts was something that Charlie would not know for a long time to come. But that night's introduction had startled him. All the long days preceding his arrival in town had been one odd surprise after another, saddening and shocking and worrisome. And so this last one, despite his earnest hopes, proved more of the same.

This was what the world was like? Not much different from the everyday misery of life on the little rented farm with his gran. He'd hoped for so much more. As he listened to the moans and thumpings and occasional harsh barks of laughter from the men, he hoped that at least his mule, Teacup, was safe and sound and enjoying a good night's slumber in the livery.

It had cost a few coins that he knew he shouldn't have spent, but he'd never indulged in anything in his life, and the money he'd earned at that last farm had burned a hole in is trouser pocket until he'd spent some.

Charlie passed some of the long, noisy night by counting out the last of it, searching his pockets over and over again, sure he'd dropped some of the money somewhere along the way. But no, when after long minutes he'd tallied the figures in his head, he had one dollar and twelve cents left. And he decided then that something had to change. He figured he'd worry about it in the morning, but morning came with little interruption from night by sleep, save for brief snatches.

He left the hotel early, the sun was barely up. The woman's cries had continued long into the early hours, then dwindled, allowing him precious little rest. Before he left the room, his eyes had once again taken in the small lace doily, a marvel of hand stitching the likes of which he'd never seen. He'd studied it for some time the night before, then set it aside.

It was white, with a pointed-edge pattern, round in shape, smaller than his palm, but large enough to fit under the dainty oil lamp on the chest of drawers. When he'd lifted the lamp to peek at it, he'd seen tiny flowers, a dozen of them arranged in a circle. It was one of the single most pretty things he'd ever seen in his life, if you didn't count all the wonders nature had up her sleeve.

Those could hardly be topped by man, he figured—a new calf, the soft hairs on its head, how it felt when you rubbed it before the calf awoke, the long lashes on its eyes staring up at you in innocence; spring buds on an apple tree, then how they unfolded over a week or so, the little leaves getting bigger and darker and tougher as the season wore on.

They were special things, to be sure, but that little doily was a corker, maybe it was because it had no real purpose? Even its prettiness was hidden by the oil lamp. How many folks got to see what some woman had worked so hard to make, hidden as those little flowers were by the lamp? He appreciated them, at least.

And so as he left the room, he spied that doily and thought to himself, "Why not, Charlie? Why not have something pretty in your life? After all, didn't they sort of cheat you out of your good night's sleep?" And so he had slid the doily off the polished top of that chest of drawers and poked it quickly down into his trouser pocket with a long, callused finger, reddening about the neck, cheeks, and ears even as he did so.

By the time he reached the bottom of the long staircase in the lobby of the hotel, he felt as if his entire head might catch fire. He shuffled toward the front door and thrust a hand into his pocket. His fingers tweezered the crumpled little doily. He would set it on the counter and leave, walk right out. It was so early, no one was there. He lifted it free, and that was when he noticed in the mirror that the desk clerk, the same man as the night before, was watching him from across the big room where he was busy sweeping the hearth of the great fireplace. How had Charlie not seen the thin, pasty-looking man when he came down the stairs?

Charlie nodded; the man watched him, but didn't look particularly angry. No angrier than he'd been the night before when Charlie had checked in. He'd looked confused then and looked more of the same now. Charlie pushed the doily back down into his pocket and struggled with the fancy brass knobs of the leaded glass doors, worry warring with fear and guilt in his brain. Worry and guilt that he'd stolen the first thing he'd ever stolen in his life, fear that he'd soon be arrested, and slim wonder, too, that maybe, just maybe, he'd get away with it.

By the time Charlie reached the livery and, with frequent glances back over his shoulder, saw no one trailing him from the hotel, he became more and more convinced that he and he alone deserved to own that doily, that it had been made and was meant for him to admire, to appreciate. He rode out of that town and vowed, just the same, to never return to Bakersfield. Just in case.

Little did he know that a few short years later, he would be a member of an outlaw gang dead set on committing a crime that made stealing a doily the very least of life's offenses.